Also by Allen French

The Story of Rolf and the Viking Bow
The Lost Baron
Sir Marrok
Heroes of Iceland
The Story of Grettir the Strong
The Colonials

Non-Fiction

The Siege of Boston
First Year of the American Revolution
General Gage's Informers
Historic Concord and the Lexington Fight

The
RED KEEP

A story of Burgundy in year 1165

by Allen French

Illustrated by Andrew Wyeth

BETHLEHEM BOOKS • IGNATIUS PRESS
WARSAW, N.D.   SAN FRANCISCO

Cover artwork: THE RED KEEP, 1938 by N.C. Wyeth,
    photograph courtesy of Wyeth Collection
Interior artwork: 1938, Andrew Wyeth
All artwork © 1997, Andrew Wyeth
Cover design: Davin Carlson

First printing, March 1997
Second printing, May 1999

ISBN 1–883937–29–9
Library of Congress Catalog Number: 96–80079

Bethlehem Books • Ignatius Press
15605 County Road 15
Minto, ND 58261
www.bethlehembooks.com

Printed in the United States on acid free paper

To Katherine,
who demanded another story

Table Of Contents

The Red Keep

I

A Raid

CONAN, very proud, was wearing his chain mail. Few boys of fifteen had such a thing in the country districts of Burgundy nearly eight hundred years ago. His father had lately sent it to him, having found it in a storeroom, part of the forgotten plunder brought home from the Second Crusade. Now anyone knew what a few years of damp would do to a shirt of mail. Parts as wide as Conan's hand had rusted away, and in many lesser places the rings were gone. Weeks of work the boy had put into mending it, with the assistance of the armorer. The fine original Turkish mesh they had not hoped to reproduce; but by cutting off all the skirts of the garment, and by using them as patches by means of coarse rings laboriously forged by Conan himself, they had made a shirt that just cleared the hips and was a good protection as far as it went. Sir Roger had been pleased with the boy's persistence and skill, for the use of the armorer's hammer was too often neglected in a knight's education. As for Conan, he declared that he wanted no long hauberk, which would limit his freedom too much. And this he maintained even though, as he sat his horse, his legs were protected merely by leather leggings.

Sir Roger, watching the boy as their horses trotted side by side, chuckled to himself. Conan was the son of a baron living some forty miles away. Sir Roger had taken the lad into his own castle, as was the custom, to bring him up to knighthood. Conan, lanky, light-haired, and frank of face, was still but a page or varlet; but he was coming on, and the easy-going knight was fond of him. The lad was all bone; he was growing rapidly, and in a year it would be difficult to put the mail-shirt on. Meanwhile, let him enjoy it.

"I don't suppose," said Conan happily, "that young d'Arcy, at the Red Keep, has such a hauberk as mine."

"Ah, but he has," replied his lord. "A very good one, bought by his father at the Vézelay fair, not a year since. A small one, of Italian make, that fits him not badly."

Conan did not care. "Well, he will outgrow his, too. But to buy a new one too small!"

"Baron Ives said," explained Sir Roger, "that his daughter would grow to it."

"Anne?" asked the varlet. "Is she a tomboy, then? When I stopped at the Keep, on my way from my home, she was rolling hoops."

"And now," replied the knight, "she goes to hunt with her father and brother. If she puts on armor, she will not be the first girl that has done so in these parts. And at need!"

"Let her use her brother's, then," said Conan. "Sir Roger, I have thought how I can enlarge mine. With the old scraps which I have laid away I can widen out the front and back. I have almost enough. The sleeves I can slit on the inside and widen with leather."

"Well, well," said the baron. "But when you are grown, the shirt will hardly come to your waist."

Conan sighed. "I never could make myself one wholly new."

The two were riding at the head of a string of horsemen, straggling at gentle pace through forest ways. The followers, roughly and variously protected by leather, with nondescript arms, rode shaggy horses. That they were all fighting-men was usual in an uncouth time when commonly only the priest and the monk journeyed without arms.

But these were on no errand of war; they were going on a friendly visit to the Red Keep, which, after a half day's travel, lay close ahead. From a little knoll in the forest, stony and bare of trees, the castle could be seen. On climbing the knoll Sir Roger drew rein, intending to stop for a view of the castle standing peaceful in its lands. The moment he looked, he shouted in astonishment. Conan repeated the shout, as did others who hurried to the spot.

The Red Keep stood a half mile away, the square block of its heavy tower dominating the lesser build-

ings. Above it hung a pall of smoke, fed by black wreaths that curled upward from the narrow windows. Not far outside the gate a huddle of huts was burning furiously. In all the scene there were no men, unless some few were unseen among a score or more of horses standing grouped close to the drawbridge of the castle. The horses and the double fire made it very clear that this was a raid, a surprise, a fight as yet unfinished.

Sir Roger shouted "Rescue!" and drew his sword. Conan, in a voice that cracked as he raised it, repeated the word and the action. "Blow trumpet!" cried Sir Roger, to hasten the laggards. "Forward!" From the knoll the horsemen furiously spurred to save their friends.

In answer to the trumpet in the woods, at the castle gate a warning bugle blew. The call was repeated from within. There were shouts and trampling; armed men, rushing through the gate, began mounting their horses. Nervously they looked, now at the forest, now within the castle. All had been fighting; and some, with streaming eyes and still coughing, had been in the smoke. "The barons — why do they not come?" There appeared at length, running, a group conducting a little clumsy figure, crooked, heavy-backed, which the men hoisted to its saddle. Next, alone, strode a tower of a man, who paused in the gate to send one rallying cry back into the castle.

"Curse you, Aymar, hurry!" cried the crookback. "Who blew the alarm?"

"I, Lord Odo," answered one. "I heard a trumpet in the wood, and horses galloping."

"And none can come who is not our enemy. Aymar, speed you!" The huge man, reaching his horse's side, gathered the reins and set foot in the stirrup. "Are you sure," demanded the dwarf, "that you stabbed everyone?"

"How could I be, in that hurly-burly in the dark? I know only that none followed me out of the smoke. I am lucky not to have smothered there myself." He heaved himself to the saddle. "Why the alarm?"

"Enemies in the forest. Away everyone — keep close to me and make for home!" Odo rode first, but not so fast that his bodyguard could not protect him. The big man rode back across the drawbridge and bellowed twice within the archway. Then growling, "Plunderers take their own risk," he spurred his great horse after the others.

The last of the fleeing band was seen by the rescuers. Pursuit seemed hopeless. "Their horses are fresh, ours are tired. Let us make what rescue we can within the castle."

Conan, at Sir Roger's side, asked, "Who are they? Who would — could?"

But he knew the answer. "The Sauval. Never to be trusted." That treacherous, bloodthirsty pair of brothers, with their band of ruffians. The plague of the whole region, always from their castle stronghold robbing and raiding.

The courtyard of the Red Keep, when the rescuers clattered into it and drew rein, seemed peaceful. The people of the castle had been getting in wood, for a wagon still stood with its horses harnessed. Conan looked twice before he saw bodies lying, and noticed trickles of blood. It had been a complete surprise.

Into sight staggered two plunderers, their arms full of loot, their heads already swimming with wine. They were speedily cut down. Conan, watching that swift slaying, stared with wide eyes, and felt his heart quiver.

Sir Roger measured with his eye the smoke coming from the keep itself, the great square donjon-tower which by the color of its red stone gave the castle its name. Such a tower was, to every castle, its citadel, its last stronghold. "The fire is dying out. Into the castle, now, and save every friend. Kill any Sauval. You six behind there, guard the gate."

He strode across the courtyard and into the keep. Conan kept at his shoulder, all limbs and neck and awkward joints, with startled, eager eyes. "Keep behind me, boy! We may meet more of those lingerers. There, they have found another. Hear him shriek. Behind me, Conan, I tell you!" For the boy was pressing on.

The baron sent some of his men down into the cellars, then led others up the stairs. In the great hall were evidences of the surprise — a woman's tapestry frame still standing by the fire, its skeins of wool on the floor. The tables stood covered with food. "Treachery," said the baron. "But Ives would never believe me. They had time to defend the upper stairs. Now to find them."

The real fighting had been on the stairs leading upward from the hall, where the newcomers cleared away the bodies. "Unarmed," commented Sir Roger. Above, in the chambers, more bodies — then defiance from a turret, shouted down. They who were there would sell their lives dearly. Assured of safety, a score of men and women rushed down, hysterical with relief. But where was Baron Ives? Where the lady? Where the son and daughter? — And where, demanded Baron Roger anxiously, was Conan?

The varlet staggered into the light. In his arms, senseless, was a slender girl. With his eyes streaming from smoke, he coughed his lungs clear, and pointed an elbow.

"In that dark passage. It is crowded with dead, but I think Anne lives. Crawl as you go in: the smoke hangs heavy."

The girl stirred in his arms, and women rushed forward to take and revive her.

The men emptied out the dark passage.

The baron, his wife, his son, his two squires. They had made a good fight, for there too were five of the Sauval. Between wounds and the smoke, all appeared dead.

But Conan whipped out his knife. "That man is alive!"

One of the Sauval was rising to his feet. His knife was in his hand. But the varlet seized him, mastered him, stabbed but once. Toward that slaying the others were indifferent; but they looked with interest on a lad whose attack could be at once so furious and so skillful.

A servitor came running. "One of the gate towers is doomed. It is full of stored wood, which is burning furiously. The portcullis has fallen, and we are shut in."

Sir Roger went hastily to look. One of the towers which flanked the gate was a raging furnace. Its stairs, floors, and roof were of wood; many beams had been let into the walls. The machinery to lift the huge grating of the portcullis being destroyed, it had fallen of itself. To be sure, it might be lifted by main strength; but since the tower, in falling, might crush the entrance archway, Sir Roger decided to

wait until it was safe to go out. He used the time of
this detention to search the other towers, gather such
property as could be transported, and make himself
known, across the battlements, to the peasants outside. For these, gathering too late, thought at first
they were besieging the Sauval. At last the calcined
tower collapsed, fortunately down into the moat.
Danger thus being removed from the gateway itself,
the portcullis was raised and propped, and the peasants came pouring in.

Their lamentations were loud. Who now would
hold the castle and protect them?

"Men," said Baron Roger, "the castle cannot be
held, for yonder corner is open to anyone's assault.
There are no masons to rebuild it; and if there were,
so many of your men-at-arms are dead that there are
not enough to garrison this place. Myself, I have not
enough men to lend you. All I can do is to take the
Lady Anne home with me. To all others I offer protection and a farm."

"What!" cried some. "Abandon the castle?"

"I see no other way."

"But appeal to the duke!"

"I will. But have you not heard? The old duke is
dead these three months past. The young duke is
but a boy, and his mother, who will rule the duchy
until he is a man, is indifferent to vassals' needs.
There are bad times coming for Burgundy."

The peasants understood him well.

A duke should sustain his vassals, his lords small

and great, as they in their turn should defend the peasants on their lands. If the duke did not aid the baron, who then would help the peasant? Some of them, listening, grew desperate.

"Then let us follow the Sauval and die taking our revenge!"

Sir Roger's answer was decisive. "I must think of my own castle and my fief. My advice is, come with me."

The night and the next day were spent in burying the dead, packing, planning. When the second morning broke an exodus began, not only from the castle, but from most of the farms round about. In the little wars of that day, the tenants were accustomed to leaving their homes on sudden notice and flocking to their lord's castle for shelter. But this was different: it was twenty miles to Sir Roger's castle, and when they might return, no one knew. Loving their homes, some would not go — Dizier of the Marshes, Sandras of the Hill Farm, Lame Denys. But others knew too well the truth of the saying that "he fared badly who had no lord to protect him." Therefore a mixed procession began its march toward Baron Roger's, of whole lamenting families, carrying away their movables, and driving their sheep, goats, and cattle.

Anne, recovered in body, but in spirit terribly shaken, traveled among her women, carefully guarded by the remainder of her men-at-arms.

"The last of her family," said Sir Roger to Conan. "I doubt if she can claim even her father's fief, for women seldom inherit. — What is that which you carry across your crupper?"

"Her brother's coat of mail," answered Conan gloomily. "Had he been wearing it, it might have saved his life. I found it in his chamber; his father's arms and armor must have been carried off. This I will save for Anne."

The baron grieved for the lost plunder, and for the empty castle. "In all this region is no such square keep as that, for ours is round, and that is of the fashion of Normandy, they say. It is doubly the Red Keep now, for the red sandstone is stained with blood." He thought awhile. "I cannot see why Ives did not go into the turret with the rest, where he could have held the narrow stairs. That dark passage with both ends open was but a trap."

"Unlucky!" Conan shuddered at the memory of that shambles. "So treacherous, and so sudden." He thought deep. "Must life be like that?"

The baron's answer was shallow but practical. "It is like that. Those farms will lie waste for a long while, and birds will nest in the castle. For though I will make appeal to the duchess, it will be useless. I hear it said of the woman that she will keep her son under her control, and enjoy her power."

"And Anne?" asked Conan.

"My wife will bring her up. Someday we may find a husband to claim her fief for her. As for me, I have strengthened myself with a score more fighting-men, and many workers on my lands. But my poor wife! If she was afraid whenever I went from home before, what will she be now, remembering this story of the Red Keep?" Baron Roger sighed, for he liked the hunt, and friendly visits. "Conan, how have you liked this fighting? It was your first."

The boy shook his head. "I hated it!"

"But you were always at my back."

"I was afraid not to be."

"Afraid? Yet you explored that dark passage alone."

"I thought I heard Anne groaning."

"But when you slew that man — were you afraid then?"

Conan explained soberly.

"I cannot remember quite clearly. But I was not afraid, for I was furious with the Sauval. And yet, did you notice? I slew him just as you taught me to do, when two men fight with knives. How could I be so exact, when I was in such anger?"

To the baron the answer was simple. "You have the making of a good fighting-man. The men saw that, and will do anything for you now. And listen, Conan: I will do for you what I have never before done for anyone so young. From this day you are no longer page, but squire. Does that please you?"

"It will please my father. I thank you, Sir Roger."

"But you do not smile. Are you not glad?"

"Yes," answered Conan. "At least I think I am. But I shall never really be a good fighting-man, Sir Roger."

The baron laughed.

II

The Prior Brings Bad News

IT WAS THREE years later. At the evening meal, in the castle of Sir Roger, a minstrel had sung of a Crusade. When he had finished, the baron called him to the dais and rewarded him, while all in the hall fell into discussion. Conan, tall and strong now, but still ungainly, demanded another Crusade. Eustace, a youth of his own age, small and slight, but bright-faced and eager, longed for the same. Stout Father Gregory, the castle chaplain, unmindful of the figure that he would make on the march, declared himself willing to go. But Anne, slender and quick, with a face that showed thought as well as a certain impulsiveness, pulled at the ribbon at her waist and frowned in disapproval.

"What!" she scoffed. "Will you do what King Louis failed in? And have you not enough to do, here at home?"

Conan answered: "Nobody wants me. I am the fourth son, and so there is no need for me at Prigny. I must make myself a place somewhere."

"There is plenty of room in Burgundy," replied Anne. She turned to the other youth. "And you, Eustace. Why should you want a Crusade?"

"To learn," he answered. "All learning is of the East. If only I had got to Jerusalem before this Saladin drove the Christians out! But I will get the knowledge of the Arabs. And at Constantinople is all the wisdom of the ancients. Then when I return, see if I know not something of healing!"

"Ah," said the chaplain contemptuously, "of healing! Of the learning of the church, nothing!"

"You know, Father," replied Eustace, "I am not pious. You could not make me a priest, for I drowsed over Mass books. But there is much to be done in the world by one who learns to heal wounds and sickness."

"Aye!" cried Anne. "You worked well at the last sickness in the village."

Eustace shook his head. "I was only trying to learn. Thirty people died in twenty days, and at the end I knew no more of what killed them than at the beginning. Perhaps a few I saved, but I cannot tell you how. And what is sickness, what brings it, what cures it? That I would know."

"Better spend your time," said the priest severely, "curing sickness of the soul. Better save folk from hell, than from mere death."

"But if he saves them from death," explained Anne, "then you can save them from hell. He is the best here in binding up wounds. Better than any of us women."

"He knows at least," chuckled the priest, "what makes a wound."

Eustace replied, "But not what is a wound."

Conan stared. "How — what is a wound? It is a bleeding cut in flesh."

"But what is flesh?" Eustace demanded. "What is blood? What causes blood to flow, and what stops it? What heals the cut? In the East, perhaps, I could learn the answers to these questions."

"Be content," reproved the priest. "Leave such silly thoughts alone, and learn how to cure."

"I could cure better," answered Eustace doggedly, "If I knew those things. But all I do helps me to learn, and Sir Roger allows me my living."

"Well he may!" cried Anne. "What you have saved him in horses alone, would pay for your living for a year. The grooms are not jealous of you, because you give them credit. But someday you shall go to Paris!"

"Ho!" said the priest. "Anne, you talk as if you were somebody!"

Anne was rebuked. Heiress of a deserted fief, dependent on Baron Roger for her living, on Lady Blanche for her clothes, she had nothing to reply, and could merely sulk. Conan, believing that he understood, put out his hand to soothe her. The feeling in her answering grip surprised him. For in truth, not being deep, he did not suspect her depths.

Anne's desires were stronger than Conan's, because more definite. She never forgot her old home. Her hopes centered in her father's empty castle, in the deserted farms now lapsing into wilderness, in the servitors that were loyal to her here, and in the peasants that still tilled their old lands. Someday she must regain the Red Keep. But Anne had learned not to say, "When I have my fief — " There had been too many delays, too much silence from the duchess. And, further, she had learned to fear that she might never regain her fief except through marriage. She was always afraid that any day the baron might call her to him and say, "Anne, this is your husband." For she was almost marriageable. And any needy adventurer, or any ambitionless old attendant on the court, might be glad to take the wife with the property.

The priest began to doze on his stool. Eustace, murmuring something about an injured man, went away. Anne and Conan remained, inattentively watching the familiar scene.

Comfort had not yet come into that corner of Burgundy. It is true that near Dijon, the residence of the duke, the richer vassals were beginning to build, within their fortified enclosures, dwellings for their personal lodging. But though Sir Roger's wife had more than once mentioned them to him, as offering some decency, privacy, and ease, he would never build one, and for two reasons. In the first place, his small fief did not provide the money for such elegance. The most that Lady Blanche might hope for from him was, someday, a little chapel, which he had promised her at their wedding.

But further, Sir Roger did not hold with modern effeminate ways. To be sure, his ancestors had lived in a wooden keep, while he dwelt in a donjon of stone; but in each case the quarters were crowded and uncomfortable, proper for a hardy and warlike race. Air and light, space and privacy, were softening to the spirit and interfered with the defense of a castle.

Therefore, at this evening meal the great hall contained not merely the baron's family and his personal servants, but almost every inhabitant of the castle, even dogs. The place was barely large enough for all. On the dais, a low platform, was the table of the baron and his family, his two knights, his four squires, and Anne. Below, according to rank, were places for chaplain and varlet, damosel and servitor, man-at-arms, huntsman, and groom. Two great fires crackled in the one enormous fireplace. Servants passed in and out. Under the baron's eye were all the members of his household except his cooks and his watchmen; he could summon anyone at any time by merely lifting his finger.

In the hall were clatter of dishes, medley of talk, laughter, and dispute. The air was close with the smoke of torches and the breath of crowded humanity. Odors were many and not all pleasant. By day there was little sun; and always there was little ventilation except by the chimneys. But no one objected to all this, or to the lack of privacy. They were used to it; it was a public life that everyone lived; no one could escape the jostling or the observation of his neighbor. The voice of each was pitched, the ear of each accustomed, the nostrils even indifferent, to the conditions.

But tonight there came a sudden hush when there pierced through the noise the blast of a horn at the gate. Everyone was attentive when a watchman came hurrying in. All listened for Sir Roger's orders.

"The prior of Vézelay, with some twenty followers." He nodded in response to his wife's gesture; everyone knew of her fear of a sudden attack by men in disguise. He ordered knights, squires, and men-at-arms to the gate, as an honor and as precaution. But he held Conan back.

"Listen, Conan. This Prior Matthew will be abbot soon. He travels in state; he expects everything of the best. Bid the cooks serve whatever is ready, and at once put on the spit poultry, game, plenty of everything. Tell the cellarer to serve the prior only my best wine. And do you take charge of the service. Everything must be done well, lad."

As Conan left the hall he heard orders given to clear it of the lesser fry. In the kitchen his orders caused great commotion. Fires were quickened, and the spits started again. "I have heard of this prior,"

said Christopher, the cook. "A lover of show. When he is abbot he will travel with his own wine and his gold and silver dishes, even with his bedding and his cooks. Now he is simple, lest he miss his advancement."

When Conan, carrying the baron's best silver basin, with a page following with napkin and ewer of water, came again into the hall, he saw at the lower tables plump monks and more than a dozen men-at-arms, already regaling themselves on the remains of the former meal. But as he went to the dais he was surprised to see in the seat of honor a burly figure in hunting dress, a man heavy but not unathletic, red of face and bluff, with a strong voice which he took no pains to subdue. He was leaning toward Lady

Blanche in the fashionable manner of gallantry. The baron was looking on a little grimly. — So this was a monk!

The prior looked coolly at Conan, and spoke to the baron. "And who, Sir Roger, is this young sprig? Your son?"

"My son is yet a child," replied the baron. "This young man is here as my squire, though his home is nearer yours than mine. He is Conan, son of the baron of Prigny."

No softness came into the face of the prior, no regret for the word he was about to speak. "So? Then I have news for him. Young man, your father is dead."

Conan stood stunned. The baron questioned anxiously. The answer was cool. "Why, he was but lately slain in a chance encounter on his borders with the Sauval. He and his men were outnumbered, yet he accused the Sauval of trespass and robbery, and attacked them. That was unwise, for Odo of Sauval is deliberate in counting odds. He must have seen that the Prigny had no chance; and he was right, for all were slain. One must reckon wisely in quarreling with the Sauval."

Anne, attentive, saw that the prior seemed to approve of the skill of the slayers, and to blame the slain. Her heart swelled with anger. But Conan's head was whirling with the sudden news. Intimate with his father he certainly was not, for five years had passed since he had seen him. It was not Conan's affections, therefore, that were hurt, but his memory of a home concerning which he had forgotten anything unpleasant. He had felt it as a background, a retreat.

"It is unwise," the prior was going on, "to keep to old-fashioned ways. The Sauval know that, and they arm their men with good weapons, not with what each man can find for himself. They say that the weapons of the Prigny, in this fight, were only knives and short-swords, while the Sauval had spears and shields."

The baron, with an anxious eye on Conan, was waiting for a chance to silence the booming words of the prior, which those below the dais heard with mixed feelings. The men of Vézelay were listening to their prior as to an oracle concerning war; but the men of Castle Fessart felt all their sympathies go out to Conan. As he stood shading his eyes with one hand, he felt someone tugging at the other. Looking down, he saw Anne, her face full of distress. "Come with me," she begged, and Conan let her lead him away. She took him out of the hall to an embrasure on the tower stairs, where by an arrow-slit the two had often sat and talked. There, at length, Conan found words.

"I can't explain why I feel so bewildered. I did not know my father well, or depend on him. At home he was busy, and often quick-tempered. And these things often happen. Why am I so upset?"

"It was the way it was told!" cried Anne. "That man might as well have struck you with a hammer.

Speaking so well of the Sauval, too! — You are all right now, Conan?"

"Quite," he answered. "But something has gone that I did not know I prized, and I begin to see that I ought to have prized it higher."

"It was so with me," agreed Anne. "I did not understand that I owed my happiness to my parents. And then suddenly it was too late. Living is like that, Conan."

He recalled that the baron had once said the same thing. "Well, we go on living, those that are left."

But she demanded, "What of those who caused us to be left, who slew my father, and now have slain yours?"

Conan turned and looked at her. Her expression was not hard, but firm and purposeful. "Father Gregory says it is not right to take vengeance — that the Bible says so. But he has not read the Bible for years, for there is none in the castle; there never has been. Only rich lords, or great churches or abbeys, have Bibles. But even if it is not right to take vengeance, is it right to let the Sauval go on killing and killing?"

"No," said Conan. "There is justice."

"There should be justice," corrected Anne. "But the duchess pays no attention to Sir Roger's demands for justice for me."

They sat silent until she asked, "Your Crusade — shall you want to go now?"

"I must think it out. But you know it is always easier to go than to stay."

"What do you mean?"

"It seems so easy, as a knight-errant, to put a thing right — and then to go away and leave it. But it is hard, living at home, to put a thing right and make sure that it shall stay so."

Anne agreed, and again they sat thinking. They knew the difficulties at home. Little private wars, larger contests between great lords, unfairness, oppression, epidemics that swept whole duchies, famines general or local — these, sometimes of tragic importance, were often to be struggled with. Even upon a single fief the problems of administration, justice, proper husbandry, and foresight, where trading was slight, ignorance was colossal, where each estate must produce practically all it consumed, where neighbors encroached, outlaws raided, where bloodshed followed a quarrel, and disease was everywhere — there the responsibility was complicated and weighty. Small wonder that a Crusade seemed a welcome change from these burdens. Conan frankly acknowledged the temptation.

But Anne rejoined, "If you feel how much is to be done here at home, then you are the very one to stay and do it."

Conan answered, "There is nothing for me to do, for I have no fief."

An answer seemed to spring from Anne's depths,

so quick, so impulsive, that she stopped it only by putting her hand over her lips. She knew a fief for him. The Red Keep could be his. He could be her husband!

Conan? Anne clenched her hard little hands. Strange that she had never thought of that solution. Yet not strange, since the baron had never mentioned it. And the reason was plain: Conan was too young, too soft. Sir Roger needed as neighbor some hard-hitting, energetic, aggressive lord, a seasoned fighter. Not kindly, changeable, self-doubting Conan. Anne relaxed.

Yet a strange tingling remained, and she looked at him with a shyness that was entirely new. Handsome, yes. Manly, too, in his way. But — yes, soft. That was why she felt protective toward him. And a chatelaine should not feel protective toward the lord who should defend her. So much Anne knew of the feudal state, so little of marriage.

She was relieved when a door below opened, and the light of torches flooded the place. A number of steps below them, the baron conducted the prior out upon a landing. The monk's dominating voice filled the tower.

"Then since you press me, Sir Roger, a day's hawking tomorrow. Who is your best man with the falcons?"

"That very same young Conan whose father's death you made known. You saw how he slipped away; he was distressed. It might be kinder not to use him tomorrow."

"Pshaw!" jeered the prior. "Teach the boy hardness, lord baron. He must learn to meet disasters. And surely you know that hawks ought never to be badly handled. I cannot bear to see clumsy work in the field."

They passed out of hearing.

"I hate him," said Anne vehemently. "I despise him, too. For I know he is only a bully."

Conan admired. How easily she put the word to what he had felt.

III

Evil Tidings

THE MONTHS rolled by, until it was January of Conan's twentieth year.

Even in the castle there was little comfort. The cold had penetrated every stone in the keep, and the lord and his people cowered like the peasant against the cold. Fireplaces warmed only the faces; backs were chilled by the drafts that rushed to the chimneys. And Conan, making his rounds as head squire on a cheerless, sunless morning, found everyone sleeping who could. It was a surprise to find the armorer busy at his little forge.

"What, Giles, at work today? — And what is this? Lady Anne's hauberk?"

"Yes," admitted the armorer. "She brought it to be mended, but I was to tell no one, least of all you."

"But what could have damaged the mail?" asked Conan. "It was whole but a few days since, when she wore it to the boar hunt."

"It was then it happened," said Giles.

Conan was astounded. "But she got not near the

38

boar. It is true she would press in too close, so that I bade her stand back, somewhat sharply. But she was two strides away from the beast when I finished him."

"Aye," said Giles dryly. "You were so busy with your short-sword that you could not see what went on close at hand. One of the men (she would not name him) cast a spear at the beast and missed him, but hit the young lady."

Conan snatched the hauberk off the anvil and looked at it closely. "No blood was shed!"

"Nay. It was a glancing blow, but the point caught the links and rent them."

Conan glared, as his sudden anxiety gave place to anger. "I gave orders that no spear should be thrown at close quarters. Ha! — Jehan was picking up his spear a little later. I thought he dropped it in the confusion, and rallied him on being so white. No wonder he was pale. Giles, that is his last hunt with me!"

"See to it," said the armorer. "But now, Conan, I cannot mend this mail so that it will not be noticed. Such fine Italian work I cannot rival. If my patching is seen, the story will come to the baron and the lady, and then Lady Anne will have no more hunting. But have you no more pieces from your Turkish mail that you laid away so carefully, years agone? I could piece in those fine links with these, and it would pass."

"Aye," answered Conan. "I could not take the shirt from the varlet who has it, for then the tale would come out. But I still have those pieces tucked away, and you shall have them."

"But you must tell no one," reminded Giles. "Not even the young lady."

"I should like to scold her," said Conan reluctantly.

"At the beginning of the next hunt," suggested Giles, "make her swear to be cautious."

"Cautious!" repeated Conan. "She promised last time, but she was going in, spear in hand, like the oldest huntsman. Oh, yes, she will swear, but she will forget herself."

"It is in the blood," said the armorer admiringly. "Her men love her for it."

"None of her vassals can have seen this happening," reasoned Conan. "Else Jehan would have had his head broken. — Now I remember, none were up with us, and they were scolding each other for not being nearer their lady."

"How they cling to that allegiance!" the armorer exclaimed. "Not one but dreams of going back to the old fief."

Conan smiled. "That vexes the baron. He wants them for his own, but they are still men of the Red Keep, every one. — Well, you shall have the links, Giles. Do your best work, and I will pay you myself, for she cannot."

The armorer shook his head. "She is as poor as a mouse. But I will take no pay for this."

Conan began searching for Anne, vexed with her, and the more so because he might not scold her. But it was she who found him, coming upon him from

behind. "Oh, Conan, here you are. Eustace wants us."

He felt the brightness of her presence. Of all that he had met so far, Anne was the only one not shape-less with wrappings against the cold. Actively going about the castle, like himself, on self-imposed er-rands from which the other damosels shrank, she had discarded her outer robe, and wore a woolen dress which she had modified from the prevailing fashion. At a time when ladies affected long trailing skirts and hanging sleeves, Anne had cut off both — for how else could she ride to the hunt? Her skirt came to the ankle; her sleeves gave just a hint of the style; the closely fitting dress showed her lithe figure to perfection, and its warm colors seemed to glow with her own life. On her head she wore a close cap which, with her red hair, framed her expressive face; she carried her cloak on her arm, and in her hand a covered basket. When all else cowered within the castle, Anne was ready to go out, and naturally assumed that Conan would go too.

"There is a sick man at Hughes's hut. Let us see what we can do."

And in a minute, with short cloak over his shoulder, and its hood over his head, he was helping her across the icy drawbridge. Over rough ground they picked their way, until they reached a line of huts with walls so low that the thatch almost reached the ground; under the snow they looked like mere mounds. Here dwelt Sir Roger's married servitors and men-at-arms, while beyond them lived, in huts which even under their load of snow seemed slight and temporary, the similar servants of the Red Keep. One of these huts Anne entered.

She stepped down, for the floor was below the ground. Conan, following her, blocked the light from the room, and when he had shut the door they were in darkness, save for the glow of embers on the hearth. Anne asked, "Hughes?"

"Ah, my lady," rumbled the hoarse voice of an old man, "it is fine to see you again."

They made out the shape of the veteran man-at-arms, sitting well-muffled in his chair by the fire. Anne emptied her basket and named to him each article, bringing out his chuckles. He was one of those who had held the turret stairs at the surprise of the Red Keep; but now he was tied to his chair by feebleness. On the other side of the fire sat Father Gregory, whispering prayers over his beads, and by the wall was another shape.

"Eustace?" asked Conan. "Is the sick man there? Who is he?"

"Here on the pallet," answered Eustace's voice. "A stranger, who stumbled into the village two nights agone, and fell, and has not spoken since. They brought him here, but, as he was slow about dying, this morning they sent for the priest and me. He is not of these parts, yet not a vagabond, for his clothes are good. He has been in a fray and was wounded, but not seriously. It is cold and exhaustion that have brought him low."

"Can you save him?" asked Anne.

"Ah, there is a certain fever that is deadly in such a case as this. It seems as if a man cannot breathe deep with it. I can do nothing but keep him warm. If he has not enough strength to carry him through, he will die, perhaps without speaking."

"He has spoken," said old Hughes. "In the night, asleep, he has cried broken war cries, then talked as if he were traveling in snow, with a message that he must tell."

Eustace, beginning to light a splinter of wood at the fire, spoke professionally. "I asked you once what is a wound, but here are more questions. What is a fever, and how measure it? And again, the pulse: what is it, and what do its changes mean? This man's is faster than my own, and very irregular. But if I judge other men's pulses by my own, by what shall I measure my own? For mine varies: it quickens when I climb the tower stairs. Who will make me an instrument to measure all pulses by? — Here, see if you know this man." Eustace held the splinter, now burning brightly, close to the sick man's face.

To Conan's surprise, in spite of the rough beard on the man's chin, the fever-flush, and the wasted cheeks, he felt that he was looking on a familiar face. He strove to recognize him.

Roused by the light, the fellow threw up a sluggish arm as if to defend himself. He muttered: "A Prigny! A Prigny!"

Conan exclaimed, "It is Chartier!" He seized the man by the shoulders, and, as the fellow's eyes opened, demanded, "Chartier, how came you here?"

"Here?" asked the man thickly. "Where, then?"

"At Fessart, just outside Sir Roger's castle. Do you not know me? I am Conan."

The man knit his brows in an effort to understand. "Not — little — Conan?"

"No longer little," explained Conan. "It is five years since I left home. But it is I, Conan of the Prigny."

The man collected himself. As if within him the waning fire revived, he spoke with effort, but with quicker voice, and clearly. "Good! I have not come for naught. Your brother — Blaise — is dead."

Conan gripped him closer. "Blaise — dead?"

"Aye — slain — a week hence."

"By whom, then?" But Conan feared that he knew the answer.

"The Sauval. We two were out alone, hunting. We came on Odo and Aymar, and a dozen men. Blaise parleyed and drew back. We turned to go. Then — I turned just in time to see! Aymar's spear in Blaise's back!"

The man's voice faded. As he fumbled at his throat, Anne, quicker than Eustace, took the wine that she had brought for Hughes and put a little between his lips. He mouthed it, swallowed, and revived.

Conan asked, "You were hurt then?"

"No — I got away — to the castle. We went and buried Blaise. Then your brother Fulke sent me here to tell you."

"You met them, then, on the way?"

Chartier smiled, a grim and twisted smile, full of the pain of his wounds and the memory of his struggle. "I met them — and left two dead. But they had lamed me — and then came on the snow."

Conan pressed his hands. "Good man you were, to get here!"

He answered with some pride, "You needed to know."

"Does Fulke want me to come home?"

"No. To stay — until your knighthood."

"Eighteen months. Chartier, you risked this for me!"

"No risk. On lands of — Red Keep — should have been safe. Those murderers there."

"There? What were they doing?"

"Robbing the tenants!" When Anne cried out, the man asked, "A woman? Who?"

She answered, "The lady of the Red Keep. Chartier, they shall pay!"

Chartier, struggling for breath, still spoke on. "Good to know. I — " He relaxed, and was silent.

Eustace rose from beside him. "As quick as that," he said. "His pulse just flickered and stopped." Anne was already closing the man's eyes, but Eustace did not notice that she, so young, was experienced in women's knowledge. He asked, "The pulse and the fever, how read them? How can I ever learn it all?"

"Gone?" complained old Hughes. "And I am left with the aches in my bones. Slew two, quoth he? I envy him."

"Patience," said Anne, and gave him her hand. The old man held it, and was soothed.

"Eustace," said Conan, "pray make the man decently ready for burial. I will have a grave hewn through the frost. — Anne, my brother is dead!"

"Was that planned?" she demanded. "Planned with a long purpose?"

"Nay," he answered. "How could it be? And I am to stay here. If I had been at home I might have saved him, or died for him."

She clutched his sleeve. "Not died for him!"

"Why not?" he asked, full of feeling.

She knew the answer, but would not give it.

IV

Anne's Plans, and Others'

THE SPRING came when Conan would soon be twenty-one. Because he would then be knighted, his father's hauberk had been sent him. He was now both tall and broad, but the mail fitted well.

Except on the field of battle, knighting required many ceremonies, and Lady Blanche planned to use them all on this occasion. Most important of all, he ought to keep vigil, watch and pray over his arms, one whole night in the chapel. But there was no chapel, so Sir Roger must build one. This he had promised years ago, but he had been too poor, until the tragedy of the Red Keep had brought to him, with Anne's farmers and laborers, some surplus riches. He had at first intended to set aside such moneys for Anne. But Lady Blanche argued against such an idea. Had not the crops, though raised by the men of the Red Keep, come from the soil of Fessart? Was he not at the expense of rearing Anne? Well, then! As the profits took shape in sundry pieces of gold and silver, Lady Blanche took charge of them. The chapel would be, for herself and her children, a sure passport to heaven.

Moreover, the ladies in castles near Dijon were building chapels. So at last two master-masons were sent for, and came from Vézelay.

Berengar was the head of the guild of masons at Vézelay, and Pierre was his grandson. The one was able, the other active, and soon they had organized at the castle a little corps of those workmen who had some skill in laying stone. For this purpose Anne readily lent her own men, lent them even eagerly, and watched through the spring every process of the work. The chapel was very small, and it grew fast.

In the household Anne took privileges allowed to no one else. She was a favorite with Sir Roger, though not with Lady Blanche. The chatelaine knew very well that Anne thought her more timid than the mistress of a castle ought to be. Moreover, it vexed her that Anne was not devoted to the interests of Fessart, but thought always of the Red Keep, as if she were a man, intending to possess it again. Impossible! So Lady Blanche said openly among her ladies-in-waiting and her damosels, who, consequently, were not jealous of the girl, but rather a little sorry for her.

But Anne took her own way. She was recognized as a lady in her own right; and though she was a chatelaine without a castle, she had what all the damosels envied even while they laughed — a troop of retainers, shabby and morose, indeed, but devoted to her to the death.

To Conan it was quite clear that when Anne lent

her men to the masons she wanted them to learn as
much as possible of the craft, in order that someday
they could be useful in building up the Red Keep.
Well, let them learn; the idea was harmless enough.
But he was puzzled why she herself should talk so
much with the two masons, until at length he came
upon the reason.

Conan had never been to Vézelay, though the town
and its abbey were celebrated throughout France. But
Sir Roger had told him much about the place. Abbot Martin, the former prior, who had brought to
the castle the news of the death of Conan's father,
was always at odds with the townspeople, the most
numerous of whom were the guild of masons. This
Berengar, as the head of the guild, was, therefore,
one of the most important men of the place. To be
sure, he was but an artisan. So were they all, but
they made many difficulties for the abbot, who had
set up a strong troop of swordsmen to curb them.

Anne talked with these men almost as with equals,

and on the very day when the chapel was finished
Conan came upon her discussing with them. Men
had come from Vézelay to escort them back; they had
taken from the castle their tools and their light derrick. These men (and here was one more of Lady
Blanche's timidities) were not admitted to the castle,
but were to lodge outside overnight, to start back the
next day. Berengar and Pierre were therefore free to
talk with Anne, and now they were bending earnestly
together over a diagram scratched on the ground. As
Conan approached, the two men went away, leaving
Anne studying intently. He saw that five crosses had
been laid out as the corners and the center of a square.

"And what is that?" he asked.

With her finger she pointed to the four corners of
the square, and named them: "Fessart, Vézelay, Sauval, Prigny."

"A map," he said. "And the center is the Red
Keep. But what has that to do with the work of the
masons of Vézelay?"

"It is for their warfare," she explained.

"What," he demanded, "do masons fight?"

She answered, "Sixty years ago the commune killed
Abbot Artaud, and only ten years ago they drove out
Abbot Pons."

"Aye," he rejoined, "and they were punished for it.
And now Abbot Martin's men are saying that they
must punish them again."

"Why does a churchman keep swordsmen?" demanded Anne. "We have heard, have we not, that he has become very friendly with the Sauval?"

"Let him," said Conan haughtily. "I despise them both."

"How can you despise them?" she demanded. "Two wolf-packs together are stronger than two apart. Conan, when you are baron of Prigny — "

"I? Baron?" he asked, startled.

"Yes, when the Sauval have killed the last of your brothers. See you not that with purpose they are wearing the Prigny down? Your outlying farms have already been harried, as they could not have been in my father's day. Look at this map. See how the Red Keep stands at almost equal distances from all the corners. He who holds it can most easily aid, or attack, any of the others. Whom would you rather have there, me and my men, or the Sauval?"

"You, of course."

"But when the abbot protects the Sauval," she persisted, "how soon will they take my castle, unless the men of Vézelay prevent?"

Her castle! Conan would have pitied Anne, but her ideas vexed him, being new. He saw that she was aiming at a strange alliance between barons and the common men of Vézelay. Impossible! Yet, not knowing how to refute her, he said weakly, "This is not a girl's business."

Anne made with her knee the ladylike equivalent of stamping her foot. "Then make it a man's!" she cried. "How soon will the Sauval be too strong for you entirely? Look forward, Conan, and make a plan. Nay, put not your hand on your sword hilt. The sword is a good thing, but the mind is better. Show Sir Roger and your brothers that if the Red Keep is built up again, each will have a defense from my side."

Always that vision! He objected, "But the rebuilding of the Keep?"

"The masons of Vézelay could do it. And they could prevent the abbot and the Sauval from sharing my lands between them."

Her castle, and her lands! "But how could you pay the masons?"

"I would pledge my revenues."

And now her revenues! Penniless Anne! He said, not unkindly, "But my dear girl, you have none."

Anne exploded. "You men are all the same. None can see beyond his nose. Go your way, Squire Conan. Fight like a bull, and when the wolves of the Sauval ring you round, think what it might mean to have a friend at your back. Fare you well!"

Conan stood blinking. She had flashed on him like a flame; her ire had made her beautiful, and her confidence in her own ideas made him feel small. He was deeply disturbed.

Anne, as she marched proudly away, could scarcely maintain her lofty carriage after the first moment. She had not meant to say so much, or at least she had not meant to say it so. If Conan were ever to be persuaded, it was not by anger. Already repenting, she was glad to see Sir Roger coming toward her, and she joined him.

But his brows were knit, and he scarcely greeted her. "Where is Conan? There is a message — ah, I see him. Come with me, Anne."

As Conan saw the baron approaching, he read bad news in his anxious visage. His mind leaped to meet it. Not Fulke! Anyone but Fulke!

"I will be plain with you," said Sir Roger bluntly. "Here are more evil tidings. Conan, your brother Guy is slain."

Anne was right, then. The Sauval were wearing the Prigny down. He was so sure, that he asked no questions.

Sir Roger burst out with an oath. Guy had been found slain with two of his men, and there was no trace of the slayers. But it was those robbers — who else?

None else indeed. "You foretold it, Anne," Conan said.

"I am sorry," she responded, as if the foretelling made her feel almost guilty.

Conan started as the fact and its meaning struck home. Fulke might be the next, Prigny itself. "I must go!" he cried. "At once!" Then, knowing that he would need the rest of the day to prepare, he decided, "To-morrow morning."

They could not persuade him otherwise. Fulke might need him. Anything might happen.

"Stay at least till I can knight you," urged Sir Roger.

But the chapel was not consecrated, and he could not stay for that, and for the solemnities. Besides, Conan had approached his knighthood unwillingly, for he had not earned it by feat of arms. No, he must go.

Anne looked at Sir Roger with concern. "But he cannot go alone. You must give him an escort."

Sir Roger shared her alarm, but knit his brows. "My men are all hard at work on the farms; much of the hay is down, and must be got in. Wait three days — four."

But Conan would not wait. Then Anne saw the solution. "The masons. He must go with them as far as the Red Keep. That is their easiest road, as well as his."

Conan was unwilling to travel in slow company. But the others urged him, and he submitted.

He had slight preparations to make. His clothes were few, he had no servant, and but one horse. He left his lance and took his boar-spear, gave away the pup that was not yet trained, chose among his three hawks the one of most promise. The things he left behind he bestowed as largesse among his friends, and in the same way (for lavish giving was expected of all nobles) he parted with the trinkets of gold and silver that were the hoardings of his boyhood.

In his one interview with the baron he opened to him Anne's schemes. Sir Roger was a man of his class, looking down on all of lower order; but to Conan's surprise he agreed with Anne.

"If the Sauval worked with the abbot," he admitted, "they would be dangerous. I see no hope in the young duke, for his mother has him in leading strings, and never replies when I claim justice for Anne. The girl is right. Though to rebuild the Red Keep seems impossible just now, we may need the help of the masons against the Sauval. Despise not these artisans, my boy. They are not like our villeins on the land, who are dull clods and need guidance. These Vézelay men are craftsmen and traders; they are richer than I. — Conan, why not go with Berengar and Pierre to Vézelay? Study there both your enemies and your friends."

But Conan felt that he must go directly home.

In the morning he saddled his horse, and in the courtyard made the beast ready for the journey. Eustace hung about and helped. He was depressed, and said: "I asked permission to go with you, but the lady would not permit. She claimed the right to my services. They have maintained me all these years, and I am not to go just when I am becoming useful. Sir Roger would have let me go, but she would not hear of it."

Conan knew that Eustace had long ago paid for his living by his services, but he knew also that in this debate the baron was no match for his wife. He told Eustace that he was sorry, for he would have liked his company, though he had refused a servant. He bestowed about his saddle his little baggage: a bundle of clothing, a sheaf of arrows and a bow, and various small articles that he would need at Prigny. The load was clumsy, but what saved him from making an absurd figure was the evident fact that he was ready for business. Armed, vigorous, and alert, however rustic his appearance, Conan was not to be mistaken for a bumpkin. There was something about him that suggested that his hand knew its way to his weapon.

Pierre and Berengar had already taken their leave of the baron, and had ridden out to wait Conan in the road. Anne came now to Conan; she was pale, and explained that she had sat up most of the night finishing a purse, which she fastened in his girdle. It was empty. Anne had nothing to give, except her sad little smile of farewell.

Furtively watching the two as they talked, her retainers, a dozen men of the Red Keep, squatted or crouched in a corner. They were nondescript and shabby, with such arms as each man could find for himself: swords of varying length, caps mostly of leather, and quilted doublets of all colors and materials. These men never took their ease; they were always observant and waiting. Some were sad, others surly; for years they had been nursing a hope that never turned into a promise. Notably they were apart, and a unit. In a grim silence they understood each other without words. The departure of one from the group occasioned no remark; the coming of another, who fitted himself into a vacant place, brought out no greeting. In that somewhat noisy place they were oddly quiet. Indeed, their silence seemed dangerous, so that a varlet who displayed in his dress some jauntiness and fashion, and looked at them as if tempted to jeer at their glumness, thought better of the impulse, and passed by.

Gloom was added to their grimness as they watched Anne and Conan. They loved the squire well because of his old-time service to their lady and his unfailing kindness to them. They would miss him. But, more than that, they had nourished a wish concerning him, and now it was going to fail. Why should not he, so young and strong, and so good a huntsman that he must become a good warrior— why should he not marry the young lady and restore the lost happiness of the Red Keep? But look at him now, starting on a dangerous journey, and yet so indifferent to Anne that he was plainly impatient to be gone.

Nor did Anne show any feeling beyond the strength and self-reliance common to firm spirits at all times, and necessary in that age. Many were stupid in that day of ignorance, or timid in that time of force. Few were tender. Strong souls acquired independence of thought, boldness of action, patience and hardiness against misfortune. Anne's life had taught her to be prepared for what she might get, not for what she wanted. She would not tell Conan that she would miss him, nor that she admired him. She had never given him reason to suspect that she saw in him more than a good comrade.

And now at last came Sir Roger, with Lady
Blanche. Conan took his leave of them — of the lady
with formal courtesy, of Sir Roger with real emotion.
At Castle Fessart, Conan had grown from a varlet to
a squire and almost into knighthood, and much of
what he knew he had learned from the honest and
kindly lord.

"I wish," said the baron, "that I could give you
some fitting gift. Particularly a new hauberk, but that
is a rare and costly thing, a year at least of a master
armorer's work. You must either take a better from a
vanquished knight, or buy one with booty."

"I fear it will be many a day before my sword
wins me such fortune," replied Conan with becoming modesty, believing his words not at all. For he
was young, and green. The baron, suspecting his
thought, smiled.

"Go and win your spurs," he said good-naturedly.
"And may you find a princess to succor, or a dragon
to slay, whichever is most to your mind." Conan
grinned a little sheepishly, for though princesses were
to be met with, dragons lived only in Asia and Af-
rica. The good knight gave Conan a gold piece, his
last after paying the masons. "Stuff it in your purse
— no, no thanks. I wish it were more. And now,
Conan, remember that you will soon be on dangerous ground. Ride warily, and take no risks. So be on
your way, with the blessing of all the saints."

Conan had not ridden far from the castle when
he found Berengar and Pierre waiting for him. Their

pack train had started well before them. Conan greeted them a little grudgingly, for while he liked these masons well enough, he looked on them as inferior to his own estate. Yet they lived, these townsmen — and Conan had never seen a town — quite as well as any castle dwellers. They were better clothed than most whom Conan knew, they earned money, and, unlike a knight who kept himself poor by his largesses, they waxed rich. With nothing to be proud of but his lineage, he grudged these craftsmen their prosperity. It even grated on him, a little, that while they doffed their caps as he overtook them, they looked him in the face with head erect.

"Messer Conan," said Berengar, "the roads have so often been beset, that we are very glad of your company."

"My protection, mayhap," said Conan grumpily.

He caught from Pierre a merry look. But Berengar answered gravely. "We masons travel to a certain extent under the protection of our commune. One who harmed us would be certain to hear of it if ever he went to Vézelay. Yet it is well to make a show of force, and with us the more the better."

Mollified, Conan rode on with them. The masons traveled light. A bundle on the saddle of each was all they had beside their cloaks, their quilted jerkins and leather hats, and their short-swords. Thus they were able to keep pace with Conan's more heavily loaded horse. With him a little in advance, as befitted his young dignity and his training, they rode forth between cultivated fields, toward the rolling woods.

But before they left the open spaces, near the wood's edge, they came upon a youth waiting by the roadside with a somewhat heavily burdened horse. Behind him Conan heard Pierre mutter in distaste, "That Jew!"

Conan had seen the young man spending the night at the castle, a light and frail figure, with a dark face delicate as a girl's, capable of varied expression all the way from caution through suspicion and alarm to terror, but without a trace of manly determination. Yet in the gentleness of the young man's nature there was something appealing, had Conan been prepared to see it. He knew only that here was one of the despised race, of almost his own age, yet timid as a rabbit. Conan expected the Jew to speak to him; yet he merely bowed low, and, letting the three pass by, mounted his own pack-laden horse and followed at a little distance.

Pierre grumbled: "He uses us as an escort. Something for nothing."

Conan had the same feeling, though with less irritation than scorn. But Berengar answered: "He follows his nature. It is the only way a Jew can thrive, to creep along behind the back of the strong."

Pierre complained, "These Jews are rich enough to hire swordsmen to protect them."

"There are rich Jews and there are poorer," replied Berengar. "But could any Jew trust his own swordsmen not to rob him? No law protects him. So the great Jews follow in the train of the nobles, the little Jews go along behind the knight. Do you not recognize this lad? He is Isaac, the son of Barzillai of Vézelay."

"What has he in that pack?" asked the unsatisfied Pierre. "It is heavy, or I misjudge."

"He carries the silks that his father will sell us, scarves for your mother and sister. Or maybe the furs and spices that the nobles must have. Pierre, these Jews serve us, but at a risk. I talked with him last night. With his merchandise the lad has come all the way from the sea, slipping along from castle to castle and from town to town under such escort as ours or no escort at all. He has been in danger all the way, and now is in the worst passage of all. Let the Sauval seize his pack, and his journey is for nothing. Should he lose his life, there would be no justice against his slayer. Barzillai can raise no outcry to reach the ears of the duke's judges. Grudge not the youth the little security that he feels, slinking along there like our shadow."

Pierre grumbled no more, and Conan felt satisfied to let the Jew follow along like a servingman. So they entered the forest belt which was to enfold much of their journey.

Conan was glad to be out of the sun. Dressed for fight, he wore on his head a cap of coiled rope, and over that one of leather. The iron cap of the knight, with its nosepiece — the best thing in that day — he had not been able to afford. On his body he wore linen next his skin, and over that soft leather. Next was his gambeson, a thickly quilted garment, made to lessen the shock of a blow on the mail, but hot on this warm day. Over all he wore his hauberk, a long shirt of linked rings, coming to the elbows and falling below the knees. Though it was slit up a little at front and back, it was a clumsy garment.

For some miles they traveled without catching sight of the pack train in front. Conan learned to like the masons as traveling companions, since they were alert, intelligent, but, in this dangerous country, not too talkative. In build they were different from him, for while he was fair and long of limb, they were dark, stocky, and slower of movement. Berengar, at sixty, was vigorous as an oak, ruddy as an apple. Pierre was slighter, ready of smile but slower of speech, always giving his grandfather the first word. Their dress was of good materials; their short jerkins were belted at the waist and allowed freedom of movement. But they wore no armor such as Conan's, and explained very simply their lack of defense.

"We are safer without armor than with it," said Berengar. "A man-at-arms challenges trouble by his very aspect. We ask for none and give none. Expecting peace, we commonly receive it."

"And if there is trouble?" asked Conan.

"We abide it," said Berengar simply.

Not so, thought Conan, with the young Jew. Isaac had been steadily following in their path, not so near that he seemed to claim equality, nor so far behind that he would appear, to other wayfarers, to be traveling by himself. In case of an affray the Jew's method would be plain: he would flee away among the glades of the forest, and make his way alone. He would not stay, not he, to defend those who had cast upon him the shadow of their protection. Conan saw this clearly. But with a touch of human warmth the young squire asked himself why the Jew should feel toward others anything but suspicion and fear.

V

Ralph the Robber

GLANCING BACK at the Jew, Conan saw that, as if to proclaim his peaceableness, he carried no weapon except the little knife at his belt which it was customary to use at meals. His backward look betrayed his habitual mistrust. Suddenly his nervous heels beat against the ribs of his horse, urging him onward. And Conan saw where there came, trotting upon their footsteps, a horseman with two footmen, one running at either stirrup. On coming into sight they put on speed, and rapidly closed in upon the travelers. As they did so, the Jew came nearer still, actually attempting to thrust his horse between those of the two masons. His olive face turned a yellow-gray. At this, Conan swung himself about in his saddle, and, with a supporting hand on the croup, studied these pursuers.

He saw upon a rangy horse a long and lean man, wearing on his head a leather cap, and on his body a quilted garment sewn with rusty iron disks. A knightly sword with a golden hilt, out of keeping with such shabbiness, jingled at his side; at his saddlebow hung a mace and a round buckler. His men seemed like himself, worn with exposure, hardened with campaigning. They were unarmored, tattered, and carried as weapons short-swords, with bows and arrows. Good runners both, they loped without evidence of fatigue.

The rusty leader paid no attention to Conan, but rode directly up beside the Jew, and, reaching out, seized his rein and jerked his horse to a halt. In a low, fierce tone he said to the young man: "You come with us now. We will take you by a shorter way." And with the utmost coolness turning the Jew's horse about, he gave it into the hands of his followers, who seized the bridle at either side and began to lead the beast away. In the rear, and calmly turning his back upon Conan and the masons, their leader followed.

But Conan's anger started at this bold defiance of his safe-conduct of the Jew. Irresolute at first, he glanced at the two masons. They had stopped, and were looking at each other. Their thought was plain: this was none of their affair. They were not indifferent, for plainly they were disturbed. But they were not ready to fight against these dangerous-looking ruffians.

Yet though Conan must act alone, he forgot the odds against him when he looked at Isaac. The youth did not utter a sound, but his glance was fixed on the squire with such terror and appeal that Conan's blood tingled. He felt a surge of heat within him; his hair

bristled along his scalp; and, with no thought, he took instant action.

He rode encumbered by the hawk at his wrist. Therefore he handed the bird to Berengar, and the old man took it, gloveless though he was. Then as Conan spurred toward the horseman, he dragged from its socket his heavy boar-spear, and shifted it in his hand to find its balance.

The horseman, stopping at the sound of hoofs,

turned his horse across the way. To the two with the Jew he waved his hand, urging them away. Then reaching for the handle of his sword, he confronted Conan. To the squire's surprise, he saw before him a face scarcely older than his own, wolfish and bold.

Conan saw that he could afford to give neither challenge nor warning. Before the sword was out, Conan laid his horse alongside the other's, head to tail. He said: "Stay just as you are. No further move. Tell me what you would do with the Jew." It pleased him that his voice came full and strong, without a hint of the anger that possessed him, nor yet of his doubt of the outcome.

He had snatched an advantage; for the horseman, with his right arm stretched across his body, away from Conan, had laid his whole side, where no plates were sewed upon his jerkin, open to the spear. He sat rigid, bared his teeth angrily, and snarled: "We have business with him. He is needed not far away."

"That is unlucky for one of us," answered Conan, "for I have business with him myself."

The man growled, "If you are a Sauval, leave him with us. You will gain by it without soiling your hands."

"Can I trust you?" asked Conan. "Where will you send my share?"

"Faithfully to the castle within the week. On the word of a free man."

Conan saw that the two with the Jew had stopped

some rods away, and that one was stringing his bow. Isaac, on hearing the bargaining, wrung his hands and cried aloud.

It vexed Conan that the Jew was not worthy of his care. But he said: "A free man, or an escaped serf? Now shall I try this spear on you, to see whether your hide is thicker than a boar's? Bid yonder villain drop his bow — " Conan added no "or — !" The threat was in the suddenly balanced and pointed spear.

Sullenly the order was given, and with equal sullenness obeyed.

"Now," said Conan, "make those fellows let the Jew go free."

Again the order was given. As the reluctant hand fell from the bridle, the Jew spurred his horse, and, forcing him through the bushes, circled around Conan and the masons to the road again. There he reined in and stayed, wide-eyed and trembling.

But the problem was not yet solved. "Now," said Conan, "your men are good runners, and maybe they could keep up with us without your horse. But if they are seen following, they will find only your dead body. Bid them stand here."

"I am not going with you!" cried the leader.

Conan answered: "You are going until I choose to set you free. Consider, friend, the weakness of your armor. Those little plates are not half so good as rings. A ring, if it caught the point of my spear, would hold it. But a plate merely turns the point onto the leather, which it pierces. I know that within fifty feet I could plant my spear in you where I please. So make no attempt to escape, but ride steadily. And do you, Jew, lead the way."

Isaac turned his horse eagerly, and behind him the others formed for the road. Conan now perceived that Pierre had been close to him, with his sword in his hand. The sight pleased Conan. "Escort this plunderer, Pierre. I will watch these two for a minute. And ride smartly."

The Jew needed no more words. Beating his horse, he urged it to a gallop. Next went Berengar, then the cursing robber with Pierre close at his flank with sword pointed at his ribs. Conan, confronting the two footmen, bore their curses indifferently until the others were well away. Then with a warning to the men not to follow, he wheeled and galloped after the rest. In a few rods he knew himself safe from an arrow, for no shaft could fly far among the low-hanging branches. Overtaking the rest, he took Pierre's place. Just in the rear of the robber, Conan kept his station for a few miles.

"You are no Sauval," said the man at length. "Else you would have shared with us."

Conan replied, "Why should any man share that which he can keep to himself?"

"The Sauval know that robbers must live. Therefore, many have settled near them. I mean to establish myself on their border, to get their pickings. Who are you, not to understand that I can be of use at times?"

"Never mind that," answered Conan, inclined to

admire the man's effrontery even while he baffled it.
"But tell me your name, so that if ever I need you I
can call upon you."

"I have left behind me in the south," replied the
fellow, "a name that I mean to forget. Here I shall
call myself Red Ralph, which will do well enough
till I get me a fief."

"A fief!" exclaimed Conan. "That is aiming high!"

"Not for me. The Sauval are growing, and they
yet may need vassals of their own."

Conan sneered; later he saw too much truth in
the idea, and was angry at it. But now he answered:
"Well, Ralph, red is your hair, and I misdoubt that
by now your hands too would have been red, had I
not prevented. I would slay you now, had I not after
a fashion promised you freedom. You are a bold
knave, to work so near to Baron Roger, who shall be
warned of you." A little puzzled, Conan wondered
how safely he could be rid of the man, and saw with
relief that the fellow's horse, as lean as his master,
showed signs of fatigue. "Lest I be tempted to forget
that I would set you free, you shall leave me now."
He called to the others to halt, and summoned the
Jew to his side. Then Conan said, "Ralph, I question
whether you came honestly by that sword with the
golden hilt."

"It is mine by inheritance!" cried the robber. In
spite of Conan's spear, he showed his anger. "Now
by God, sir squire, you shall not take it from me!"

Conan answered: "Now by Saint Michael, who is

only an archangel but good enough for me, you shall part from the sword here and now. Unbuckle the belt, and hand the sword over to the Jew."

The hardy rascal folded his arms. "You shall kill me before I give the weapon of my fathers to a heathen."

"As you do not deserve to wear a knight's sword," said Conan sternly, "you shall not carry it away. You, Isaac, unbuckle this fellow's belt and take it from him, sword and all."

It was a study of hate and fear to see the angry robber stiffly erect, his eye now upon Conan and his spear, now upon the frightened Jew who bent from his saddle to unarm him. Rumbled threats rolled from the lips of the marauder, but he made no move. Isaac trembled so that his delicate fingers, made for skill, lost their deftness, and he fumbled long at the buckle before the strap fell apart and he held the sword in his hands.

Meanwhile, Conan studied the face before him. Still young and not ill-looking, intelligent, and as yet not wholly evil, the robber's visage was already deeply marked, not merely by the weather, but by the struggles of the mind. The brow was habitually knit, the thin lips were firm and down-drawn. "A bold man are you," said Conan, "to try to take this Jew away from under my hand."

"It was then or never," answered Ralph. "I could not know that you, not yet a knight, would be so ready of your hands. — But a bolder man are you, messer squire, to take my sword and give it to this Jew while I still live. What will he do with it?"

"Why," answered Conan lightly, "there is a market for such trinkets, is there not, Isaac?"

Ralph broke out fiercely, "By every devil that this Jew serves, if he sell my sword he shall pay with his life, and you too, noble as you are, though I follow you long."

"Nay," said Conan wondering, "you speak like a noble yourself. Is the sword really yours, then?"

"Noble I am," answered Ralph, still furiously. "That was my grandfather's knightly sword, and with it I have avenged my father's wrongs and my own. I will yet get it back. For I can get a knife to cut the heart out of this Jew, and can follow the sword wherever it goes."

"Isaac," asked Conan, "will you take the sword on these terms?"

"Oh, my lord!" cried the frightened Jew. "I would not carry it a mile."

"Fasten it to my saddle, then," directed Conan. "Ralph, the sword shall be mine." This he said with a touch of pride, for the sword was precious and wonderful, but also with conscious defiance of a fate which might result from holding such a weapon.

The fury left the young robber's glance, and Conan perceived in him the rare ability to master his passion as he looked at the subject in a different light. "Then two strong men will someday meet," Ralph said fearlessly, "for be sure that I will ask it at your hands. Yet till then keep it as having won it of me fairly: I thought no one would take the Jew from me, once I had him in my grip. Keep the sword, then, as too fine for me just now, since it has made me much trouble already, with its golden hilt. But since I shall surely follow it, tell me your name."

"I am Conan of the Prigny."

"The Prigny? I know not the name."

" 'Tis known," replied Conan simply. "Go your way, Ralph; and if you think of me hardly, remember that I held your life at the point of my spear."

"And shall I thank you for not taking it?" snarled Ralph in sudden harshness. He turned his horse, and, roughly spurring the jaded beast, rode back upon the track.

Conan turned to his companions. The Jew was fawning, Pierre smiling, Berengar frowning. The old man handed back the falcon which, as it fretted on the unaccustomed wrist, had scratched him deep. "Messer Conan," he said grimly, "you should have slain the robber while you could. Better for the countryside, better for yourself."

Conan made the simple avowal: "In cold blood, Berengar, I could not do it. Once he was in my power, I had to spare him. What do you know of him?"

"Nothing. He is a new wolf come to make his lair here."

"I know this," said Isaac. "Two days ago he marked me on the road, and but for my company he would have seized me then. Yesterday, when I saw him again, I feared he was following me. Last night he must have slept outside Sir Roger's castle, and watched for me today. It was his last chance, for tonight I should be at home in Vézelay."

"You have yet to make it," said Berengar, still grim.

"Isaac," asked Conan, "you have traveled from the south sea always thus in peril of your life?"

"Sometimes in company, my lord, but often not."

"By heaven, you are braver than that robber!"

"Not all are quite evil," replied Isaac. "They rob, but do not slay."

"That red man," said Berengar, "would have left you under a bush with your throat cut. You owe your life to the young squire."

Isaac would have thanked Conan again, but his manner was servile, and Conan waved him into silence. Berengar spoke again. "Messer Conan, time passes. Had we not best be on our way?"

It was sensible. Turning to the road, they spurred their horses on.

VI

A Bit of Folly

THE ROAD passed beyond Sir Roger's boundary and soon became unfamiliar to Conan, who
in years had not traversed it. The region is still called
the Morvan; even today it is sparsely inhabited, with
few towns above the size of hamlets. In that day
villages were fewer still, and the travelers on their
journey rarely saw a human face. The district is not
mountainous, but steeply rugged and unfriendly.

By pushing hard, the little group of four caught
sight of the rear of the company of masons and
followed along behind them, never really in their
company, for they too were traveling fast. Hours
passed, and the sun was already low when Conan
thought he recognized a landmark.

"Is not this," he asked, "part of the lands of the
Red Keep?"

"It is," replied Berengar. "We are on the domain
of the Lady Anne, and the castle itself is not far in
front. Your own Prigny will then be but a few hours
farther on. What will you do, Messer Conan: go on

to your home, or turn with us to Vézelay to see for yourself some things which may concern you?"

"I notice," said the squire, "that you and the baron make the same suggestion to me. Did you discuss it between you?"

"We did," replied Berengar frankly. "We men of Vézelay see that the abbot may call in the Sauval to help suppress us. Here would be Baron Odo's opportunity, for he would bargain for the Red Keep. If he holds that, he has driven a wedge between Prigny and Fessart, and can keep them from aiding each other. Leaving Sir Roger in peace, Odo would go on wearing the Prigny down, till he would not only have command of their lands but would be within striking distance of two trade routes, from which he could collect rich tolls to increase the cost of everything to us in Vézelay. All our people understand that."

Conan was stirred by Berengar's use of Anne's own phrase, wearing the Prigny down. "But if my brother is warned of what is planned," he asked, "is not that enough? Why go to Vézelay?"

"A wise man," explained Berengar, "studies his enemies when they are off guard. See for yourself this abbot who wishes to be a little king. Learn for yourself what the Sauval are like, yourself unknown."

"Myself unknown!" cried Conan, displeased. "And why?"

"Because if you told your name, designs would be concealed, and yourself perhaps flattered and deceived. — Do not be angered," for Conan drew himself up. "Churchmen are deep politicians. And as to making yourself known to the Sauval, who so often come and go — why, there are dark corners in the streets where swordsmen may lurk at night, ready to stab in the back."

"It would be safer, then," said Conan, "to ride directly home from the Red Keep."

"Not so," replied Berengar. "Much of the way borders the land of the Sauval, on roads that are commonly watched. Be suspected, and — there has not been a mile in all the road we have traveled today where a man could not be disposed of unseen, and his body hidden."

As Conan remembered Ralph and the Jew, he felt his flesh creep. Yet (and this was not at all what Berengar expected) the young man felt also that his pride was challenged. Still doubtful of his own courage, not yet quite able to distinguish between bravery and recklessness, he was glad of an interruption that gave him an opportunity to express himself.

All day the falcon had fretted on his wrist, for the motion of riding had roused it to expect hunting. Most of the time Conan had kept it hooded to still its complaints; but for the last half hour it had ridden with its eyes free. Now it suddenly straightened itself, ruffled its neck, and shook its wings.

In that region where once had been good farms, there was now much growth of shrubbery and a multiplication of game. A covey of small birds rose be-

fore the horses; and the falcon, though bound to
Conan's wrist, struggled to pursue them.

"Ha, good bird!" said its master. "It is hard to see
the game and not strike it."

"Keep the bird still," muttered Berengar, though
under his breath. "This is no time for sport."

The small birds settled, but a better prey, a partridge, came flying low. The falcon flapped again,
and screamed. Conan's blood responded, and he prepared to loose the bird. "One good flight!" he cried.

"Not here!" answered Berengar. "Not now!"

But Conan tossed the falcon high. Catching the impetus, the clever bird darted for the prey. The partridge, warned by the falcon's scream, wheeled quicker than the hawk, and dived into a copse for safety. Above the tangle of low treetops the falcon hovered, voicing its anger. Conan's whistle and the cast of his lure were ignored. The bird soared in ascending circles, plainly looking for prey.

Berengar muttered to Pierre: "These noble youths! They have no understanding."

Pierre, however, was likewise intent on the bird, and when it suddenly poised, gave a halloo. Something had caught its eye; it sailed away from the watching group.

"There!" said Conan. "In a minute it will be satisfied. Go on your way while I bring it in. I will meet you at the Red Keep."

Berengar and Pierre turned on the path of the pack train, which was already out of sight. "It is useless to tell him to abandon the bird," grumbled the old mason. "A hawk is as valuable as a horse, and the rules of the chase are as the laws of the church to these hunting-men."

Conan, galloping through the brush with his eyes on the bird, saw it dart away, then swoop, strike, and evidently miss. For a few moments the master, riding hard, lost sight of the falcon. Then it rose into view, screaming loudly, hovered while Conan's trained ear caught the crying of frightened birds, then stooped

like a stone and disappeared. There was silence among
the birds, and Conan, laughing, knew that his hawk
had its prey. He galloped in search of it.

When he came to a little clearing, and pausing,
whistled, a little movement in a tree caught his eye.
Halfway up an old and dying oak, on a stubbed
limb, the falcon sat; tearing its prey. To Conan's whistle and call it paid no heed, but with a grumbling in
its throat continued to send down floating feathers,
or sank its beak into the body of the bird and glared
above it. Conan threw up the lure, but the busy
falcon appeared not even to see it.

The bird was young, and though Conan had
thought it fully trained he knew too well the nature
of hawks not to recognize an emergency. If he were
not to expect from it such fits of rebellion, he must
at once recover it. But to do so was not simple.
Often he had climbed a tree for a falcon, but then
he had been in his hunting clothes, lightly dressed.
Now he was encumbered with his armor, and time
pressed. But Berengar was right: Conan had no
thought of abandoning the bird, for it was valuable,
he had put much time into its training, and his pride
was roused by its willfulness.

Leaping from his horse, he unbuckled his sword
belt and hung the weapon at his saddle. Over his
head he pulled his hauberk, and threw it on the
beast's back. The gambeson followed. Then leading
the horse under the tree, Conan clambered on its
back, poised himself erect for a moment, then sprang

for a lower branch. Catching it, he swung himself up till he gained a foothold. Some twenty feet above him the hawk still sat. Conan climbed carefully nearer, fearful lest it fly away. But the falcon was still absorbed in tearing its prey. With relief Conan laid his hand upon it, slipped the hood over its eyes, and secured the legs once more.

And then, as he looked down, he shouted in anger and command. From below the tree his horse was moving away, on its back a ragged, crouched figure, hammering with its heels. At Conan's shout a bearded, sneering face looked up in mingled fear and triumph. The horse broke into a gallop. Conan shouted again. The face turned away; an impudent hand waved. In a moment the steed and its scarecrow rider were out of sight among bushes, and Conan could hear only the thudding of hoofs. He stood there furious, helpless, the victim of some petty outlaw.

Blaming the thief, the falcon, but not yet himself, he began to descend. Had any of the branches been weak enough to be broken off, he would have tied the bird to it by the leash, and dropped them both together, as he had done various times before. But there was no branch suitable for the purpose, and he clambered down hurriedly. The bird encumbered him; yet he reached the lowest branch and was about to leap to the ground when he felt — again to his anger and disgust — the branch give way beneath him.

His leap was hurried and awkward, as he held one hand, with the bird, above him. He landed unbalanced, plunged, and fell headlong. With relief he knew that he had injured neither bone, joint, nor muscle. But either some fallen stick or the struggling bird had torn his forehead, and he rose with blood trickling down into his eyes. It was some minutes before, with plucked leaves, he could stanch the blood and feel it ceasing to come. And standing helpless, his hawk on his wrist, looking along the track made by his departing horse, he knew that neither thief nor bird was at fault, but his own heedless self.

On his head he had only his cap of coiled rope, on his wrist his angry falcon, on his body the suit of soft leather that would not turn a knife. He clenched his empty right hand as he saw that the sun was descending low. Accustomed since childhood never to stir without weapon at his side, he felt impotent as never before. He must have at least a cudgel. And he began to look for something which, with his bare hands, he could make into a club.

A glitter in the grass — ah! Lying where it had fallen from his horse was the sword of Ralph, the outlaw. In a moment Conan snatched it up, and, joying in its weight, girded it to himself. Then feeling that he had some protection, he loped on his own backward track.

He was lightly dressed, the afternoon was growing cool, and, though the bird on his wrist encumbered him, he made good progress. Soon he was back at the narrow forest way. Before long he saw, as he followed the masons, the stony knoll from which, so long ago, he had seen the Red Keep afire. He caught but a single glimpse of the castle now, standing without sign of life. He quickened his pace, and increased it again when, after a half mile, he saw before him the edge of the forest and the open space beyond. So eager was he to overtake his companions that he ran without caution, and suddenly found himself beyond the shelter of the trees, on level grass. And there, close by, Berengar and Pierre sat on their horses, confronting a dozen men who, two of them on horseback and the rest on foot, were in position to prevent either advance or retreat.

Of the pack train of masons there was no sign; they had gone on their way unseen. But a little to one side was Isaac, his bridle held by a footman, evidently detained while the others examined the two masons. The young Jew was pale but outwardly calm; he knew no other method than ready submission.

Had Conan been wise, he would instantly have fled. But he had never in his life run away from anything. Instinctively he confronted every emergency with the combined strength of hand and weapon — too seldom with his mind — and now it did not occur to him even to pause. Following his impulse, he advanced toward the masons, prepared to help them, never even in doubt.

He felt a warning of danger when he recognized the nearer horseman, known by description far and

wide. He was short and crooked, sitting cramped on
his horse, wearing defensive armor and a dagger, but
carrying neither spear nor shield, which were too
heavy for him. There hung at his saddlebow a little
light battle-ax, for most men a one-handed weapon,
but fitted with a double handle for his use. A cripple
and weak, he was gray-haired, though scarcely forty,
with unyouthful face heavily lined. Odo of Sauval!

Behind him loomed his gigantic brother, Aymar,
in hauberk and steel cap, and heavily armed. Conan
slowed his step.

Though intent upon questioning the masons, Odo's
sharp eye measured Conan, and a movement of his
hand, pointing him out, brought about a prompt shifting of the group. Two men moved to hem Conan in,
so that when he reached Pierre's side, these men
were in position to cut off his retreat. It was a re-
markable example of discipline, the men obeying the
slightest move of Odo's finger, a proof of ascendancy
in character alone. Not Aymar, but Odo, was the
leader of the Sauval.

As Conan came into the line of Pierre's vision,
the young mason cast a single glance at him, and
not knowing him, turned away again. Conan failed
to remark this, for his eye was on Odo, and his heart
had quickened its beating.

In a quiet voice Odo spoke to Berengar. To those
who had heard true tales of him, this quiet manner
was terrifying, so harsh were the judgments which

he had been known to utter after the mildest questioning.

But though he was well known to them by reputation and by sight, neither of the masons betrayed any fear. They sat their horses in quiet confidence that the protection of their commune, which they had already invoked, would extend to both them and their property, against even this leader who levied heavy tolls.

"Building a chapel for Baron Roger of Fessart?" said Odo. "What of the money that he must have paid you?"

"Some was paid in advance," replied Berengar. "The rest is in my purse, eight pounds Burgundian, made up of various coins, a golden chain, and a pair of rings."

"And you have paid no toll today?"

"None. We passed by no castle, nor met anyone."

"But I find you crossing my land."

Berengar showed surprise. "We are on the fief of the Lady Anne d'Arcy, who gave me her permission to pass."

Odo smiled dryly. "She is unaware that I have taken this place under my protection since she seems to have abandoned it. — Now if I let you pass, you masons, will not a little friendly present from you to me seem right?"

"Quite right and reasonable," returned Berengar with something of the same dryness, "if upon your

next entry into Vézelay you bestow an equal present
upon the guild of masons."

A flash came into Odo's eye: he was unaccustomed to such retort. But he merely said: "That is to
be considered. And if I ask no gift, it is understood
that friendship subsists between me and your guild?"

Again Berengar was surprised. "Friendly feelings, my lord."

"But this Jew," asked Odo, still mildly. "Your commune has no claim on him?"

The shrewd question met the case, for no Jew was member of a commune. Berengar acknowledged this. "Yet, my lord baron," he said manfully, "the commune will not look kindly upon new tolls where never were any before, nor an interruption of free travel so near our boundary."

"He is only a Jew," said Odo lightly, "and he shall merely give me the choice of his goods. — Tell the commune," he went on, "that its members may come and go as freely as ever." His eye still fixed on Berengar, he seemed to meditate upon his own words, as reviewing his exact meaning. He had not definitely bound himself. Then Odo suddenly tossed his head as dismissing the subject, and Conan found the eyes of the Sauval fixed on him. The glance was hard as steel.

VII

The Trap of the Dark Passage

ODO ASKED: "You ragged villein, bloody of face, whence do you come, striding so freely?" His tone threatened no violence, but his description angered Conan.

It was not till he saw Pierre again studying him without recognition that Conan began to understand the figure he cut. He had torn a sleeve of his jerkin when he fell, his cap was askew, his hair awry. The blood from the cut on his forehead had been smeared on his temple and cheek, and he had failed to wipe it all off. With such looks, his confident manner was quite out of keeping, and from the tall Sauval came a loud laugh.

"With a hawk on his wrist and a knight's sword," he barked. "And yet a scarecrow! You fellow, where have you stolen those things?"

Odo turned and looked at his brother. "Aymar, did I give the word to you?"

Aymar covered confusion with a louder laugh. "Only look at the fellow!" But he said no more.

Conan saw Pierre's effort at recognition suddenly

succeed. But the young mason closed his lips tightly and turned his head away. It was a warning — to be silent, not to betray himself. Conan saw his meaning.

"Is the fellow another of your company, old man?" asked Odo lightly. But Berengar himself had not recognized the new figure, and Odo, expecting no answer, went on. "Fellow, give over that falcon. He is not for such as you, and I will relieve you of the guilt of stealing him."

"And give here the sword," blurted Aymar, greedily.

Afterward, Conan perceived the opportunity to submit and deceive, but not now. His falcon and his sword? His anger boiled. He drew back, and looking Odo in the eye, unhooded the bird and disentangled the leash from his wrist. Rather than give up the bird he prepared to let it fly free. To Pierre's quick gesture of appeal he paid no heed.

"Well, then," said Odo indifferently, and pointed with his finger to the two retainers who stood near. "Take him, you two." He leaned upon the pommel of his saddle, and with cruelty in his eye, prepared to enjoy what he should see.

The two retainers closed confidently in upon Conan, coming together from the right. Insulted that such fellows should offer to lay hand upon him, he turned upon them with such fury that the nearer stopped, irresolute. The second sprang, only to be felled by a backhand blow.

Odo pointed a finger at the daunted man. "That coward," he said in a voice of ice, "shall hang. Aymar, take this hawking vagabond and cut his throat."

Conan had seen feudal justice meted out by Baron Roger, and was used to summary and harsh treatment. But this was murder. His anger chilling into horror, he stepped backward, holding up his hand. "Wait!" he cried.

But Odo smiled. "A little late," he said.

And the burly Aymar spurred forward, at the same time waving on his men. "Careful of the bird!" he warned. The falcon's life was more valuable than the man's. Seeing that he must fight, and desperately, Conan summoned his courage.

As Aymar spurred at him, intending to bowl him over with the shoulder of his horse, Conan stepped aside. With trained skill he launched the bird square in the face of the baron; then, kneeling, he let man and steed pass by. With the next action he clutched his sword. It rattled from its sheath with a balance and weight that gave him joy, and with the swing of his drawing he lashed backward at the horse's leg in the hope of hamstringing it. He missed, yet the point nicked the leg, and Conan heard the beast begin to plunge and kick as it carried its rider on. Overhead he heard the scream of the liberated falcon. With Aymar, for the moment, out of the way behind him, he looked for enemies in front.

An attack from his left was blocked by the masons on their horses. In front of Odo two retainers promptly placed themselves, as if trained to protect him from attack. But other footmen closed in; even the man who held Isaac's horse dropped the bridle and rushed forward with drawn weapon. Wearing no armor, Conan felt that the odds against him were overpowering. He hesitated, in a moment's doubt and fear.

Then Pierre, snatching out his own sword, urged his horse a little forward, blocking off a pair of footmen. "Back!" he cried. "Safe conduct! Baron Odo, I appeal to you!"

But Odo, with a little lifting of the lip, sneered and was silent.

Behind him Conan heard Aymar cursing and struggling with his horse. His only chance was now. Two men were coming from his front; and from the right the coward, hoping to redeem himself, with hissing breath was rushing in. Brandishing his sword, and shouting, Conan took one stride forward. It was a feint. As the two stopped and raised their shields, Conan turned to his right and struck. The sword hand of the coward leaped from the wrist; the point of Conan's blade struck in the fellow's temple, and he fell. The man had at least saved himself from Odo's sentence. Through the gap thus opened in his attackers, Conan stepped to momentary safety.

Aymar was between him and his best protection, the woods. Yet Isaac was not far away, and between them the man who had guarded the Jew. As this fellow dashed at him, Conan gave him his point in

the throat, a trick long practiced and now serviceable, for the common use of the sword being to
slash, the man was not prepared. Coughing out his
life, he sprawled at Conan's feet, and the squire
stepped over him toward Isaac. He thought to run
by Isaac's stirrup to safety. But the Jew had already
flogged his horse to speed. Though the eyes of the
two met, and Conan saw that Isaac knew him, in
the Jew's glance was only terror. He galloped away,
not to be overtaken. Conan felt a bitter contempt.
This was the lad that he had saved!

Yet because of that rescue, Conan now had the
outlaw's sword in his hand. It was a king's weapon,
heavy but well-balanced, long, sharp. It gave him
confidence. As he saw that Aymar, turning his horse,
was still able to cut him off from the woods, he
swung about in flight.

Least encumbered of all who were there, he raced
ahead of the shouting men, toward the castle. This
stood on a little peninsula between two ravines that
led down into a gorge where no horse could catch
him, nor footman either. If he could escape by either
side of the castle — ! For a few moments he strained
for speed, until he saw that the distance was too far.
Hearing at his left a pounding of hoofs, he looked
and saw that Odo, still with his two attendants, was
galloping to cut him off on that side; then glancing
to his right he saw that Aymar, at last at full speed,
was able to cut him off on his other side. Pierre, still
shouting and pleading, was riding not far from Ay-

mar, but not offering to use his drawn sword. Conan
feared that he was going to be herded into the castle, as into a trap.

Directly behind him were the remaining footmen,
and he took one look at them. They were coming
straight at him, all but one, who had paused to bend
a bow. Trap or not, it was the castle or nothing, and
he bent to his run.

But of the archer he had a wholesome fear, for he
knew how dangerous was the bow. Trying to guess
the moment for dodging, he suddenly swerved to
one side. A swish in the air told him that his trick
had succeeded. His swerving brought him toward
the edge of the moat, and for a moment he thought
of leaping into it. But he dared not take the jump
blindly. Hearing behind him the increasing thunder
of hoofs, he risked one more look.

It was well that he did so. Scarcely twenty yards
away Aymar was coming, and standing in his stirrups, was just about to throw a javelin. The cast was
perfect. The weapon flew true and swift, and in the

effort to dodge it Conan slipped and fell. The javelin seemed to brush his clothes as it flew past.

Roaring, Aymar snatched his sword from his side, and spurred at Conan as if he would override him in his passion, whatever the consequence to himself. Then Pierre, who had been riding step for step with the knight, deliberately pulled rein and swerved into him. Whatever had been Aymar's intention, the mason spoiled it. Barely missing the prostrate figure, the two horses toppled on the edge of the moat, then fell into it together. Conan, scrambling to his feet, peered over the edge.

The moat of the castle led right and left away from the castle gate into the two ravines. It could not hold water, but springs kept it always wet. Conan saw, some six feet below him, a depth of shining mud, out of which showed the tops of jagged stones. In the mud both horses lay sprawling. Aymar's, lying still, was evidently hurt. Pierre's horse was struggling violently, trying to regain its feet.

Bellows of fury came from Aymar. He had fallen clear of his steed, and floundering in the mud, was endeavoring to rise. His sword was still in his hand; his eyes, glaring at Pierre, showed that he would deal with him as soon as he was on his feet. Conan saw that the mason was entangled, unable also to find firm bottom in the mud. He leaped down, and wading in the edge of the mud, took Pierre's hand and drew him to firm footing. A single moment Conan hesitated then, wishing to attack Aymar. But the baron was at last on his feet, and from the level above were plainly heard the shouts of the approaching footmen. Crying "Follow!" Conan scrambled up to the level, and running to the drawbridge, crossed into the castle. Once in the courtyard he turned sharply to one side and drew Pierre with him, out of the reach of arrows.

"Well done, Pierre," he said. "You saved me. But now we are in for it."

Pierre, breathing hard, took a fresh grip of his sword. "What now?" he asked. "Do you know this castle?"

Conan looked about him to refresh his memory of the few hours he had spent in the castle five years ago. The plan of the place was a blunt triangle, and they had entered it between the two low towers that formed the stubbed point. Now they were in the grass-grown courtyard, which widened as it spread away from them. At the farther corners were slender towers capped with pointed roofs; but overtopping them, and occupying most of the farther side, was the great keep, square, massive, narrow-windowed, with its flat top guarded by battlements. But for its air of desertion, the castle seemed unchanged and as strong as ever. But Conan knew that behind and above him the right-hand gate tower had crashed down into the moat, blocking off from the rest of the ditch that part from which he had just escaped. He had a thought of fleeing over this pile of debris; but a glance showed him that the lowest remaining part of the tower was too high above the courtyard to be climbed.

He could escape from a window — if he could find one big enough to let him pass, and if he had a rope. He could barricade a door or passage — if anywhere in the whole castle remained a single stick of wood or piece of furniture. Little by little, he had been told, the castle had been stripped of fittings. Doors, shutters, even the two great gates that once had closed the entrance, all had been carried off. Only the portcullis, the heavy wooden grating shod with iron and walled up in its grooves, remained in place, propped up above a man's height. He could remove the prop and let it fall — and he went to the entrance to see if he had time. But the thought had come too late. Just stepping on the drawbridge was the archer, backed by swordsmen, and behind them came Aymar, muddy, dripping, bellowing his fury.

Conan drew back and faced Pierre. His mouth went dry; his knees became weak. He said thickly, "This is not knightly war: it is murder."

Pierre said only, "War is always murder."

Conan's reluctant breath came more deeply; then as he wondered in which corner he should be hunted down, his anger once more burned. "Into the donjon!" he directed. "But stick together!"

They darted across the courtyard and into the entrance of the keep. The tales had been correct, for the door was gone. The lower story was a great vaulted cellar, around the pillars of which, for a little while, they could flee and fight, but hopelessly. "Upstairs!" commanded Conan, and they ran up a stairway, into the great hall.

Here again a vaulted ceiling echoed their tread. The place was entirely bare. No ragged hanging dangled on the wall; there was no broken parchment in the windows. But from the court below came the trampling of their pursuers. With a cry, Pierre ran to a window on the opposite side and leaned out. He turned back with frowning face. Conan knew what he had seen: far below, in the ravine, tumbled rocks.

"We must go higher," said Conan. "And still the stairs are too wide for defense."

The upper story showed a corner turret, with its stairs leading to the roof. Pierre pointed, with a question, and Conan remembered that five years ago those stairs had been barricaded, with stout men behind to defend themselves. But without a barricade there was little chance for unarmored men. He shook his head.

"The chambers, then?" asked Pierre.

But each of the rooms was doorless and bare. A minute or two of fighting, and the end would be sure. Conan said, "No."

"What then?" demanded Pierre, desperate.

Of the remaining place Conan thought with horror. He saw the mouth of the black passage; he remembered the corpses brought from it one by one. And now the trap for the dead baron was to be the trap for himself! Well, he would die fighting!

Below, in the banqueting hall, they heard the shouts of the pursuers.

"In here," said Conan. They entered the passage which, when once the corner had been turned, seemed completely dark. But presently, growing accustomed to that lack of light, they perceived that light yet filtered in from both ends, leaving the place heavily dusk. "Here we will wait," said Conan, "back to back, so. This is the narrowest place of all: they can come at us only one by one. And yet if we crouched by the wall, one walking erect and feeling his way might miss us. If they send but one in and he passes us they will think we are not here."

"But if we are found?"

"Then fight! Keep low. Strike upward. If we can overcome enough of them, we may make our way out again. But if I fall, wait not for me."

"Nor you for me," replied the young mason. "How strange it is I am not afraid of death!"

"I am afraid," said Conan simply. "Hist! They are coming up the stairs."

The Sauval came with little rushes, a few steps at a time, with pauses for watching and for listening. Then one said, "Now!" and they rushed once more, and stood still in the outer passage. The two hidden men could hear their breathing.

Aymar's harsh voice said, "You three, try those stairs to the roof."

Feet padded swiftly up the stairs and down again,

with but the slightest pause for inspection. "Baron, the roof is empty."

"These rooms next," said Aymar. "But they will be empty, too. I know where these men are."

The rooms were searched, with shuffling and with sudden cries of "Ha!" Evidently Aymar stood still in the same place, for they reported to him, "Empty!"

Aymar spoke, and the fugitives knew that he meant them to hear. "They are in that passage, and we have them surely. You three hold that end, and enter when I enter this. Raoul, follow me. Are you ready?"

Conan whispered: "He is coming from my end, and will come quickest. If he passes me, I will strike his man, and we can rush out to the stairs. If he and I fight, defend my back. Now!"

Footsteps at either end of the passage; the dim light was cut off; iron clanked. Aymar's voice echoed right there in the vault. "Are you ready?"

"Yes," came a gruff answer, with an oath.

"Forward, then!"

Shuffling began.

Conan and Pierre were each upon one knee, ready to spring up, but were close pressed against one wall, with shoulders turned flat against it. Their heads were bent, to allow a man's groping hands to pass over them. Conan gripped his sword, but knew that it was too long for fighting in that narrow space.

Aymar was moving more quickly than his men. Sensing their reluctance, he snarled: "Come on! They have no armor." His sword rattled against the walls as he strode freely onward. He was passing Conan when, stumbling a little, he lurched and brushed him. Instantly, with a roar, he turned to strike. The sword rasped sparks along the roof, down the wall, but the blow was futile.

Conan made one quick thrust upward, felt it turned by the mail, and dropped his weapon. He sprang; his hands sought and found the baron's throat, within the mail, above the gambeson. When his thumbs met on the throat, and his fingers gripped the hairy nape, he squeezed, and clung.

Aymar hammered with the pommel of his sword. But Conan, his head guarded by his rope cap and his hunched shoulders, took no harm, though the strokes were cruel. Worrying his hands home, he took the hammering grimly. Then Aymar dropped his weapon, lifted Conan from the floor, and braced against one wall, hurled himself and Conan against the other, trying to break the grip.

Conan took the shock and kept his hold. For a moment more he yielded, until he himself was braced. He bit his inner lip clean through, and with the power of fury dashed himself and Aymar forward. Aymar's head struck the opposite wall; still braced, Conan thrust onward with all force, to finish that throttling. He felt that he could hold himself thus against any force that Aymar could exert.

But to his amazement, the very wall against which he was pressing gave way, slowly, so that Aymar's body yielded almost beyond his reach. Conan looked up. Fresh light invaded the passage; and in the opening of the apparently solid wall he saw his adversary's head lolling backward. Aymar was senseless.

Conan released the Sauval, whose body crumpled to the floor. He groped, and snatched up a sword, to be ready for the next attack. Instead, he heard the running of men in full flight.

Even beside him there was no struggle. A fallen man was groaning, and someone was panting heavily. "Pierre!" cried Conan in alarm.

"Finished one, I think," replied the mason. "Yes," for the groaning stopped with a gasp. Then evidently Pierre faced about. "What? The wall has opened!"

"I cannot understand it," said Conan. "A miracle."

"I understand it well. Messer Conan, here is our salvation. Slip through, and replace the block."

"Go first," directed Conan. From its weight he knew that the sword which he held was Aymar's, and putting his foot on the middle of the blade, he snapped it. Feeling farther, he found his own, then wormed his way through the opening.

Conan found himself in a passage narrower than the other, lighter, but lower, for his head brushed the roof. He leaned back into the larger passage and gave one look at the huddled form of his antagonist. "Is he dead?" asked Pierre. "Give him one thrust." But not yet hardened to slaying, Conan could not do it. He knew only that Aymar, still unconscious, could not know the method of this escape. And he heard the war cries of men encouraging each other to return. He drew back his head. "How do we close this?"

Pierre showed him the great stone which, pivoting, had given them their entrance. "Simply swing it back." It was not so simple, for when nearly in place, it resisted them. Pierre felt along its edges. "Clever! It is beveled and grooved. Now lift, and push again."

They lifted as they pushed, and the stone slipped over the obstruction, into place. Pierre stood admiring. "See, here are handgrips if we wish to open it again. You must have been pushing upward before. The miracle was, Messer Conan, that you pushed right there."

"Quiet!" warned Conan. "The men are coming back."

Muffled through the wall, they heard tramplings, calling, cries of astonishment. With his ear to the crack, Pierre listened till the sounds died away. "They have dragged our two to the light. Now to get away."

"But how?" asked Conan. "Is there a passageway out?"

"Doubtless," answered Pierre. "Let us find it."

"Why not stay till they have gone?"

Pierre shook his head. "My grandfather will wait till he has news of me. With these men angered, his life will not be safe. We must get out quickly."

VIII

Escape

THE LIGHT which entered the passageway in which Conan and the mason stood, came from a narrow slit in the stones. This showed only sky. Stone walls were close on three sides; at the fourth there was blackness. Toward this, Pierre confidently walked. As he melted into it, Conan followed, till the dim light was gone. Then Pierre said, "Steps!" and in another moment Conan was feeling his way down a winding stair. Turn after turn he followed, wondering how far down this would lead, until Pierre gave the word to halt. Another dim light entered below, and peering down, Conan saw the mason's face pressed to a little loophole.

"Come down," Pierre said presently, "and see for yourself."

The slit gave no width of vision whatever; but it so happened that it revealed what Pierre wanted. In the section of the view thus opened, Conan saw first the towers of the gate, one broken down, the other still with its conical roof. Beyond was the field over which he had raced ahead of the Sauval. On the

farther edge of this was Berengar, waiting on his horse, and peering anxiously under his hand at the castle. Considerably nearer was Odo, also mounted, but alone. He had sent his guards into the castle. In the crookback's face was no such anxiety as Berengar's attitude expressed, but rather confident expectation.

"Let me only get my hand on you!" growled Conan.

Again he followed Pierre down. The stairs came to a passage which led level for awhile, perhaps along a side of the keep. Then Pierre warned him of stairs again. This time they seemed interminable, and the footing more rough than before, while more than once Conan's cap struck against some stone of the roof. At last, always in pitch darkness, a sloping passage led downward from the stairs' end. Its floor became slippery, and putting up his hand, Conan found that the roof was dripping.

"Under the moat," said Pierre simply, but always leading on. Soon the passage, leading upward, became dry. "Now," he said, "we are well away from the castle."

"Will this take us far?" asked Conan. "I have heard that such passages sometimes run for a mile."

Pierre, stopping, halted Conan with his hand. "We masons think such stories merely legends. The Lady Anne's father must have been trapped because he was seeking this escape, but was followed too close. Pity that he did not have enough time."

He led on again, but the end was not far away. They found themselves in a little chamber, out of which they could find no passage. Pierre said: "Feel for a stone with handgrips. — Ah, I have it already! Come and help me. Lift as you pull." But it did not give way. "What resists?"

Conan felt around the edges of the stone. "Tree roots are entering here, but not many. Ready? Now heave!" Braced, and pulling with all their strength, they felt the stone yield and saw the light stream in.

Pierre checked the swing of the stone. "Gently. We must not be seen." He peered through the crack, swung the stone wider, then gave place to Conan. "See, we are safe."

Just outside was a screen of leaves, sheltering a path that was long untrod. Stepping out, and peering through the leaves, Conan saw the castle beyond the ravine. The path ran along the face of the steep descent, and trees and bushes, even in winter, would mask it from observation. Pierre came to his side, and after a little hacking at the tree roots they swung the stone back into place. Conan studied the spot carefully, to know it again. Then, following the path, they were led away from the castle, and making a turn, found themselves clambering steeply up among a ragged growth of trees. Through these, always studying his path, Conan led the way to the edge of the clearing.

The meadow was just as before. Not far away was Berengar; and nearer, by the edge of the moat, was Pierre's own horse, cropping the grass. Aymar's was not to be seen. Some fifty yards in front of the drawbridge was Odo, scanning the castle and listening, with the beginning of impatience. The two listened as well. From the castle no sounds were heard.

"Take my horse," said Pierre. "We three can get away together."

"Not so," replied Conan. "That is a fine horse of Odo's, and I mean to have it for my own. Moreover, we must not be seen riding away together. Separately we came, separately we depart. When we are mounted, we must ride away in different directions. Go with Berengar, but without haste; and I will circle around and join you. Run to your horse, now, and I will help myself to Odo's."

They ran from the bushes. Directly at Odo, Conan

sped silently upon the short grass; he was almost on the point of touching him, when Odo turned. Without start or show of surprise, the Sauval raised his hand, holding the little battle-ax, and struck swiftly, skillfully.

But Conan caught the handle of the ax, and the shock forced open the baron's grip. The ax stayed in Conan's hand, and with his left hand he caught the falling wrist.

For a moment the two looked at each other. The Sauval was passive, and except for a little flush that mantled under the sallow skin, his expression did not change. He stared coldly, haughtily. Even when thus caught, he was commanding and superior; it was his only defense, and he used it well. But Conan's eyes did not fall, as so many had done, before that unwinking glance. His hand clenched and his arm stiffened.

"Come down!" he said. He put force into the jerk of his arm; and Odo, snatched from his saddle, soared with spread cloak and landed on his back. Conan let him fall heavily and stood over him. He poised the little ax. But not even now was the baron jarred into the loss of self-command. He looked up steadily and silently into Conan's eyes.

Conan tried to force himself to anger. Through his teeth he said, "You deserve this!" The weapon threatened; but Odo lay still, and it did not fall. Turning the little weapon toward a stone, Conan struck smartly, and the whole edge of the blade sprang away. The rest of the weapon Conan sent spinning into the bushes. He set his foot on the Sauval's throat, and still Odo did not move, nor change expression. Conan pressed lightly, laughed contemptuously, turned, and sprang into the saddle. Looking down, he saw that Odo still lay motionless, still unblinking. It was in Conan's power to override and trample him. He despised Odo, and tried to lash his anger into crushing him. But he could not. Turning the horse, he struck the beast with his hand, and riding without the use of Odo's short stirrups, galloped away.

As he approached the woods he looked and saw that Pierre and his grandfather were entering them in quite another direction. He drew rein, and viewing the castle he saw emerging the group of his assailants, supporting the tottering Aymar. That they might see him departing alone, he waved derision at them, and heard their hearty cursing. Then galloping into the woods, he circled till he found the road, and following after the masons, soon joined them. He held out his hand to Pierre, and the young man took it. In the eyes of both shone the light of comradeship. They rode along together.

Pierre asked, "Did you slay the baron?"

Conan answered, "I could not do it."

"It was a mistake," said Pierre, almost fiercely. "I would I had gone with you and slain him with my own hand!"

"Then," said Berengar, "you are no true mason. What have we to do with the lives of the strong?"

"I have just had to do with them," replied Pierre. "Do you blame me for that?"

"No," replied his grandfather. "Had I been younger, I should have struck in, too. But no needless killing, Pierre, to bring on our quiet family the vengeance of those nobles. As it is, you are a marked man." He turned to Conan. "On the other hand, messer squire, you made a mistake in not killing that poison snake."

Conan was chilled as he recalled the reptilian glance of Odo's eyes. "You think I shall be sorry?"

"As surely as you live!"

They rode on silently another mile, in the growing dusk, until at a fork in the road Berengar drew rein. "Messer Conan, there is the way to your home. We take the other."

Conan protested. "But you advised me to come to Vézelay."

"To come unknown," explained Berengar. "But now you have been seen. When the Sauval come next, they will know you."

Pierre laughed. "Not when once he has washed off that blood."

"Am I so marked, then?" asked Conan.

"Look in the pool of yonder spring."

Dismounting, Conan looked into the water and viewed his face by a late gleam in the sky. Not only were his forehead and cheeks now stained, but blood from his bitten lip had marked his mouth. This was the savage mask that had not daunted Odo. But when Conan had washed there were left but a few red lines on his forehead, close under his hair, and a swollen lower lip.

Berengar was positive. "Look at his height and his long blond hair. I tell you he cannot be mistaken, once he mingles with the knights."

"Then," said Conan, "let me mingle with the artisans only. Take me among your workmen, and let me stay until I have found out what I need to know."

"What, you, a knight, among us of the commune!"

"Not yet a knight," reminded Conan. "Berengar, it is a better plan than the other."

There was silence, while the masons looked at one another. At length Berengar said, "Let it be so." And together they took the road to Vézelay.

After but a few more miles, hastily traversed, day seemed to come again as they left the woods and came to cultivated land. Light was still in the sky when, at a turn of the valley road, Pierre pointed ahead. Before him Conan saw a sight that made him cry out with astonishment.

Climbing the heavy hump of a hill was a mass of buildings which completely covered it. Their walls, roofs, and stubbed towers rose, rose, until at the summit was planted the bulk of a great church, its high towers and sharp spires clear against a layer of violet in the sky. It was encircled by battlemented walls, and other such were visible at the foot of the hill,

beneath which vineyards and gardens spread out into the valley. All over the hill, lights, at different points, were cutting the growing dark.

The country-bred Conan drew his breath, and gazed openmouthed at the town and abbey of which he had so often heard. Hundreds of years they had been here, burnt and rebuilt so frequently that the making of the modern church was almost in living men's memories. Believed to hold the relics of the Magdalen, the church was the focus of countless pilgrimages, from the offerings of which it had grown rich. Thus had been built the vast edifice, far too big for its monks and the people of the town, but not for its pilgrims. Today in its emptiness the church stands above a town which has dwindled to a few hundred souls, an isolated community, away from all the common streams of travel. But Conan saw it as the objective of busy roads, an active and prosperous center, already recovered from its disastrous contest, a dozen years before, with abbot and king. Here men still told of seeing Philip of France, when he came to hear Bernard preach the Second Crusade. Vézelay was busy, and above it in the church the footsteps of the pilgrims were continuous, while services and masses, the ringing of the bells or the intoning of the priests, the perpetual ebb and flow of the devout, rarely ceased from matins to vespers.

As Conan was still marveling at a sight so strange to him, the three travelers overtook another, who was riding a horse so jaded that, with drooping head, it could scarcely plod. The rider, bent and dejected, was paying no attention to his beast, and it could only have been the knowledge that food and shelter were near that kept the animal to its weary journey. Pierre, riding first, recognized the rider and spoke sternly.

"Isaac, this day you lost your chance to prove yourself a man!"

Starting from his dejection, the young Jew turned, recognized Pierre, then, looking wildly farther, saw Conan. He looked closely, cried in a strange tongue some few syllables, then, dropping his face in his hands, began to sob without restraint.

Pierre, taken aback, said no more, and the three travelers passed on. After they had reached the base of the hill and were beginning the ascent toward walls that stood close in front, Pierre drew nearer to Conan and asked, "Will you follow my advice?"

"Most certainly."

"Then because that handsome horse will surely be

remembered as the Sauval's, leave the beast with me, and go forward alone on foot. Grandfather and I will stay and have a word with that young Jew."

"Good. Where shall I meet you again?"

"When you reach the gateway, hold your head down and keep your face in shadow, as if very weary. The guard will ask your purpose. Say you are a pilgrim. Tell them you are a mason, and ask for the house of the master of the guild. Pass on up the straight street, turn to the right when the street divides, and linger under the first heavily shaded doorway. We will come and guide you farther. One thing more — wrap with this scarf the handle of your sword, for it is very noticeable."

It all went simply, according to Pierre's plan. Conan walked on, and coming to the gate of the town was allowed by careless warders to pass as the pilgrim he pretended to be. Going up the steep street he sought the heavy shadows, and lingered at a barred entrance until the masons approached on their horses and beckoned him to follow. He went with them through a gate into a courtyard, where, as soon as the gate was shut, Pierre turned to the dark house and shouted joyfully. Shutters and doors opened, light streamed out, women and children came running, and there were happy welcomes, with hugging and kissing. When the women turned their inquiring eyes on Conan, Berengar said simply, "A guest," and led him indoors, where food was almost immediately ready.

Conan, in the warmth of the house, felt the fatigue of his day. A bowl of soup was like a drug. He begged for a bed, and while the masons sat down for a long talk with the family Conan was almost immediately asleep.

IX

A New Life

A S THROUGH several drowsy wakings Conan at
length struggled into full consciousness, he began to put together the things that he saw and heard.
The women of the house had long been awake; he
smelt food, and from the clink of dishes had been
aware that people were breakfasting. It was not that
which roused him, in spite of his customary appetite.
Remembrance of the events of yesterday suddenly
swept over him. Not his fighting and escape occupied
his mind, but the significance of the fact that he had
found the Sauval patrolling the lands of the Red
Keep, almost as if they owned them. Forgetting food
and his usual briskness, he still lay, and, for the first
time in his life, tried to think.

Naturally, therefore, he wished for Anne. For five
years she had been his daily confidante, and up to
now his method of thinking had been to discuss
things with her. Not that they always agreed, but her
opinions always influenced him, and usually he came
round to them. As, in spite of her absence, he was
doing now.

He felt that he had done well in coming to Vézelay. Here he could, he must, learn what was going
on. If people plotted, he must counterplot. But with
whom, and how?

Pierre, coming at last with a tray of food, found
Conan lying with knitted brow. Breakfasting, he still
was thoughtful. "Pierre," he said, "you must help me
to think. I don't see my way."

"Well, then," began Pierre, seizing the opening,
"we have been discussing. Do you really mean to
pretend to be one of our workmen?"

"Of course," said Conan. "That is settled."

"You must associate with us and our men," warned
Pierre. "And at times, not to be suspected, you must
put your hand to the tools."

"I have worked with tools before now," replied
Conan. "Every squire, even every knight, to some
extent is an armorer."

"But that is honorable, at need," Pierre pointed
out. "We masons" — and here Pierre raised his head
— "are humble folk, and our work is ignoble."

Conan smiled. "That is a fine pride with which
you assert your humility. But if in stepping into your
degree I serve my family and the Lady Anne, it will
not lower my nobility. So as a good friend, Pierre,
who has fought back to back with me, give me your
advice."

"First, then," said Pierre, "before you leave this
room you must cut your hair."

Now Conan himself began to rear his head in

pride. Then he controlled himself. "I see," he agreed.
"It will betray me. Well, then, trim my hair."

"I will fetch my mother," said Pierre.

As he let the woman cut his hair, Conan felt that
he was stepping down from his proper station. The
artisan kept his hair distinctly shorter than the knight;
and here was Conan, who but yesterday had felt
himself superior to these craftsmen, lowering himself
into their class. As the first clipped lock fell into his
lap, he sighed. Pierre, muttering to himself, abruptly
left the room; and the woman, as she plied her scis-
sors, alternately implored Conan's pardon and mumbled appeals to her saint. When she had gathered
the fallen trimmings, Pierre came again to the door.

"Burn them," he directed. "Burn every hair. I have made the fire brisk. And, Messer Conan, here are clothes for you. I got them of our tallest journeyman, telling him that yours were worn out in your pilgrimage, so that he readily sold me his extra suit."

When Conan was attired in his new costume, he hardly knew himself. The knight of the day dressed commonly in long robes, and even his armor was the long hauberk. Looking down at his unaccustomed shanks, Conan felt himself like a varlet again. True, between the knight's robe, ending well below the knee, and the craftsman's kilt, ending just above it, the difference was scarcely a foot; but that difference showed the gulf between two social classes.

"By Saint Christopher," said Pierre, "who was the tallest saint I know, you are too noticeable! If the men do not look upon you, the ladies will. Bear your head less haughtily; put on a hangdog look, lest your rank be betrayed after all."

"Nay," said Conan. "If the burghers of Vézelay have not a self-confident carriage, then you are no true specimen of them."

Pierre laughed. "The men of our commune are indeed a truculent lot, and perhaps you may pass for one of them. Now, Messer Conan, forget that you ever carried a sword. A knife must be your only weapon for awhile. But, meanwhile, I feel that your robber's sword must be disguised."

He brought the weapon out from its corner. "The pommel and the guard are too handsome and bright.

Give me leave to disguise them with a coating of wax. It will readily melt off again, in boiling water."

With Conan's consent, then, Pierre dipped the ball of the pommel and the bars of the guard into melted wax. After repeated dippings he coated it to his liking, and then, dusted it with ashes from the hearth. " 'Tis not so bad," he said, looking at it critically. "But if you should wear it, fret not the handle too much with your hand, lest the wax rub away, and the gold show. — And now, why not go out and see the town? If you make acquaintance, say that grandfather has hired you while you are here on pilgrimage. If you see Isaac, do not greet him. I have warned him not to appear to know you. And by the way, I have sold him the baron's horse. It was concealed last night outside the walls, and now is gone southward already, with a trader, all neatly managed by Barzillai, Isaac's father. I have the money whenever you want it."

"I must buy me a knife," said Conan. "So give me a little of it now."

Pierre began to unbutton his doublet. "But had you not gold?"

"A little. But when I climbed I tied my purse at my saddlebow, and it went away with the thief that took my horse."

"In all common sense," cried Pierre, "none would have thought you would not have buttoned your money close to your skin."

Conan explained. "Remember that every poor man

thinks he may demand alms of a lord, who thinks shame to refuse him. If it took me as long to give my largesse as it takes you to get at your purse, what a figure I should cut! The knight must always be ready to give."

Pierre's purse was in his hand at last. "I see." He offered a handful of coin, and Conan took but a little.

"Keep the rest against the time I may need another horse. Now let me go and gawk about."

"As a pilgrim," suggested Pierre, "your duty is toward the church. It will be proper for you to give thanks to the Magdalen, who certainly, or some other saint, guarded you yesterday. For me, I prayed hard to her while waiting in that dark passage in the castle, and my candle is burning to her now."

Accordingly, Conan left the house. He was so conscious of his changed appearance that he carried himself badly, and was so afraid of self-betrayal that he wore a hangdog look — the very pattern, at least at first, of a loutish journeyman mason. Gradually gaining confidence, as he realized that he was not observed, he began to study the place and the people. Finding that he was going downhill while of course the church was at the top, he turned and walked up.

Conan marveled at the town. He walked in a narrow street which led uphill in a slightly winding course. House abutted upon house; walls were high, doors were studded with iron, and the small windows were barred. Here and there little towers swelled from the house fronts and rose above them, the means of defense of the burghers against the abbot. They reminded Conan of the tales he had heard of the bloody struggles of the commune against Abbot Pons, successful until the king intervened. These towers had then been destroyed; yet they had risen again, witnesses of the dauntless spirit of common men.

The street gave every proof of the town's prosperity. In its confined space jostled many people, so various in appearance that Conan felt sure he would not be noticed. He heard unintelligible dialects, saw strange costumes, and passed among people of all degrees. Here tripped a dainty lady with her attendants, and if she cast a glance at Conan it was only in appreciation of his thews. There workingmen passed him unnoticing. Peasants gave him his path; but a reverend scholar, evidently despising him, advanced upon him so steadily that Conan was almost too late in remembering to give ground. It was well that this occurred, for a couple of squires of his own age next bore down upon him with a like assurance. Chuckling to himself, Conan gave them room.

Within a few minutes he met as many people as commonly he saw in a day at Fessart. As still they came, he was astonished that so many more should keep advancing to meet him. He wondered that so many women sat spinning at doorsteps, so many children were underfoot. How could all these folk support themselves on this crowded hill? Of manufacture and trade he knew nothing.

He learned a little of them when he found the street of the armorers, and bargained for a knife. The man had weapons of all kinds, some new, some old, some foreign. Conan bought an old knife of Italian make, worn, but of splendid steel. Were it sharpened, he could drive it even through a mailed coat.

Conan resumed his climbing of the hill, up the narrow street. At a shadowed turning, there appeared in front the tower of a church, crowned by a spire, bright in the full sun. It appeared like light in darkness, or like that Arabian temple which a returning crusader had described to him, suddenly appearing, flooded with sunshine, at the end of a deep and narrow gorge. As Conan moved on, the center of the façade appeared, with a wheel window and a great double door. And finally appeared the second tower and spire.

The square in front of the church was occupied by many people, priests of all kinds, monks, knights and ladies, burghers, craftsmen and peasants, and travelers of all qualities, down to the minstrel and the vagabond. Going to the famous shrine were many Christians, to give offerings, to implore help, to fulfill old vows or to make new ones. Drawn by the strong tide of people setting toward the church, Conan passed through the sculptured portal and an enormous enclosed porch and entered, by a second great doorway, into the church itself.

Before him stretched, two hundred feet and more in length, a building amazingly high and vast. The

striding piers, of creamy tan, rose to whitewashed vaults; but the piers were linked, and the vaults were supported, by great round arches built of alternating stones of a whiter cream and a deeper tan. From small windows, soft light came to reveal these tints, while deeply cut moldings gave relief and change to the vast and solemn building.

As Conan's eye, after seeing all this, began to look for details, he saw that every capital was carved with storied figures. A flying dragon caught his eye; farther on, knights in hauberks were in combat on foot; while another knight rode his horse, holding his hound in leash and blowing his horn. Here were not only Bible stories, but also legends, grotesques, and marvels.

Conan spent an hour in admiration and wonder. Finding the altar to the Magdalen surrounded by many devotees, he said there his own prayer of thanks and lighted his candle. But as he left it he thought of Anne, and wished for the human comfort and counsel of her presence.

At length, by a side door, he went out and found himself on a terrace, beyond which rose a squat structure, burly and formidable, battlemented, and with a frowning portal. By description he knew it to be the abbot's palace; but seeming more like a fortress, it beetled above the steep fall of the hill, and protected the abbot and his semi-military family. Feeling secure in his disguise, Conan gawked along in front of it, noting with trained eye its readiness for defense. He reached the door and lounged past, only glancing at four men who, with shields and spears, were sprawling on stone benches. But a bark from one of them halted him.

"Fellow, this place is for your betters. Out!" The man pointed back, past the side door of the church, to an open gate admitting to the square.

Conan stopped, removed his cap, and scratched his head. Then mumbling, "Oh, very well," he turned to go away.

At that moment there strode through the open door a heavy figure, passing out between the men, who sprang to their feet with hasty salutes. Conan, stopping and bowing too, glanced up. This was the prior whom he had once known at Fessart; he was abbot now, a little stouter, much more important. Abbot Martin was in undress, his robe kilted up by a belt, his legs free for a hasty stride. He was followed by a monk, but behind came a pair of men-at-arms, heavily weaponed.

The abbot paused and scanned Conan. "A pilgrim? No, you are a man of this place."

"Only in his clothing, my lord," answered Conan. "Mine was in rags, so I bought this of a mason with whom I lodge. I am to stay and work with him."

"Away, away!" ordered the abbot impatiently, about to go on. Then he paused again. "And you remain here? Pilgrims soon go home."

"A homeless man," replied Conan.

"Homeless men," remarked the abbot shrewdly, "commonly have a reason for not wanting to go home."

Conan, groping for an answer, recalled the only homeless man he knew, a peasant's son who after a brawl had fled from Fessart. "Why, so have I, your grace," he said. "A — a girl."

"And another man," suggested the abbot.

"Aye, indeed," agreed Conan, in surprise well put on.

"And mayhap," went on the abbot, pleased with himself, "the use of a knife." As Conan was about to protest, he added, "I know the story, or fifty like it." He surveyed Conan's tall form. "Such men commonly join my guards." The remark was half a question.

Conan tried to gain time by scratching his head. Ought he to seize this opening? He mumbled, "If your grace — "

The abbot's eyes were now keen, for he was always on the lookout for guardsmen. "What, fellow, what? My pay is the best. And what know you of masonry?"

Conan thought again of the fellow at Fessart. "I am a peasant's son, and can lay stone. Here I can learn to cut it."

"With whom do you lodge?"

"One Berengar."

The abbot appeared to change his mind. "I know the man. Well, learn of him. Someday you may be the more useful to me. Your name, fellow."

The peasant's son at Fessart saved Conan again. "Luke," he answered readily.

"Well, Luke, learn your trade. Brother Theodore, give this fellow somewhat." And the abbot was gone in a moment, followed by his men-at-arms.

Brother Theodore gave Conan not copper but silver, and the squire, wondering, went and found Pierre, and told him the story in detail.

"This I learn from it," Conan said. "You can deceive people if your story is simple, and if they have a scheme already in their heads. But what was the abbot's scheme? How can I be more useful to him if I know your trade?"

Neither of them could explain it.

X

The Abbot's Scheme

DAYS WENT BY, while Conan learned to shape stone, and mastered the simpler arts of masonry. Very soon he found himself working on the great church, where repairs were constantly going on. He worked always with Pierre, and the men accepted him as an apprentice. They called him Luke, and jested at his clumsiness, but learned that he could best them all at quoits or wrestling. Good nature and simple manners made him welcome among them.

Conan learned about Vézelay, its people and its gossip. Pierre brought him any important news. But that for which he waited most was slow in coming, until one morning Pierre drew him aside with a sober face.

But Conan smiled. "So the Sauval have come at last?"

Pierre, surprised, asked, "How did you know?"

"Your face was troubled. But trouble is what I want. — They are here, then! How many?"

"Both brothers, with at least twenty men. Never

so well armed: they equip their men notably. Where do you think they lodge?"

"With the abbot."

"How should you guess that?"

"How not, if they and he are plotting together? Now, Pierre, we must listen for every bit of news."

"Aye, and watch for it," said Pierre. "For my plan is to go to work on the buttress opposite the palace door. But we may have to keep the peace between our men and the Sauval."

Pierre did not need to explain his meaning. One thing that Conan had learned, to his satisfaction, was the state of friction existing between the commune and the abbot's men, but amounting to hatred between the men of Vézelay and the Sauval. The robber barons and their men infested the roads near the town, put peaceable workmen in fear of their lives, pestered quiet travelers, and laid taxes on goods. The last was most important, for the price of living had recently gone up. To have the Sauval and their followers dwelling in the palace would be an insult.

The next day Pierre went to work at repairing the stonework opposite the palace. That morning he took with him only Conan, not caring to have too many of his men so near the guard. The abbot, the Sauval, and a whole train of the fighting-men left the palace early and went down into the town. Pierre kept hard at work as they went by, but Conan watched covertly. "The abbot," he reported to Pierre, "pointed you out to Odo."

"They know me well enough," said Pierre. "Was it not you they looked at?"

Conan was sure that it was not.

An hour later the little procession came back. The men-at-arms, jaunty, swaggering, undisciplined, went first into the palace. Watching as before, Conan saw that the abbot and the two barons remained outside. "They are coming over here," he reported.

"If they mean to punish me — " began Pierre.

"Nay," replied Conan, "they have sent their men indoors. Suspect nothing; be natural."

"Natural!" objected Pierre. Then hearing steps approaching behind him, he turned and faced the three.

The abbot, coming first, was somewhat as Conan had first seen him, in hunting clothes, handsomely trimmed. Odo, following, was dressed as smartly without sign of war, and with a feathered cap. Deformed as he was, and clumsy on his feet, there was something about him that suggested power. But Aymar, coming last, wore his hauberk even here, a mighty man, ready at all times to maintain himself with his hands, always scowling and threatening.

The abbot addressed both Pierre and Luke by name, and said: "I would talk privately with you, Pierre. Luke is to be trusted not to talk too much?"

"Certainly, my lord," replied Pierre.

"The business must be kept quiet for awhile, till it is settled. But as you have built at Fessart, what say you to other building elsewhere? There is a castle needing repair, some leagues away. Will you take a score or two of your men and do the work?"

Conan knew his meaning, but at first Pierre, missing it, looked at Odo. "Is it your castle, my lord?"

The abbot laughed and answered for him. "His and yet not his. Not Castle Sauval, but the Red Keep."

"Strange!" exclaimed Pierre. "Are the Sauval to receive that fief?"

Aymar growled, "Ask no questions, fellow." The abbot, with reddening face, said hastily: "That is expected. Do you know the condition of the castle?"

"If I do not," cried Pierre with feeling, "it is not the fault of the barons of Sauval. For I was penned there a fortnight since, and I marvel yet that I escaped."

"Why then did you interfere?" And the towering Aymar, taking a step nearer, looked down upon Pierre. His face was heavy-browed and dark; his voice, when he thus raised it, was raspingly harsh. He had none of Odo's smooth purposefulness, but an unthinking readiness to violence, like a growling mastiff.

But Pierre, in growing anger, did not blench. "Why, for fair play toward a wayfarer like myself, whose life you would take only because you coveted his hawk and sword." Pierre was hot. "If I thanked the saints that night it was first because my life was saved, and next because I saved that man's."

"Barely," roared Aymar. "Barely, villein!"

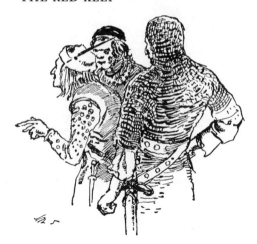

"Peace, Aymar!" Odo spoke in a cold voice that struck his brother to silence. Odo turned to Pierre, and asked, with no anger nor threat, but as in casual interest, "That fellow was in your company, then?"

"The Jew was in my company," replied Pierre. "But that man simply appeared from out the forest."

Odo nodded, and asked with the same mild interest: "How did you get out of the keep? My men believed you trapped."

Pierre had controlled his anger. "Your men were stupid. And the moat was nearly dry."

"Try it again!" cried Aymar suddenly. "Give me one more chance at you!"

Pierre laughed scornfully, "If ever I am in the Red Keep again, I deserve to be caught for my folly."

"Well," said Odo mildly, "that castle is to be mine, and the abbot has recommended you to me as the man to repair it."

Pierre's indignation waxed again, as he faced Odo with folded arms. "It is likely, is it not, that I would trust myself and my men on the work? How much do your men love the commune? And if I brought my men home alive we should never see payment."

Odo looked grieved, and made an appealing gesture toward the abbot, who took his cue and spoke. "Think again, Pierre. Since the castle is to be repaired and occupied — "

In seventy-five years of quarreling with their abbots, the Vézelayans had learned plain speaking. Pierre interrupted. "But the rights of the Lady Anne?"

Frowning, the abbot waved his hand. "That is too high a matter for you. But since someone is to repair the Keep, why not you of Vézelay? Shall we have to send to Avallon? Take your best men, as many as you can. Build up the fallen tower, and finish as soon as possible. I will guarantee the safety of you and your men, and promise you high pay."

But Pierre, outraged at the proposal, grew red in the face as he sought for words. It was plain that he would refuse. Then Conan struck in.

"Why," he said, "the thing can easily be done."

The attention of the rest shifted instantly to him. The abbot smiled, Odo studied him, Aymar stared. And Pierre was stricken with amazement. Conan, laughing, took him by the arm.

"Why, how you look! This means money, man. You must do it. Of course you must." But as he spoke, smilingly, his grip on Pierre's forearm tightened once and again. It was the only signal that he could manage.

Pierre, in spite of his indignation, accepted the warning. Overborne and surly, he took the best course, and grumbled: "It would be difficult. The question of transport — provisions — safety — "

The abbot, seeing consent coming, humored him. "You may work it all out yourself."

"The men may not agree — "

"They will with good pay."

"There must be quarrying — "

Conan laughed aloud. "Are you always this way when much money is offered? My lord abbot, leave him to me. It can be managed."

"Good," said the abbot. "Luke, advise him further. Pierre — come to the palace with your plans. Can you come tonight?"

"Tomorrow night," replied Conan.

The three went away.

Pierre was already gathering up his tools. Conan helped him, and followed at his shoulder as he walked away. They reached the square, Pierre always frowning. When out of sight of the palace he wheeled on Conan.

"In heaven's name, expound this to me. What do you mean, building up the Red Keep for the Sauval?"

"For ourselves," corrected Conan. "Man, this is the very thing I could have wished. Do you not see?

We could never build up the castle by ourselves against the attack of the Sauval unless Prigny and Fessart stripped themselves of every man for our defense. That is impossible. But if the Sauval set us at work, and believe we will be true to them, and so leave us in peace — then let my brother and Sir Roger throw in but forty men each when the tower is high enough, and none can put us out but the duke himself or the duchess his mother."

"They?" exclaimed Pierre. "Little they care!"

"They must care if Sir Roger once holds the Keep in the name of Anne. Then he can force them to deliver the judgment that has been delayed so long."

"But the commune," objected Pierre. "Its policy has always been to keep out of quarrels between the barons."

Conan replied: "Since we may not explain to anyone our true reason for this, let us fall back on another policy of your craftsmen, to line their pockets at no matter whose expense. The pay, man, will make them take part."

Pierre was still a little sulky. "I notice that you count on me for this."

Conan laid his hand on Pierre's shoulder. "Since we are comrades, you must be for it, even to the point of fighting by my side again."

"If grandfather will only permit," said Pierre, beginning to smile.

Answered Conan, "He must!"

It turned out that Berengar, consulted on the plan,

allowed himself to be won over to it. He protested that his reasons were not Conan's. "I may not concern myself with the affairs of your barons. We have always said, let them cut each other's throats. But this time there is a threat to Vézelay. We cannot have the Sauval so near or so strong. So I agree. Yet Messer Conan is right, for the heads of the commune, other than ourselves, cannot be consulted. The whole story would surely get out. Now, how shall it be planned?"

The two masons fell to figuring on their men, their provisions, the quarrying of fresh stone from the ravine by the Keep, the time needed to build up the tower.

"Think not," warned Conan when this last point was reached, "that the Sauval will allow us to build the tower to the very top. When they think it high enough, so that none can take the castle by storm, they will descend upon us and hold the Keep. We must deceive them on the time for finishing, and have our friends there first."

"I see," said Berengar, admiring, "that you have a mind for war."

"It is as plain as a naked sword," replied Conan. And to his mind it was.

But the old mason had an idea of his own. "Then be ready to deceive these robbers. Have your scaffold built outside, and keep it there till the last minute. Let it be supposed that only from the outside can the tower be built. But meanwhile, little by little, have stone brought inside the gate, and an inner scaffold prepared, by means of which the tower can be finished, even if you throw down the outer scaffold and close your gates."

"Good!" said Pierre.

"I never should have thought of that!" cried Conan.

The old mason chuckled. "It is as plain as a naked sword!"

They made their plans, and prepared to consult some of the masons, feeling that should they secure the help of the younger unmarried men, enough of the older would join them to secure success. The next day, when the masons were to be together for work, Pierre planned to gain their consent.

XI

The Country Knight

PIERRE BROUGHT together, for work on the church opposite the door of the palace, as many of the younger men as he could manage. For they were the more adventurous, the less conservative, and the less likely, probably, to look too deeply into the abbot's plans. Before they went to work, Pierre laid the scheme simply before them. They discussed it at intervals during the morning. The idea of high pay was tempting — but how high? The question of safety came next. Would there not be brawls and danger? Would not the wandering Sauval constantly interfere with the work?

"Two things must be settled," said Conan in Pierre's ear, "The men must see good profit and feel absolutely safe."

About the middle of the morning the abbot issued forth, his men before him, the two barons with him, their men-at-arms following. All were on foot, except the abbot and the barons. The workmen glanced to measure that warlike array. When it had passed, the men were silent. Each was frowning a little.

138

"They are unwilling," said Conan again, "to try this scheme unless they feel quite secure. We must manage that."

At the noon hour the men threw down their tools at the first stroke of the great bell above them, and began to cluster around Pierre. "Tell me this — Tell me that — " The question of safety had become more important to them than pay. There could be little talking until the bell ceased its clamor. While it still reverberated Pierre looked appealingly at Conan. He must do the arguing. Conan felt doubtful: he knew that only he was wholeheartedly for the scheme, while yet he could not give his reasons.

He stood up to speak, a little doubtful just what promises he could safely make, when his ear caught the sound of horses' tramping. The men themselves cocked their ears, and looked toward the gate. One asked, "Is the abbot returning?"

"Nay," replied Conan. "These are fewer men, but more horses."

The other laughed. "What, were you trained for war?"

"But use your ears," Conan replied.

The man craned his neck. "True. There are no footmen, but more riders. A dozen, I guess. And look at them, lads! Here is the country knight come to town."

It was so. The tall knight who led the little file of riders was in the oldest of hauberks, which apparently, so did it thrust out about his knees, was underlaid by the stiffest and newest of gambesons. The hauberk was neither rusty nor bright: it had been merely kept from damp, and showed the dark gray of old steel. The horse was no longer young, and never had been fiery; it was simply a big, sleek, well-fed beast, with the mark of the collar plain on its heavy shoulders. Knight and steed alike looked capable of long endurance and hard labor; but neither looked fitted for the explosive shock of battle. They seemed so slow that even Aymar de Sauval would be lightning by comparison.

Yet Conan's heart, as he looked upon the knight, gave a quick throb. For he knew the man. That head, with its fair hair, faded by the sun, curling from under the rope cap, that face with the blue eyes dark and steady and the mouth with an unobtrusive obstinacy — why, that was his own brother Fulke, the quietest, gentlest, most tenacious of all the Prigny; not the best fighter, but the best fitted to care for the peasantry and the fief.

Yet his place, as husbandman and guardian of his people, was at Castle Prigny. What was he doing here, where politics and schemes beyond his ken were breeding, and where violence might be expected at any minute, now that the Sauval were in Vézelay?

So, over that older and wiser brother of his, whose face he had not looked on for eight years yet knew on the instant, Conan felt a yearning as from old times; yet also he felt protective, as if he were the elder and Fulke needed his care.

The country knight was followed by nearly a dozen

servitors, all sober, solid men, decently and properly dressed in country fashion, all simply armed with sword and buckler and riding horses of the farm type, well-fed, well-broken, with no sign of dash or spirit.

"As I live," remarked Pierre, "he has chosen all his solidest liege men, who could neither chase a Sauval nor withstand one in an onset. They have no armor and not a spear, and must be mountainously slow. How long would it take Red Ralph to get past the guard of any of them?"

But though, amid the snickers of the masons, Conan saw the truth of Pierre's scoffing, he also saw beyond it. The quick guerrilla system of the Sauval was good in rapid assault, and if it succeeded by surprise, it would justify itself. Yet Conan, as he looked from face to face among his brother's followers, felt his spirit rise in defense of them. Dimly he remembered each one: they had come to the castle to consult with his father; they had held him on their knees; they were loyal followers of the Prigny. All strong men, all masters of small farms, slow thinkers, slow doers, they were, nevertheless, of a massiveness hard to overthrow. He could see them making an iron ring through which an attack of twice their number could not break. Conan's heart swelled in response to the appeal of home.

The country knight drew near, and Pierre saw upon his shield the falcon of the Prigny. He looked quickly at Conan, who nodded.

Fulke of Prigny drew rein before the group of masons, and spoke to Pierre with the courtesy of a stranger asking his way, not with the arrogance of the baron demanding service.

"That is the palace opposite? I desire speech with the lord abbot."

"That is the palace," replied Pierre. "But the abbot is down in the town."

Conan spoke, holding his head down. "I hear his trumpet this moment."

"He is coming, then," said Pierre. "You may have speech with him here."

"Thanks," said the baron gravely. "I will wait. But tell me — is it true that the barons of Sauval lodge here at the palace?"

"Aye," replied Pierre. "They are probably with the abbot now."

The knight spoke rather to himself. "So much the better." He motioned to his followers to rein their horses back, off the narrow road, and placed himself before them.

Pierre looked at Conan with concern. "They are but a dozen. What if the Sauval fall upon them here?"

"We must be ready to strike in," replied Conan. But he saw that his brother had placed his men well, in an angle of the palace wall. There was strength in his position.

The trumpet sounded again, announcing the coming of the abbot. For he went like any temporal lord.

The monks still filed silently about the abbey grounds, with arms crossed and heads bowed. But that was because the abbot left their governance to the prior, who was something of a martinet. To him the abbot handed over what he considered small affairs; but following the politics of the abbey and working for the increase of its property and influence, the abbot dressed and lived in the great world.

So now he came riding in at the gate behind a score of his men, who, in handsome livery, swaggered along the road, sneering quite openly, as they passed, at the unfashionable country riders. But when the abbot came abreast of these, in surprise he drew rein.

Odo, too, looked at the Prigny, with an eye cold and expressionless, as usual. Aymar, however, seeing the falcon on Fulke's shield, was immediately bristling, shifting his sword nearer to his hand. And the Sauval men-at-arms, who followed, drew close and stared in threatening silence upon the few men before them, as wolves are intent upon fat cattle.

At the gate behind them, crowding to watch but not entering, were a score or more of townsmen and women, and among them Conan saw masons who had been working on the steps of the church. He caught by the shoulder an apprentice who stood by.

"Slip out to the gate," he said. "Bid our men come in, and warn those other guildsmen to be ready if we cry Commune." The lad obeyed immediately.

"Why, Sir Fulke," said the abbot, with a little smile, the courtly counterpart of the sneers of his men, "what do you here, so far from your own fief? Do you need aught, that you come to Vézelay?"

The abbot's men, who had passed, now came crowding back, to stare upon the scene, and thus a curve was formed from wall to wall, hemming the Prigny in. The masons now began to come forward, some thirty of them, by old policy favorable to whomever was against the abbot. They were armed only with their knives and tools, yet their rallying cry would double their numbers in a minute.

And Conan, knife in hand but held close along his forearm, took his place not far from Odo, ready to leap and snatch him from his horse. Odo, under threat of the knife, would be a hostage for Fulke.

This little stage set itself in but a few moments after the abbot asked his question, and before Fulke, deliberately scanning the ring in front of him, answered.

"Yes, lord abbot, I do come to Vézelay because I am in need. And in the presence of your guests I will ask my question." He spoke in a deep and competent voice that had in it the throb of deep feeling. And that feeling suddenly broke to the surface when he demanded almost fiercely, "What has become of my brother, Conan?"

Conan thrilled. Here was family feeling, a bond between him and this almost unknown brother. But the abbot gazed at the Prigny in surprise; and though the Sauval glanced quickly at each other, it was in surprise also.

"A fortnight and more ago, so I lately learned," went on Fulke, "my brother left Castle Fessart on his way home to me. Three days ago a vagabond was caught, riding my brother's horse and wearing his armor. Unluckily, my men who caught him were young, and when they had learned this much, they slew him. Otherwise, before I slew him myself, I might have learned from him if he were an outlaw preying by himself, or whether he were in the pay of those who have a hatred for my house."

It was a bold defiance at the end. Fulke's right hand rested on his hip, his left on the hilt of his sword. And a growl came from his men, as if to emphasize his almost open accusation.

So open was it that Aymar, answering to defiance as surely as fire to a spark, straightened himself in his saddle, and bellowed:

"You mean us! You mean us!"

"Yes," replied Fulke, "I mean you. I ask, lord abbot, that these men give an account of themselves. Two brothers I have lost, though I have no proof as to the means of their deaths. Now the third has disappeared. Let these men tell me what has become of him."

There was a jeering note in the rumble of voices that rose among the Sauval followers. They found amusement, saw no pathos, in the coming of the lord of Prigny to admit his injury and demand an explanation that would never be given and a reparation that would never be made. It was childish to admit a hurt and make a demand where there was neither sympathy nor power to punish.

For the abbot said smoothly: "You know, Sir Fulke, that I am suzerain neither of the Sauval nor of you. Carry your complaint to the duke at Dijon. He has at last come to manhood."

"But what manhood?" demanded Fulke. "He is still under the thumb of his mother and her old counselors."

"And be sure," cried Aymar, "that you have proof! We have done nothing, yet you put the blame on us."

"Give me information where I am to seek my brother," demanded Fulke. "Or else take oath before the altar that you know nothing of him, either you or your men."

Aymar shouted: "I have no information. I will give no oath. I am minded to punish you for this insult." He was lashing himself into a fury. "Give me leave, my lord abbot, to avenge myself, and I will remove these men from your presence."

The men of the Sauval, with another growl, drew close. The crisis was complete. Should a weapon be drawn, at the next moment a great brawl would be in progress. Nor did the abbot make a move for peace. Perhaps he thought an affray would be quickly over. But Conan, looking about, saw that the masons, with hammers, crows, and knives, could strike upon the backs of the Sauval. More came streaming from the gate. He made sure of his own position, within arm-sweep of Odo, sitting on his horse.

Did Odo suspect a foe behind? He sat his horse unmoving, but with a little lifting of his voice he made it cut across the angry murmurs.

"Men — be still!" His men turned and looked at him; their weapons, already partly out of their sheaths, slid quietly back again. The ice of Odo's character chilled his own men, even his brother. Sulky, yet obedient, Aymar dropped his hands.

"This is no place for these matters," went on Odo. "The baron of Prigny should know better than to turn his question into a public accusation. Sir Fulke, let but the abbot give us audience tomorrow, and I and my brother will satisfy you that we know nothing of your brother's disappearance. Meanwhile, keep your men under control and let them give no provocation to mine."

"I will meet you before the abbot, Baron Odo, as soon as audience is given. And I know that no other method than mine would have brought you to any explanation. Lord abbot, when shall this meeting be?"

"Oh, tomorrow, tomorrow," replied the abbot hastily. "I will send you word. But get your men to lodgings and keep them there."

Pierre spoke up, and the abbot turned quickly to him. "And let the men of the Sauval also keep in their quarters, lord abbot. If they are allowed to leave these grounds there may be brawling in the quiet streets of Vézelay."

"Aye," retorted the abbot. "Quiet streets, quiet streets! Until your commune chooses to ring its bells."

"We will police our own streets," replied Pierre steadily. "Vézelay will not be a battleground for outsiders, whatever may be permitted here in the abbey. And, Lord Odo, if we masons are to serve you, respect our rights and our decencies."

"I have respected them," answered Odo coolly. "Else had there been bloodshed by now. — Lord abbot, let us proceed."

XII

Red Ralph Again

"THAT ENDED well," muttered Pierre to Conan, when they were again by themselves.

"But why?" asked Conan. "When was Odo mild except with a purpose? I would I could get my brother forth from Vézelay, and at once."

"He must stay for audience with the abbot."

"That gives them time," replied Conan, "to waylay him here, or ambush him on the way home. That could be done quietly. Pierre, if any of the Sauval leave the town in numbers we must be told at once."

"The town guard will tell me everything," said Pierre. "But shall you not warn your brother?"

"At the first chance."

But the work was no sooner finished that afternoon than the men fell upon the two with questions about the Red Keep. Every form of doubt was brought up, the chief that the Sauval could not be trusted. The debate was in full swing when Conan, supperless, went out to find his brother.

It was still a bright evening. If he went openly to Fulke's lodging he might be seen by the Sauval. It seemed good luck, then, when he happened on the country knight strolling in the town. His men left behind, according to agreement, he yet wanted to see the place, which he had not visited in years, and was looking about him with interest. But wherever the lord of Prigny wandered, he was pointed out by those who had heard of him. This is he that braved the Sauval! Women stared from windows, people gazed from doorways. Conan was forced to loiter behind, in the hope of catching him alone.

But he had not counted on his brother's keenness. Conan had not dogged him fifteen minutes, loitering along from corner to corner, when Fulke turned on him and loudly demanded his purpose.

"I tell you, fellow, I will have no spying on me. Go your way, or else you will feel the flat of my sword."

And seeing that the knight's lifted voice brought more people to doors and windows, Conan slunk away. He would have to change his plan. As soon as darkness came, the unlighted streets would be deserted in spite of the expected moon. Then he would knock at his brother's door.

He realized, with a start, that it was almost time to go to the abbey with Pierre. Hurrying back, he found Pierre and Berengar discussing, and with them he went over their figures — again how many men, how much time, what wages? And what security?

"Ask more, ask more," repeated Conan. "The abbot must give it. And otherwise the men will not go."

Pierre hesitated, because many of the men needed the work and the pay. "If we ask too much they will get men from Avallon. Or even Semur."

"They dare not," reasoned Conan. "Those towns are too far away, and too near Dijon and the duke. This must be done quietly."

Still not of one mind, Conan and Pierre went to the abbot's palace. Here, through the iron-studded door, they were admitted into the guardroom, and then conducted to where the abbot and the two Sauval were sitting in a small and private room.

Pierre laid down the conditions and his difficulties. The clearing of the moat, the quarrying, and the building, would take uncertain time. Thirty men at most were all that he could hope to muster. In forty days the work might be finished. Otherwise, anything up to fifty. The castle would have to be provisioned for them, for the men could not provide their own food. Lime and lumber must be ready. The drawbridge must be made workable. Horses must be provided for the men and tools.

"Come to the point," said Odo at last, coldly. "What pay?"

"Double pay for the forty days," said Pierre firmly, using Conan's suggestion. "After that, triple."

"Triple!" cried the abbot.

Having committed himself, Pierre spoke confidently. "I cannot get the men on any other terms. Most of them have never been ten miles from Vézelay, and the longer we stay the more I shall have to fight their homesickness."

Odo remarked indifferently, "Pay them, my lord abbot."

The abbot, after his one protest, agreed with more willingness than Conan expected. Does he plan, then, Conan wondered, not to pay?

"Here is a list," said Pierre, "of what we shall need. The lime must be stored under cover." He turned to Odo. "And this, my lord, is necessary. I must have your word that, once we are at work, you and your men must withdraw and not return, or be seen near the castle, until the fiftieth day, or until I send you word that the castle is ready. For if you or your men approach the castle, my men and I will go home."

Aymar, as he heard the words, started with a growl. But the lifting of Odo's hand restrained him. The baron, sitting hunched in his chair, slowly nodded. "It will be done. Is that all?"

"One more thing," said Pierre boldly. "You are secure in all this, for you take no risks. But my men stand to lose their work unless their pay is made sure." He turned back to the abbot. "My lord, our wages must be paid in advance."

"In advance!" cried the abbot. "That is unheard of!"

Pierre shrugged.

The abbot was choking with words of protest, but Odo smiled. "Abbot Martin, the money will be well laid out, for you stand to gain many times the amount. Pay them, my lord."

And the agreement was made. But while Pierre was making his last explanations to the abbot, and Aymar was listening as if he understood with difficulty, Odo rose, as if with him the subject had come to an end, and, making a sign to Conan to follow, walked to an embrasure. Here a torch had been placed in a socket, and as Odo took his stand, the light fell full on Conan's face. Behind the baron, Conan saw, through the window, the moon already up above the mists of the land, and shining coldly. Equally cold was the look which the baron turned on Conan. His eyes seemed lidless, and his stare like ice.

"Fellow," he said quietly, "what is your interest in all this? You are not one of these workmen. Are you not of the land?"

"A countryman, lord baron," explained Conan. "behind me, at home, I left things a little hot for me. So I am learning this trade. A man must live."

Odo watched him with a steady stare, as of slow, inward-thinking calculation. "Must live — and you call this living? Now I saw you had some influence with the masons. You helped to bring this about?"

"Without me," replied Conan boldly, "it would not have happened."

"And why with you?" asked Odo keenly.

Conan smiled, as well as he could imitate it, the slow smile of the peasant who thinks himself shrewd. "Simply money, my lord," he said. "Why should it go begging? And these townsfolk — what care I for their fear for their skins? I rather like a risk. And the sooner I earn a little money, the sooner I get away."

"To your home?" asked Odo.

"Nay," replied Conan. "Home is closed against me for awhile yet. But out of this dull masonwork to something more like life. The abbot took me not into his service, but some lord will."

"You will be serving the abbot if you build this castle." While Odo spoke, he was studying Conan keenly. Conan, smiling and nodding, withstood the icy stare. Odo seemed suddenly to come to a decision. "When this castle is built," he said, "it must be manned. What, will you then take service with me?"

"Readily," answered Conan. "What could be better?"

"These workmen," went on Odo, his voice level and contemptuous, "haggle over small pay, even when it is doubled. With me there will be money, wine, freedom. Can I count on you?"

"Aye, my lord," said Conan quickly, eagerly. "Depend on me."

"But say nothing to yon mason."

"Understood, my lord."

"Your pay," said Odo slowly, "may as well begin now. Nay, say nothing. Fellow, notice in my following a man named Ralph, red of face and hair, and bold in speech. If he bring you messages, they are from me. If he slip a purse into your pocket, take it freely. On your way out now, he will have speech with you. — Enough." Odo turned away.

Pierre had finished his talk with the abbot. Everything had been made clear, and particularly about the money. The whole sum, even to the fiftieth day, was to be paid over to the masons' guild, anything unearned to be returned. The masons would prepare, and as soon as they were told that the castle was provisioned they would start. Pierre and Conan took their leave.

"You were right," said Pierre, as the door closed behind them and they were in the next room. "The terms were not too harsh. If they had been easier it might have been a mistake."

Conan came out quickly with his own remark. "Pierre, Red Ralph is here in the palace, in Odo's pay. I am to speak with him on the way out."

"In heaven's name!" exclaimed the mason. "He will know you."

"Nay," answered Conan. "All think that I am dead. And I cannot avoid him. Go you home, and I will follow when I can."

Pierre and Conan were conducted again to the guardroom. Here, in a corner by a window, sat a striking figure which, but for Odo's mention of Ralph, Conan would not have recognized. His rusty garments, his nondescript equipment, were gone. He

was arrayed in a sleeveless robe, fashionably shaped, gaily colored, and whole. The bright sleeves of a mail shirt emerged from the shoulders. His dagger had a polished silver hilt; and even his sword had a hint of fashion, being less long, less broad, less heavy than the weapon of a paladin which Ralph had yielded up to Conan. Yet it had, Conan felt sure, no such balance and temper as the one which lay hidden under the mattress of his bed.

Ralph was idly knocking with a drinking mug upon a table, and frowning. He cast a surly glance at them as they entered, and held up a finger at Conan. The next gesture flicked Pierre onward. The two parted, and the outer door closed behind the mason.

"Now," thought Conan, "we shall see if he knows me!"

But everything was in his favor. The flickering torches cast shifting shadows on his face; but, more than that, Ralph's own mind was busy elsewhere. He filled a mug from a beaker, and, pushing it across the table, invited Conan by a gesture to sit. And still for a few more moments he sat frowning and thinking deeply until, with a toss of the head, he cast off thought and looked Conan in the face.

"Luke is your name?" he said, with that bold voice which Conan knew well. It seemed as if he felt himself superior to any, hesitant before nothing. What, thought Conan, would be his stand before Odo? "Drink, fellow, if you will. For me, I find no pleasure in it tonight. — So the abbot left you among the masons rather than take you in his guard? He and Odo look far ahead. Are you ready to be useful?"

So that, thought Conan, is why the abbot changed his mind. "Useful? Aye," he said.

"If you wish persuasion," said Ralph carelessly, "pocket this."

He thrust across the table a clinking purse, which was evidently heavy. But Conan, who had been raising his mug to his lips, lowered it again, and pushed the purse back. "Pay me nothing now. What will my mates think if I am found to have money? When all is done I will claim my real pay."

Ralph, nodding, took the purse back. " 'Tis well thought. And your real pay is to be service among us? Good! Now listen, Luke. You know what I am promised?"

"No."

"Why, command at the Red Keep."

"What, Aymar is not to have it, then?"

Ralph laughed scornfully. Bragging was his weakness. Self-confident even in adversity, a little success had puffed him up. "Aymar has no judgment. Always rough and violent, except under Odo's eye. Now as chatelain at the Red Keep, so much nearer the main roads than at Sauval, is needed one with discretion, to plunder travelers gently."

A second time Conan lowered his mug. "What is this gentleness? With the Sauval, that is new."

"Odo is deep," said Ralph. "Once he has the Red Keep he will change his tune. For look you, when he begins systematically to stop all roads, he must levy tolls rather than rob, else too great outcry will be raised. Now Aymar understands only robbery and murder; nor was there a single man in all Sauval that could follow a different policy until" — and Ralph unconsciously swelled his chest — "they stopped me on the road."

Conan wondered, later, about that encounter. The cruel Odo; the bold, indifferent Ralph; the threat of death; the scornful offer of service; take me or leave me, but I am your true instrument. Odo must have felt the need of a brain to serve him, as well as a fist. Quick promotion to this place of trust.

At length Conan took a pull at his mug. "I wonder," he said then, "that you fear him not."

Ralph sat taller. "What, I fear anyone?" He laughed. "This very evening I refused to do him a service. Oh, I know he will never forget it. But am I his dagger-man?" He subsided, suddenly, into the thought which had absorbed him when Conan entered. Conan wondered at himself, sitting here in this abode of enemies and piecing together the bits that he heard. Ralph roused himself. "No, I will plan for him and fight for him, but not soil my hands. Others have always done my dirty work, and shall I do his?— Luke, tell me what agreement was made with the mason."

Conan explained in detail. Toward everything Ralph was indifferent, until Conan spoke of the condition that the Sauval should keep away from the castle till the tower was finished. "Ha!" he said then. "I did not know the masons could be so clever. But after all, what matters it? We — well, let that be. But now, what time is really needed to finish the work?"

"Fifty days — why not?" asked Conan. "When they can get their pay, why should they not spin the work out to the last minute?"

"Aye," agreed Ralph. "The crafty knaves! But come, let our craft meet theirs. Listen to me. There will come a time when the castle can be held against ordinary attack even though the tower be not finished. Let the tower be but a story above the curtain wall and the entrance, and it can defend its corner. Let us descend upon it then, pen the masons in, make them finish the work, keep news from leaking out, and we can laugh at complaints. Well, Luke, what should be the safe height of the tower, and in how many days should you reach it?"

"I know not the place," replied Conan. "But the masons fear the very thing you say. I have heard them discuss and discuss it. Take a week from your fifty days and call it forty-three, and you will have the time you can strike in."

"That will bring you five gold pieces," said Ralph with satisfaction. "But now look further. Things may go quicker than you think. There may be less quarrying, or whatever. Will you do this? If before that forty-third day you reach that safety point, will you slip away to Castle Sauval and give us the news?"

Conan looked glum. "That is different. But what fear you? Why not wait till the end, and have the thing done without troubling yourselves? The abbot pays, not Odo."

"Aye," agreed Ralph. "And takes the best of the lands as his share. But I know not what is in Odo's mind, except that the young duke is grown up, and some say he is restless under his mother's firm hand. Let Sir Roger have cause to complain before the castle is in our hands and there might be trouble. Possession, possession, is what Odo must have!"

And possession, possession, thought Conan, is needful to me. "Very well, then," he said, "put it out of your mind. At the right time I will come and warn you. But that fellow Pierre is suspicious."

"For that reason," explained Ralph, "I have needed to agree thus with you. To lull him into thinking he is safe, we Sauval will keep out of his sight. And for yourself, Luke, when once we have the place I will use you under me. There must be a bailiff to oversee the farms."

Conan raised his mug. "And for that I am fitted. Who better?" He drank. Now, he thought, let me only get away! But how? Over by the door two of the abbot's servitors were chatting on their bench. The place was too secure, too much locked away. Then he heard footsteps in the passage outside, and a man, opening the door and thrusting in his head, demanded if Ralph were there.

"Aye," replied Ralph surlily. "But what are you doing here? You have your orders, and the time is drawing on."

There seemed to be other men beyond the door. Their leader said: "Jerome is gone. He will bring him soon. And we want you with us."

"Not I," said Ralph contemptuously.

"Yet speak with me a moment," urged the man. Reluctantly, Ralph went to the door. Whisperings followed, and then an outburst of Ralph's wrath.

"No, I have refused. I offered to pick a quarrel and fight him; but this must be secret. And I will not stab in the back. What are you afraid of? You are five — too many, for three would be enough. You are wasting time. Go and lure him to the cave, or you lose your chance."

He thrust the man out and shut the door behind him, opened it to shout, "Drop him over the wall!" and slammed it hard. Grumbling in his throat, he came back to the table and sat himself down.

Conan sat frozen. What man? What cave? What slaying?

Ralph was angry, with the others, with himself. "A man has his decencies, Luke. I have my standard and I will not step down from it. Yet the world is to the strong and power is to him who takes it, never mind the means. Why should I not — ? Yet I will not! I will not!"

He sat with sunk head, rapping with his knuckles on the table. Conan's cold heart suddenly beat, his head burned. This man to be decoyed — was it Fulke? He must get away!

He pushed back his stool. "I must not stay too long. Pierre will ask questions. Well then, is all understood?"

Ralph roused himself. "I will depend on you. Fail me not."

"You are safe," said Conan, rising. He felt his voice come unsteadily, and knew his knees to be shaking. With effort he controlled himself. He wanted to strike Ralph down, to rush out and cry Commune! But there were two doors, two guards. He stood, waiting to be dismissed.

"Go, then," said Ralph. "No — wait!" He looked at

the door, seemed to think, then waved his hand. "Yes, there is time. But go quickly."

The heat in Conan's head made him feel that he was reeling. He walked toward the door, he knew not how. The guards rose and opened it for him. One walked with him through the passage to the outer doorway, where the second pair of guards opened it.

"Away," said the man. "Run, unless you want trouble!"

Conan ran.

XIII

Paid Murder

THOUGH CONAN ran, he seemed to stand still, so slowly did his feet move. Everything struck sharp on his senses. The night was bright from the moon, and the heavy shadow of the palace was marked on the grass. To his right rose the bulk of the church, its spires thrusting into the dark, dark blue of a sky spotted with a few blazing stars.

Where to go? A cave? The "cave" that he knew was here, just outside the gate of the palace wall, a vaulted chamber underground, an empty storehouse. Doubtless, others in plenty were to be found on that hill, bristling with buildings, honeycombed for centuries with cellars. Would this trick of decoy and murder be played here so close at hand, all but on the abbot's own land? Yet what more likely? And knowing no other place to go, Conan hurried out the gate.

He longed for time. He wished he might run to Pierre's house, and rousing the masons, have the tocsin rung. But time was short. Yonder was the cave, its open mouth showing. Where were lurking those waiting knives?

And here he was at the mouth of the cave. Under its black arch, steps descended. There was no sound from its hollow, nothing to show that men were lurking there. He looked about. The moonlight glinted on roofs; shadows were everywhere deep, to hide assassins. No one was stirring. Yet —

Footsteps! Conan put one foot on the first stair of the cave, stepped down a little way, and waited, with only his head above the roadway level. He looked toward the sound, toward the town. Out of shadow came hurrying shadows. There were four, perhaps, in a group, not running, but hastening, without speech, with one purpose. Danger! The warning was enough, and Conan turned and ran rapidly down into the darkness of the vault.

If men were waiting there, he invited death, though his knife was in his hand. But he had to take the chance. He reached the bottom, touched the wall, skirted it, alert for any sound. He turned a corner, came upon a door, tried its latch, shook it. It was fast. He went on, came to the second corner, and turning, stood with his back to it, facing diagonally across to the stair by which he had come.

He had thought himself in darkness, but now, after a moment, he saw that there were moonbeams striking down the narrow stair. By their pale light he measured the place. It was dry, a granary waiting for its winter store of wheat. The faint odor of its last golden treasure came to the nostrils. But Conan, back to the wall, scanning the place, thought only of de-

fense. The cave was some thirty feet square, and its
heavy roof was upheld by a rude vault which, though
coarsely made, had stood through the centuries. Four
square piers sustained it. Their blackness confused
the eye, and only the faintest of light was diffused
anywhere, except at the foot of the stair.

Conan silenced his breathing as he heard footsteps at the ground level. A moment; then the light
was cut off, and a heavy foot struck the upper stair.
Then scuffing, cursing at missteps, one man after
another came stumbling down. Conan counted four.

What if they should make sure that no one was there before them?

But confident that they had no neighbor, they took post each by a pillar, and waited. The darkness swallowed them; their breathing, at first audible, quieted; and but that Conan had seen them take their places he would not have known they were there, though so close at hand. Accomplished ruffians, they were carrying out the details of their training with an agreement and smoothness that spoke of practice.

And Conan felt anger — the anger of the swimmer who, because of the recklessness or ignorance of another, must risk his life to save him. "If Fulke had but showed caution, I should not be here." Then he felt a little hope. Perhaps Fulke would not come.

But then came footsteps above, and when they paused at the top of the stair, Conan heard his brother's voice. "Why stop here, fellow?"

The answer came clearly. "Lord baron, I brought you here for secrecy. But if I am seen, and Baron Odo is told, I am a dead man. By all the saints, lord, come down here below, and I will tell you how to rescue your brother."

"You say he is in the dungeons?"

"Yes, close at hand."

"Fellow, if you are lying — !"

"The truth, baron, the truth I tell you!"

Fulke had not lost all his caution. "Go first, then. And remember, my dagger is in my hand."

Had Fulke gone first, a shove would have sent him to the foot of the stair. With apparent confidence, his guide took the steps before him, while with care, and peering, Fulke came slowly after.

"It is very dark," he complained at the bottom.

"It is still too light, lord. Come a little farther into the shadows."

Fulke took but a short step. "Now," said he sturdily, "this is far enough. Tell me your story."

Conan saw that shadows were moving. Knowing that Fulke could not see as well as they, the men were about to seize their chance. And so Conan acted. He took three silent strides, and with the swing of his arm his knife slid home — as smooth, as keen as glass — between the ribs of the nearest. With a push he threw the man off his blade, and smothered his groan with a shout that echoed in the hollow roof.

To all but himself, the noise was startling. The attackers were arrested in their spring, and Fulke stepped back against the wall. Conan, leaping forward, seized the smooth-tongued decoy, stabbed deep, and sent him reeling among his mates. Then catching Fulke by both arms, he dragged him back into the shadows.

"Quiet!" he hissed in Fulke's ear. "Wait your chance!" Then as the men whirled in a sudden tangle of striking arms and straining bodies, and while their cursing smothered other sounds, Conan pushed his brother toward the stair. "Run!"

Conan feared, as he stood still to give his brother a clear course, that the fighting men, disentangling, might fall on him. But the knight sprang up the stair to safety. And as the wrestling men swayed away, Conan jumped for the stair-foot. He dreaded to feel a knife in his back; but no man struck at him, nor even saw him. For when he had rushed up the stair, and turned at the top to listen, he heard from the cave the snarl, the panting, and the scuffle of men in desperate fight.

Ralph was right: Odo had sent too many men. With grim satisfaction, Conan listened. He beckoned to Fulke who, returning to his side, heard with awe the gasping and straining of that struggle. Then a high scream pierced all other sounds, and as it echoed, the fighters must have fallen apart. Only hard breathing and a slowly dying sobbing came from the black vault. Conan, turning to look in his brother's face, found him shaking, staring down into the hole.

"For God's love!" he whispered. "For all the saints — !"

"Away!" urged Conan, and hurried him from the spot.

They ran from the place. But out in the little square, where the front of the abbey rose high in the air, Fulke stopped directly in front of the central doorway.

"By yonder Christ of judgment," he said solemnly, "I had no hand in that death!"

"And yet," responded Conan grimly, "because you took that risk, two blackguards now are dead."

Fulke turned upon him. "Two?"

"Mayhap three," answered Conan.

"But who are you?" demanded Fulke.

"Did you ask that of the man whom you followed but now?" replied Conan. "I can tell you as good a lie as he. Come away from here, where the alarm may be raised at any moment, and I will tell you all you want to know."

He led his brother across the front of the church and along a lane that slanted down the hillside to a silent terrace. Below, and beyond house tops, the valley lay sleeping, bathed in pale light. And there Conan faced his brother.

"Look at me," he said. "Do you remember me?"

Fulke peered at him. "You are the man that followed me this evening. I thought you meant me harm."

"I meant to give you the news I bring you now," answered Conan. "But look at me again. Before this day have you never seen me? Think of me as a boy. Think of my hair as longer." And as Fulke still peered, uncertain, "Do you not remember me, Fulke, at home?"

The brother caught him by both shoulders. "Conan!"

Conan embraced him warmly in return. "Fulke, Fulke, it touches me to the heart that you should come here in search of me. I meant to cause you no anxiety. Now listen, while I tell you why I am here, and what is to come."

Conan told his tale and explained his plans. "You see," he finished, "this scheme is for all of us, for you and me, for Sir Roger, for the men of Vézelay, and for the Lady Anne." At the use of her name he paused — all this had been Anne's own scheme which he had brushed aside! And now he had come to it. He went on, "When it is time to strike, I can count on you?"

"To the death!" replied Fulke. "Name the day and the hour, and I will be at the gate of the Red Keep."

"I will send you word when we start. Forty days from that day, bring every fighter. — And now, Fulke, go rouse your men and bid them to horse. I will tell Pierre, who will arrange to let you leave the town quietly. Send to the abbot any message you like; tell him that you will not stay to be treacherously killed. But get away, you and your men, in advance of anything more the Sauval can attempt."

XIV

Rebuilding the Red Keep

PIERRE HAD little difficulty in enlisting men for the work at the castle. Various older men flatly declined, and the wives of others would not let them take the risk. But double pay attracted the younger or the adventurous men, and Pierre assembled a picked lot of good workmen.

Conan made sure that every man would have some sort of weapon and armor. But in the street of the armorers, beside a good bow and arrows, he could find nothing to suit himself. "I would even buy a hauberk," he grumbled to Pierre, "but there are only two in all the town, and both are too small."

"Try Barzillai, the Jew," advised Pierre, "the father of Isaac."

"Isaac?" said Conan. "I want never to see the fellow again." But as his need was great, he went to the house of the Jew. Isaac admitted him; but Conan, looking on him without greeting, asked for his father. And though the young man hovered within hearing, Conan ignored him. The father, a quiet, respectable, elderly man, treated Conan as a stranger, though once or twice, from a momentary expression on his face, or a look that passed from father to son, Conan felt sure that he knew who his visitor really was. Barzillai had but one hauberk, a beautiful mail which called forth Conan's exclamation of astonishment and admiration. But he was much too big for it. As his only other choice, the Jew then brought out "an old thing," a *broigne,* which was a leather corselet covered closely with iron rings. It did not cover the arms beyond the shoulders, nor the legs below the hips; but it fitted, and Conan took it. Going the next day to pay for it, he found Barzillai alone. Isaac, said the Jew, had departed on a journey to the south.

For the first time Conan felt a softening toward the young Jew. "Barzillai," he asked, "are you wise to send your son on such journeys? The risk is very great."

"I meant never to send him again," replied the man. "But he would go. We have a great debt to pay."

"Life is more than money," said Conan.

"So is this debt," answered Barzillai gravely. "Therefore I let him go. But this shall be his last trip."

Word came at last from the Sauval that everything at the castle was prepared. On this, Conan sent a letter to Sir Roger, explaining the whole situation and begging him, as he loved Anne and valued his own safety for the future, to be at the Red Keep with a strong force on the right day. So much done,

Conan started with the masons early the next morning.

They stopped at no castle, and avoided each ham-
let. Such travelers as they met gave them wide room.
They were too large a party to be stopped, and too
well escorted by a dozen of the abbot's swordsmen.
Nor were they worth robbing, for all they carried
were clothing and tools, with the spars of a light
derrick on the backs of mules. So they passed on
their slow way, until the afternoon was well begun,
and the Red Keep was soon to be looked for.

It rose at length above the treetops, a square, rusty
mass, together with its lighter turrets. At a distance
it was gloomy and forbidding. In another two miles
they came out upon the clearing, and the men saw
the castle before them. Some were saddle-sore, and
glad to be at the end of the journey. Conan heard
them commenting on the fallen tower, with its heap
of stones sloping downward into the moat. It would
be a difficult piece of work to rebuild it. No, it would
be easy. For himself, he felt the keenest interest and
the highest hopes.

As they approached, he detected the signs of recent repair. Fresh wood gleamed in patches on the
old drawbridge, which was fitted with new rope.
Chains would have been better, but in so short a
time they could not have been prepared. Beyond the
drawbridge the entrance of the castle stood open:
new gates had not been installed, for drawbridge

and portcullis seemed enough. As Pierre and Conan, riding in advance, approached, a small group of men appeared in the portal, men of the Sauval, ready to deliver up the castle. The conference was brief. Pointing to the uninjured gate tower, the men said, "The lime is there," and pointing to the keep, "The provisions are there." They were quickly on their horses, and departed.

Pierre's first thought was for the comfort of his men. Exploring the one good gate tower, he found its lower story crammed with bags of lime; there was no room for beds. In the court, convenient to the well, there was a place for open-air cooking, while in the keep was the old kitchen, for bad weather. Unpacking utensils, he soon had his cooks at work. In the hall of the keep he barracked his men, allotting to each a definite space. Then he went to the ruined tower, to estimate the work that lay before him.

Meanwhile, Conan's thought had been defense. The drawbridge could be raised by its windlass; he meant to have it lifted every night. The portcullis, he knew, was movable in its grooves; its chains had not been renewed, and it remained propped by a beam. In case of danger it could be dropped, though two strong men could hardly raise it again, with a third to prop it. Though the gates had not been renewed, at need the entry could be barricaded.

Satisfied so far, he sought Pierre at the time when Pierre was seeking him. Each had a proposition to make. Conan, the more headstrong, spoke first. "The guardroom in the standing tower must be partly emptied to make room for watchmen." Pierre, on the other hand, said, "We must set all our men to work at once on quarrying and clearing the moat."

He was right, and Conan gave way. In their enthusiasm they were ready to begin that moment, and reluctantly concluded that they must not — workmen, in all ages, disliking to begin a task out of hours, and able in that primitive period to tell time by the sun with surprising accuracy. Tomorrow must do. But the two were presently down in the moat, exploring round the edges of the great pile of fallen stone, concluding that much was unharmed and deciding, to their relief, that the foundations of the tower seemed undamaged.

To Conan's plan for guarding the place, Pierre raised practical objection. "The Sauval cannot think of coming down upon us for a long time yet, when they begin to fret for us to finish. If we spare even a single man as watchman the work will go slower. Raise the drawbridge at night if you will, but give the men their sleep." Again Conan thought it wise to agree.

They were still exploring and discussing when they were hailed from the wall. "Supper is ready. Are you going to stay there all night?" They bolted their meal, and made one more exploration before dark, looking for the spot in the ravine where they should quarry. Discussing with two experienced quarrymen, yet keeping them away from the spot where the secret passage emerged, they decided upon a place which was not only convenient for hauling but where they could cut away a tongue of stone which projected toward the castle and might someday provide too good a footing for a besieger's mangonel. Moreover, it would allow quick cutting.

The next day departed the abbot's men, taking with them all the horses but those which were needed for hauling the stone, and Conan's own. Already the masons were at work, some quarrying, some building scaffolds, some clearing away the broken stone and sorting the good from the bad. Conan felt better when, toward the end of the day, the unbroken wall began to stand up from the heap. A couple of days more, and it would be so high that it could not easily be scaled. It made him uneasy that the scaffold had to stand there, making it simple for anyone to climb. But that danger must be met when it came.

With the undamaged pieces of old stone, Pierre began to build the wall of the tower. The old wall had been six feet thick, but the new he diminished to four, to save time. He intended to make the whole tower thinner than before, leaving rough bondstones on the inside, by means of which it could someday be thickened. Nor would he build a stair; wood would have to serve until stone could be added. Broken stone, if undamaged by fire, he built into the

middle of the wall, but inside and outside it was
cased with good blocks. Thus time was saved. It
pleased Conan to see the outer pile of broken stone
begin to lessen, but he knew it would be long before
the moat would be clear.

The men, in their new situation, did not feel at
home. Few had worked away from towns, and none
had ever been in a place like this, unguarded except

by themselves, and always with the possibility that at any moment the men of the Sauval might come riding from the surrounding woods. The masons felt uneasy.

As a consequence, on the third day there was a case of sickness. A man declared himself unable to leave his bed. Pierre, concerned, questioned him, while Conan listened skeptically. From the first day, the man declared, he had not felt well. He was lame everywhere, and his head ached. Now his strength was gone. He must go home, or he would die in this distant place.

Conan felt that he understood. "How will you go home," he asked, "if you have no strength to work?"

The man answered eagerly, "I can travel."

"There are no horses to spare."

"I can walk."

"But you do not know the way."

"You must give me a guide, then."

"There are no guides," replied Conan. "Or if there were, the country is not safe for two or three. Man, you would be murdered for the clothes you wear. Or if the Sauval came upon you, what would they not do to one who breaks his promise to them? Get up, and go to work!"

The man declared that he could not work.

"Then," said Conan, smiling, "try a little starvation. For if you do not work you shall not eat."

Pierre interposed. "But he is sick!"

Conan laughed. "Homesick. Let him work, or

starve, or risk the journey home." And he would let
Pierre say no more.

Homesickness can be a real malady; but after half
a day of thought the man dragged himself to work,
and slowly recovered his strength. From that time he
worked harder than the rest. It was plain to them all
that the better they worked the sooner they would
be home. Conan was well satisfied.

But at the end of ten days, when the work was
progressing rapidly, he began to feel restless. He had
not become a skilled mason, and at times he felt
himself a hindrance. But he found a chance for relief
when the men began to complain of the lack of
fresh meat. That evening he went out beyond the
castle and tried out his bow.

"You are going hunting?" asked Pierre, who came
to watch.

"The men want meat. But what I need is to get
to know the peasants. We must know who live near
us, and make them useful in giving news of raiding
or spying parties of the Sauval."

It was a wonderful day for him when first he rode
out alone into the country. The freedom delighted
him: this was the life he loved. But as to getting
game, he soon learned how much handicapped he
was without dog for the deer or falcon for the fowl.
Long before his coming, the deer heard his horse
and fled. And the wild fowl kept beyond his reach.
All he could do, on that first long day of hunting,

was to note where the deer were likeliest to be found, and to learn the lie of the countryside, and the few paths still traveled by men.

Yet when he approached the castle, though still within the cover of the woods, he came upon the track of a horse. It was not his own; it had been made that day. He traced, in a circuit well within the forest, the course of the unknown rider, who from time to time had tied his horse in order to go on foot to the edge of the clearing.

He told the story to Pierre, in secret. "It may have been one of the Sauval, or just an outlaw. But an outlaw could serve as spy for Odo. I must be on the watch for him."

"I will watch likewise," promised Pierre.

On the second day Conan tried other tactics. Riding out to where he thought he had good chance of game, he hid his horse in a thicket. Then on foot, with bow strung and arrow ready, he slowly quartered up the wind. Before noon he came upon a little herd of deer feeding, and dropped the fattest. He returned to the castle, carrying it on his horse, in plenty of time for the masons to have good steaks for supper. The store of meat, he saw, would free him from hunting for a few days.

Thus able to do what seemed most important, Conan set out the next day to discover the old inhabitants of the fief, or to find new squatters on the old holdings. Of the latter, he felt sure that he had discovered one when he caught a glimpse of smoke rising from a ruined farmstead. Here there had been once not merely fire but violence; for the gate, which had not burned, had been cut down from outside by axes, after which it was only too likely that the owner had perished in the flames of his dwelling.

It was from the remains of this building, where a roof had been rudely made around the old chimney, that the smoke rose. As Conan approached, a hound bayed at him, and standing before the ruins, challenged him. At the sound of a surly voice the hound crouched and was silent; a man appeared, and stood on the defensive while Conan rode near. He had shield and javelin, and when Conan stopped, demanded what he wanted.

Conan answered: "I saw smoke, and came to see who lived here. What sort of country is this, where men live among ruins?"

The fellow was of perhaps forty years, long-armed and powerful. Lowering out of eyes deep sunk between heavy brows, he sneered, "Men without wives live as they can."

Conan mistrusted him. Unkempt and ragged, he held habitually his jaw thrust out, his head forward. The squire was tempted to rejoin that one of such charms and neatness of person could surely find a wife anywhere. But he answered, "This should be a good place to live, for the fields lie well to the sun."

The man sneered again. "Do you take me for a serf? There is game to be had, and that is enough. But who are you, asking questions thus?"

"I am on my way to the Red Keep," explained Conan. "Can you tell me how to go?"

The man betrayed himself. "What, lost? But you slept there last night."

So this is a spy, thought Conan. It is well that I rode not too close to where he was lurking. He looked again at the man's face, and thought it dark and treacherous. "Certainly I was there," he admitted. "But how did you know?"

"Oh, I know," the man taunted. "You were carrying a deer."

"Aye, yesterday," Conan agreed. "But the hunting is bad today."

The hound, which had been watching with true watchdog instinct, now gave a suppressed yelp. The master turned angrily upon it, struck it with the butt of his javelin, and bade it be silent. Conan saw that it was a young female, with her spirit not yet broken by bad treatment. He held out his hand to her, and she started to come to him; but a kick from her master, which if it had struck fairly might have broken a rib, sent her yelping away.

"If I had that dog," said Conan, "I believe I should have better luck with the deer. Will you sell her?"

"She is a good hunter," replied the man. "Why should I sell her? But if you will give me your horse, I will give you mine and the dog."

Conan pictured to himself the fellow's little pony, and declined. The man urged him. "I have a good horse. Come and see." He gestured toward a little lean-to beneath a tree.

Conan thought, "I will never give him a chance to get behind me." He said aloud: "Some other day. Is that the direction of the Red Keep?" He pointed at random.

The man sneered. "Go your way. You know as well as I."

Conan laughed and backed his horse away. The man made no farewell, but Conan waved a hand as he turned. Then galloping, in a moment he was out of range of the fellow's dart.

XV

Friends and Enemies

AS CONAN rode away he was troubled by the man he had just seen. The fellow was too strong, bold, well-armed. How many others of his kind were living this wild life on the deserted farms? And were they not known to the Sauval, and useful to them as spies?

Such men would make life much more difficult for the few remaining vassals of the old baron who remained on their holdings. Of these, much talk had come to him through Anne and her followers at Fessart. In their ancient steadings, walled and compact, some had held their families together and tried to make their livings from the fields and flocks. It had been for most a losing struggle. Some had soon fled; others, stubborn and unmanageable, had been burnt out and a few of them killed by the Sauval; still others had kept their places by submitting to the levying of heavy tribute. Had the rough and stupid Aymar had his way, he would long ago have harried them from their homes. But Odo perceived that the peasants were of some value, and it had

even been said that in the past year or two his plun-
dering had been lighter. He took only part of the
harvest, or of the increase of the livestock.

But if outlaws squatted on the vacant lands, they
could carry on their own private robbing. That Odo
would try to control them was evident. But nimble-
footed and elusive, it would be easy for such men to
play a double game — to act as Odo's spies, and to
rob and flee if they chose.

As Conan skirted a marsh, he heard the conver-
sation of geese in the sedges. He made ready his
bow and arrow, and pressed his unwilling horse nearer
the mud. The beast snorted, and the geese, rising
heavily from their feeding, scattered in confusion.

One of them, flying directly toward Conan, and discovering him, seemed to hang motionless in the air as it tried to turn. At that moment the arrow transfixed it, and the bird fortunately fell on firm ground. As he hung the heavy fowl at his saddlebow, Conan thought that with it he could buy his welcome at the farm he meant to visit. He unstrung his bow, much satisfied with the weapon, returned it to its case, and rode on his search.

On coming into sight of the farm buildings — low, thatched structures heavily walled about — he must have been seen by childish eyes, for he heard warnings cried shrilly from one youthful sentinel to another. He saw little figures running, converging on a meadow where men and women were haying. These drew together and watched him approach, gaining confidence when they saw that he was alone. As he drew near, two men advanced to meet him, evidently the farmer and his son. When Conan drew rein before them, he saw that they regarded him with suspicion, but not with fear.

Conan held up his goose, and asked, "Can I buy a meal for myself, and water for my horse?"

The men stared at him, amazed. He was so much more prosperous and better-armed than they, with high carriage and speech, that they must have expected him to demand service, rather than offer pay. Looking on the smiling Conan, they found nothing to say. But without waiting for them to think, Conan handed the bird to the older man, who obediently took it, and, feeling its weight, was the more dumbfounded. So much achieved, Conan sat, and smiled, and waited.

The peasant stammered, "But food — "

"Water for my horse," Conan explained. "For me a cup of milk will be enough. You can give me that, can you not?"

The man mechanically answered, "Yes."

Immediately Conan dismounted. Understanding the people with whom he had to deal, he gave the reins to the younger man, who took them as obediently as the father had taken the bird. Conan stood rubbing his hands. "Is that a goose or a swan?" he asked the peasant. He knew the answer perfectly well.

"It is a goose," replied the peasant, and added, after a moment of slow thought, "a good fat goose." Then he became suspicious again, and eyed the strange guest.

Conan, submitting to the scrutiny, talked with the son. "You have a good well? Do not give too cold water to the horse; we must not chill the beast."

The "we" brought them together. The young man answered, "Certainly not," to show that he understood the care of a horse.

Now the group of women drew nearer, but the older peasant waved them away. "Back to work. We will talk with this man ourselves." He led the way to the house, and Conan followed, while the son trudged behind, leading the horse.

The peasant opened the yard gate, and while the

son took the horse to the well, the father carried the goose into the house, into the dark depths of which Conan did not care to enter. But presently the man brought out milk and offered it to Conan. While he sipped, the man began to question him.

"Few strangers come this way. What brings you?"

"You have heard that men are at work repairing the old castle? Well, I am a hunter for them."

Interest and thought began to show in the dull face of the father. The son, with more intelligence in his eyes, drew near to listen. "You are one of those men?" asked the peasant. "Well, who is to hold the castle, once it is finished?"

"They say," replied Conan, "the Sauval."

The man threw up his hands in despair. "Then we shall be their slaves all our lives!"

"What," asked Conan, "do they not treat you well?"

"Their way of treating us well," answered the man, "is by allowing us to live at all. The peasants on the Sauval lands are miserable. And we shall have to fight whenever there is a feud."

"And that is most of the time," added the son.

"But that is not the law," objected Conan. "Only forty days in a year shall a man serve."

"There is no law here," the man said simply.

"And if our women be not safe now," asked the father, "what will they be then?"

As if in answer to the question, there rose a distant screaming in the field. Both the peasants rushed for the gate; and Conan, snatching his bow from its place on the saddle, followed. His quiver was on his back. He heard the two men shouting furiously, and hurrying to the gate, stood and watched.

The fields lay open before him, and not two hundred yards away the women and boys had been working together. Now they were running and screaming after a horseman who was darting away from them. Toward this man the peasant and his son were also running. At first Conan did not understand; then, as the horseman swerved, Conan saw that he held in the crook of his arm a struggling woman. She was striking at him with her hands; but he, crushing her close, easily avoided her blows by movements of his head. Then, seeing the running men, he shouted aloud in triumph, and, swinging his horse again, made toward them. Beside him ran his barking dog.

The man was a skilled rider. Managing his horse by the pressure of his knees alone, he rode in a curve that would bring him within a few rods of the men he was robbing, and whose shouts and frantic running gave him pleasure. Easily controlling both the steed and the woman, he raised his free hand, and yelled at them in derision. Conan recognized him now, the squatter whom he had lately visited. And this was his method of getting a wife! Conan had strung his bow, and now snatched an arrow from the quiver.

As he nocked the arrow and caught it in the fingers of his bow hand, the man, sweeping past the peasants, raised his fist high aloft and shook it mockingly. He could not have offered a better mark. Conan's action, as he took one stride forward, raised the bow, and drew the arrow to its full length, was all but instinctive. He made no pause for aim. The arrow flew in a low arc. Above the quilting of the man's jerkin, exactly in the armpit, the arrow struck. Pointing but a little downward, it would have had to pass through the whole width of the chest to injure the woman. The missile seemed to bear the man from the saddle, so instantaneous was his collapse. Man and woman fell together. The horse ran on for a few rods, and stopped. Then from the ground the woman rose, unhurt, and scudded toward the house.

As Conan stood feeling for a second arrow, he kept his eye on the heap of clothes that had been a man. It writhed, sank down, lay still; the dog, sniffing at it, started away; the peasants, rushing in with lifted fists, stood over it, but remained still. And Conan stood, surprised that his act, so simple and easy, had brought death.

The woman darted past him; he heard the house door slam, and from behind it her hysterical screams. The other women and the children, cautiously rounding the group in the field, streamed hurriedly for the shelter of the gate. Conan walked down into the field, and stood over the man whom he had slain. He could feel no regret. As well grieve at the killing of a wolf.

The young man spoke. "She is my wife, just married. I heard the arrow whistle over my head. But for you, we never could have caught him. I do not know how I can repay you." His voice was full of feeling.

Conan said only, "It was good fortune."

The old peasant was practical. "His arms. Will you take them?"

"No," replied Conan. "Can you not use them?"

"The Sauval took ours away," answered the man. "We will hide these. What of the horse?"

The beast, a light and spirited animal, stood stamping at a little distance. When the young man went to take it, it shied away at first, but in a moment let him take its bridle. He led it to Conan. It was young and strong, and well kept.

"He groomed it better than he did himself," said Conan. "Can you not use the horse?"

Both peasants spoke eagerly. "Yes, we can use it."

"Keep it, then," said Conan. "Hide it from the Sauval, if you can. If they see it, tell them you caught it in the field. As for me, the hound is all I will take for myself."

The dog, whimpering, stood but a few yards away. Its ears were down; its tail was between its legs, but pathetically wagging; its eyes were full of anxiety. Conan dropped on one knee and called to it. It came forward, drew back, advanced again, but only a step. Then it sat down, threw up its nose, and howled. Mournful and complete surrender to fate. When Conan went and patted it, it thrust close to him and whimpered.

Being a female, it had understanding, and gave itself to Conan entirely.

"Now," said he to the men, "bury this body deep, and conceal the spot. For perhaps the Sauval used him as a spy. Be silent about him, you and your womenfolk."

"We will," said the peasant humbly. "We thank you for this rescue. Now, lord, tell us your name."

"I am called Luke," answered Conan. "Now do you gather for me, before I come again, all possible information about the doings of the Sauval."

The son asked shrewdly, "Why do you want that, if you are working for them?"

"Perhaps," Conan replied, "I am not working for them. Perhaps the Lady Anne will take the fief. Would you grieve at that?"

"We would fight for her!" cried the young man. But his father said, "We belong to her."

"Be ready if she comes, then," warned Conan. He took his horse and rode away, to escape the gratitude of the women. By the side of the dead man hesitated the dog. But when Conan called it darted after him, and they went away together.

XVI

Peasants and Outlaws

NOW THAT he had a dog, Conan was well off, for the beast knew how to follow the deer and made hunting easy. It was simple for Conan, having studied the habits and paths of the deer, to set the dog on a trail, ride across country and station himself at a runway, and, when the herd came dashing in single file, to drop the stag of his choice.

He divided a fortnight between this easy hunting and hard labor at the castle, but then felt the need to know more of the peasants. His next visit to the people whom he had served brought him quickly into friendship with them. The old man, Louis by name, had talked with his nearest neighbor and was able to report that none of the Sauval had been seen on the fief since the rebuilding of the castle had begun. When Conan expressed a wish to know this neighbor, the son, Gerard, offered to guide him, and the two set out together, the young peasant proudly riding the robber's horse.

Conan asked, "Do the Sauval commonly ride here often?"

"In little parties, frequently, except these few weeks past. If Lord Odo comes, it is always with a big party. They do not hunt, nor these two years past do they rob so much. But they watch the crops, and seem to mean to levy on us regularly, as if they were lords of the fief. My wife is always afraid they will take me away to fight for them. Last month they took Alard of the Marsh Farm."

"Are there many of the old vassals still on the land?"

"A score, where there used to be three times as many. I would go away, for Sir Roger would take us in at Fessart. But my father and mother have vowed to wait the return of the Lady Anne. This repairing of the castle fills them with both hope and fear."

The quick, earnest glance with which Gerard made the remark, was a hint at a question. Conan answered it. "Tell them not to fear. But a great change is not to be had for nothing. Would you really fight for the Lady Anne?"

"We would both die for her," answered Gerard readily, and added simply, "it would be worth while to die for her. Let her take the fief, and our family could live without fear. The women and boys could carry on the farm, for the lady would ask only reasonable dues. But now, when we have to give a half of the harvest, if not more, there is always starvation before spring."

"What of the other farmers?" asked Conan.

"It is the same with all. None live without fear,

and all live poorly, because of both the Sauval and the outlaws. These do not work; they hunt and rob. I wonder that you, lord, ride about alone."

"I must," answered Conan simply. He knew that his days were full of danger; but swiftness of movement, constant varying of his route, and extreme watchfulness were his safeguards. In spite of them, an arrow any day might finish him. But it was a risk that must be taken. He asked, "But why do you call me lord?"

"You are not a mason, nor a common hunter. You are young, but you have the bearing and speech of a knight."

"Call me Luke."

Gerard smiled and shook his head. And Conan saw that although in Vézelay, when working as a mason or going about on foot in a craftsman's dress, he could pass for an artisan, here, when he was armed and horsed, his true nature declared itself.

"Here we are," announced Gerard. Before him Conan saw the usual farm buildings, low, thatched, and walled about. Gerard pointed to a scorched roof. "There was a whole band of outlaws here early in the spring. Sandras, the farmer, fought them off. They shot blazing arrows into the thatch, but luckily it was damp within, and the fire went out." The story was told without resentment and without emphasis, as an everyday fact.

"A whole band of outlaws?" asked Conan. "Where are they now?"

"Odo scattered them. Some he slew, some he took into his service. It is plain he regards the fief as his own. We believe that the outlaws are but few now, and live but here and there, singly."

Recognized by Sandras, working in his yard, Gerard and Conan were admitted and welcomed. Sandras told the same story of the Sauval, and showed the same interest in Conan himself and in the meaning of the work at the castle. But Conan told him little, feeling sure that whatever he had said to Gerard would quietly be passed to the other peasants. A state of expectancy, but particularly of caution and secrecy, was what Conan wanted to inspire. He spoke, therefore, warningly, but with reserve, told of his desire for information about the Sauval, and made it clear that he did not want them to be told of him.

While he talked, members of the family evidently made errands to the yard to snatch glimpses of him. The women filed past without waiting; the children stood and stared till sent away. But one, a fair-haired lad of perhaps thirteen, stayed at a distance and peeped from behind cover, till Conan, feeling an attraction for the bright face and noticing that the dog fawned upon the lad, made a sudden start and caught the boy before he could dart away. The father's eye lighted up as the boy was brought into the open.

"He is my third," he said. "Our herdsman and someday our hunter. He likes animals and they like him; dogs go to him, as yours did. He has a hawk and flies it sometimes, here, near the house. But I will not let him go far away."

"A hawk?" inquired Conan. "What, boy, did you catch and tame him?"

"No, no," answered the boy. "They breed in wild places where my father will not let me go. This is an escaped hawk, and I saved its life."

Conan asked, "And how was that?"

"It escaped from its master with its jesses on. And when it lighted in a tree the hanging thongs tangled themselves in a branch and the bird could not get away. When it tried to fly it was caught back, and I heard it shrieking. It was hanging, tired out and bruised. If I had not come and climbed for it, it would have died there. Do you wish to see it? Shall I bring it?" And at a nod from Conan, the lad darted away.

"This is my hawk," thought Conan, and he was right. The boy came back bearing the familiar bird which, showing no wildness, sat contentedly on the lad's hand, which he had not gloved.

"Strange!" thought Conan. "I never liked to handle that bird without a glove. Has the boy gentled it?"

But when he took it and held it, seeking to attract its attention, it would not sit quiet on his wrist, but moved restlessly, began to dig with its talons, and stretched out toward the boy. Conan was not surprised that the bird did not recognize him, for such is the nature of hawks; but he was astonished that the bird would be content only with its new master. He gave the bird back to the boy, and watched as it shook its feathers, settled down quietly, and began to preen itself.

"We believe," said Sandras, "that this is the falcon of the young lord of the Prigny, who was slain here by the Sauval some weeks past."

"Ah, I have heard," replied Conan. "Tell me what you can of it."

He was told that it was a mystery, but that the main facts were plain. The young baron of the Prigny had been returning home from Fessart; he had a hawk with him, was well-armed, had a good horse. On the way he dropped out of sight. It was not till lately that men of his brother, the Baron Fulke, came on a vagabond, once known as a starveling kind of footman, who wore a hauberk and rode a good horse. He declared that he found these; nevertheless, horse and armor bore the crest of the Prigny, and the men slew him. Now he was one of those whom the Sauval suffered to live on these lands. And whether the vagabond had slain the young lord, or the Sauval had slain him and given away his equipment, the guilt lay with the Sauval. They had protected the vagabond, and so his sin was theirs.

Conan, interested in the new version of his death, asked, "And this was the dead man's bird?"

There could be no doubt, answered Sandras. No one else could have lost such a valuable hawk.

Conan patted the lad's shoulder and sent him away.

When he himself departed, Sandras pressed him to return, and so eagerly that the squire marveled, not at first perceiving that he had brought hope, the thing most needed in all that unhappy countryside. Only on hope and loyalty could the future be built.

Thinking this out, Conan rode back toward the castle without his usual watchfulness, and was recalled to himself only when he observed, as he passed a drying watercourse, fresh footprints in its soft border. They were those of a man on foot, and the tracks, after crossing the stream, turned along it toward the castle. Leaping from his horse, Conan knelt and examined the footprints.

They were plainly not made by one of the masons, for he knew well their decent, self-respecting, cobbler-made shoes. These marks were evidently made by a man wearing skins turned up in crude fashion around the feet, and doubtless lashed somehow at the ankles. Conan could see that these tracks had been made within a short time, for the mud had not begun to dry. Here was evidence that another of the outlaws was scouting near the castle. He must follow this man.

As Conan straightened up, beneath his very face there passed, as it were, a dark streak, and he heard the whistle of an arrow. Without pause to look or even to think, he leaped into the thicket, and, running bent and noiselessly, zigzagged his way so lightly through the cover that when he had completed a half circle he found that he was behind his assailant. The man was clearly visible, peering through a screen of leaves to where he had last seen Conan, and hoping for a second shot. Too late he heard the rush from behind, and turned only to be borne down and flattened to earth by Conan's angry charge.

The struggle was brief. The man, though lean and tough, was presently pinned down, with Conan kneeling astraddle of his chest and holding his wrists. The bow lay broken beneath him. Conan looked down into a thin and ratlike face, which snarled up at him in fear and hate.

Conan asked, "Why did you try to kill me?"

"You were tracking me." The answer came with difficulty, from a chest cramped by Conan's weight. "You would kill me."

"I have not killed you, even now," replied Conan, "though it would have been simpler. — What are you spying here for?"

The man took a little courage. "To see what is going on at the castle."

"How did you know that anything is going on?"

"It is spread about."

Conan spoke at a venture, hoping to surprise the truth. "Men do not come five leagues just to look at the repairing of a wall."

"It is not so far," returned the fellow. "Only four leagues."

Conan was satisfied. "That is far to come on foot,

just for nothing, at the risk of your life." He waited a moment, then asked suddenly, "The Sauval sent you?"

The surprise in the man's eyes, and then the tight closing of his lips, showed Conan that he was right.

"What were they to give you?" he asked, and next, "what did they want to know?" But the fellow would not speak.

Conan reflected. The face showed the man: he was vermin, never to be trusted. Sure that the Sauval had sent him, Conan was yet uncertain what to do. He might let the man return and report, for the walls were not yet very high, and the Sauval might be satisfied. Yet the story of this encounter might let them know they were suspected. No, he could not let the spy return. In some disgust, Conan looked around for a thong, and saw the string of the broken bow.

He held both the man's wrists, rose, and helped him to his feet. "Put your hands together behind your back," he commanded. "I must tie you."

The man resisted, but he could not fight Conan's strength. "What are you going to do to me?" he asked, as slowly he was turned about and his wrists drawn together.

"Take you to the castle and keep you close."

"You will slay me on the way!"

"Then why am I not slaying you now?"

The man would not believe, and as Conan was fumbling with the string, snatched himself loose, and

fled. Javelin in hand, Conan pursued him, calling to him to stop. But perhaps thinking that with his light weight he might go where the heavier Conan would not dare to follow, the fellow tried to cross a near-by marsh, leaping from hummock to hummock of heavy grass. Not venturing to follow, Conan saw him rapidly passing beyond the reach of his weapon. "Stop!" he called.

But the man stumbled, and plunged at full length. His gasp of fear was stopped as he dove into the mud; he struggled frantically, lifted his face, and shrieked. Beyond the hummocks, he was not visible to Conan; but the squire leaped to the rescue. Yet in the sudden silence he knew that the agony had ceased, and was not surprised when, beyond the last hummock, he saw only the mud, churning in one spot, slowly, above its victim.

With difficulty he leaped back to solid ground. The man he dismissed from his mind as he thought of the Sauval. "Now what will they do? Have they more spies, or will they come themselves?"

XVII

Sturdy Peasants

MORE DAYS PASSED, and steadily the work progressed. Sometimes Conan labored, anxious to hurry the building; sometimes he hunted for meat; again he scouted for spies, and found none; or he visited more peasants, to widen his acquaintance and strengthen Anne's following. The evening came when he and Pierre walked upon the wall which connected the keep with the new gate tower. With the fall of this tower, part of the wall had been torn away. This had now been rebuilt to its former level, though it lacked protecting battlements. Along it a footway led from the keep to a door in the new tower, above whose archway the unfinished wall rose to a height of several feet. Conan and Pierre walked through the door, climbed flimsy stairs, and stood upon the new wooden floor of the third story of the tower. Around them stood a semicircle of ragged wall, scarcely above their waists; and outside rose the gaunt scaffold, over-topping it by nearly a man's height.

Conan walked to the wall and looked out over

the country. The view was lovely and peaceful; but there was doubt in his heart.

"We have built as high as Ralph wished," he said. "I fear to build higher. For, if the Sauval come, it will not be enough for us to lift the drawbridge and drop the portcullis. They can climb the scaffold."

Pierre replied, "We can defend it."

"Aye," agreed Conan, "a few can defend this wall. But still I am uneasy. I am for throwing down the scaffold, even though we have not yet built the inner frame that Berengar bade us prepare."

Pierre peered over the wall, down at the moat. "There is no heap of stone there now, for them to cross on. Pity the mud is not deep enough to drown them!"

"It will hold them back," said Conan. "Aye, Pierre, it is time to close ourselves in. Tell me, have we enough stone?"

"We have nearly enough to finish the tower."

"Very well, then," said Conan, with decision. "It is fortunate that we have already brought much of it into the courtyard. Tomorrow quarry no more, but begin to bring the cut stone into the castle. I would it were in now. Take down the scaffold and bring it inside. Here is two days' work. But when it is done, I shall feel safe."

"You worry too much," said Pierre. "It is still a week before the Sauval should come."

"And four days only to the coming of our friends. We should be safe. But we have trusted much to fortune, and I fear to trust her too long. Tomorrow we begin to work for safety. I myself must make one last visit, to one of the best of Anne's old vassals. After that, I will stay with you to the end."

The next day, therefore, quarrying ceased. Pierre told his men frankly that he feared interruption from the Sauval, and meant to finish the work from within the walls. All the men readily fell to dismantling the derricks, taking down the scaffolds, and bringing into the courtyard the stone that had been quarried. "There is almost too much of it," said Conan. "I would we had six horses to haul it, instead of but two. — But drive the work, Pierre. I will be back by nightfall."

He rode on his way, therefore, in the direction of Prigny, toward the steading of Dizier of the Marshes, of whom he had been told. This was a harsh man of unyielding courage, now terribly inflamed against the Sauval because some two months since they had seized his son to serve among their men-at-arms. Dizier lived two leagues away from the Keep, his farm buildings nearly surrounded, and well defended, by the marshes which gave the place its name.

Although Conan had arranged for Sandras to prepare Dizier for his coming, he thought it wise to arrive with a present in his hands. Therefore he delayed on the road long enough to hunt, and came to the marshes with a fat buck behind him on his horse. He picked his way across the marshes by a path that had been described to him, wide enough for but

one, saving half the circuit of the marsh. As he rode, he could see the natural causeway which led to the farm gate from a different direction. On that side, beyond the causeway, the farm folk were working in the field; but Conan was seen at a half-mile distance, and the hasty hoarse blasts of a horn warned the workers. Though they could see that he was alone, they were so cautious that they withdrew behind their walls at his approach. Conan's path led him to the general entrance, the only place where there was firm footing near the walls.

At the open gate Conan was confronted by the owner, whom he knew by description. Dizier, a short man of enormously strong frame, leaned on an ax and sourly demanded his business. Behind him were two half-grown boys with spears in their hands, eager and excited.

"I am named Luke," said Conan. "Has not Sandras sent word of me?"

Dizier's face did not change. "He told me little, except that you are a friend."

"And that is little?" asked Conan, smiling. "Are friends so plentiful, then?"

Dizier replied roughly, "I make my own friends."

"Then make friends with me. Here, I have brought you a present. Boys, lay down those spears and carry in this stag."

There was a pause of unbelief, while even Dizier stared his amazement. Rarely the peasant expected meat, except when, in the late fall, he killed such of his animals as he could not feed through the winter and laid up their flesh in brine. That here two hundred pounds of good fat meat should be brought as a free gift made Dizier almost gasp.

But fighting for his better judgment he came a step nearer to Conan, waving back the boys. "What is it for?" he demanded. "From whom do you bring it?"

Conan had determined to speak more openly now, so near was the time to its end, so sure was he of peasant faithfulness. He answered, "Let us say the Lady Anne."

Instantly Dizier was at his side, looking up, and demanding, "Are you really from her?" A pathetic hope looked out from his changed eyes. But when Conan hesitated to speak with perfect plainness, the peasant drew back. "Then you are against her! Either the one or the other!" His face was hard again. "You and your masons are stealing her castle from her!"

"What, for ourselves?"

"No, for the Sauval. They brag of it."

Conan saw that it was time to tell the truth. "They brag best who brag last. Listen, Dizier, and keep this secret. If you and I work together, the Lady Anne will come into her own. Trust me!"

Dizier came a step nearer, his face showing that his heart harbored loyalty to the unforgotten past. "Can I believe you?" he demanded searchingly.

Conan held out his hand. "I am for Lady Anne to the death!"

Dizier seized the hand and wrung it. He spoke with difficulty. "I could not believe Sandras; it seemed impossible. Now that I have seen you, I know you to be honest. Luke, tell me the plan."

"It is simply that Sir Roger of Fessart and Fulke of the Prigny shall take the castle before the Sauval think it ready for them. They will hold it for the lady."

"When do they come?"

"In four days."

Dizier's eyes shone. "And what can I do?"

"Watch. Send me warning of anything suspicious. We may call on you to fight."

The peasant gripped Conan's knee. "I will fight gladly. We will keep the Lady Anne in her fief!" But then his face showed doubt. "If only the young baron of the Prigny were not dead. We needed him to marry her, and take the fief and hold it."

Conan tingled. He who had once dreamed of winning a princess listened willingly to this talk of a different marriage. "Well," he said as indifferently as he could, "the man is dead."

Dizier beckoned his young sons, and they came running. Conan dismounted, and the horse was led into the yard to a shed, where the stag was lowered to the ground. With cries of delight, women and children came to look upon the beast. But Dizier stayed by Conan, with his wife and a young woman, as well, whose strong face was full of sadness.

"This is my daughter-in-law," said Dizier. "Outside in the fields, two months ago, my son stood off the Sauval so that the women and children could escape. But they took him and carried him off. We hope that he is still alive, but we know nothing of him."

At the mention of her lost husband the young woman became thoroughly aroused; her eyes shone and her mouth became hard. The eyes of the older woman also glittered with anger; she muttered and growled threats like a man. Here was living resentment. No wonder that with women like this, and with children doubtless cast in the same mold, Dizier could maintain himself here alone in spite of every hardship.

While the younger ones frolicked, anticipating a feast, and women hacked collops from the flesh and ran to build up the fire, Conan talked with Dizier. He asked of the peasants living farther toward Prigny, what man-strength they had, how willingly they would turn out to fight. And Dizier assured him that they cherished the old loyalty.

In the midst of this happy relaxation of the hard labor of the farm, Dizier suddenly started and turned his head. Conan heard the sound almost as soon as he — the galloping of horses, rapidly approaching. Dizier's face turned white under his sunburn, as he looked about on his household, who stood fixed in fear. "No watch!" he cried. "The gate!" He turned to Conan. "Hide yourself!" And he rushed toward the gate.

There leaned against the eaves of the house, close to where Conan was standing, a few dozen heavy poles or light spars, forming an accidental shelter. No door was near, so behind these Conan stepped, taking his dog with him. Here, he hoped, he might remain hidden from the arrivals, who were, he felt sure, men of the Sauval.

Dizier was too slow. He had but begun to swing the heavy gate when the first horseman appeared in the opening, leaped, as it were, into the very middle of the farmyard, and there drew rein. He and his horse, in that sudden halt, were like a statue frozen but animated, still but threatening. A steel cap gleamed on the rider's head, the ringed armor was polished bright, the brass bosses on the shield sparkled. The man held his head high like a conqueror, and his eye, as he looked about him, glanced in triumph. Dizier surprised and caught! In the high head, the haughty eye, Conan knew the man in spite of the nasal of the headpiece. It was Red Ralph, once the ragged outlaw, now more dangerous still as the trusted man of the Sauval.

In the next moment Ralph's followers appeared, crowding through the gate. There were four of them, and one was on a led horse, riding without arms or headpiece.

At sight of this man the young woman, wife of the missing man, gave a broken cry, and then stood trembling, her eyes fixed on the unwilling horseman, whose eyes roved all about the place until they saw her. Then his pale face flushed, and it seemed as if he could not look away, so eagerly did his eyes fasten upon her.

Ralph waved his hand to Dizier, and laughed. "What, old fox, trapped without a weapon in hand?" Dizier, his knife at his girdle, but helpless against the other's sword and shield, made no answer. Next, Ralph saw the fixed glances that held the young woman and the guarded horseman. "Husband and wife!" he cried, and laughed. "What, do you know each other again?" The prisoner turned his head to him with an angry growl. And as Ralph laughed again, the woman leaned against the house, her hands holding her heart.

She was close to Conan, who spoke to her guardedly. "Do not look this way. Go, get scythes and pitchforks, and arm the other women and boys." She started as she understood, then took a slow step toward the door of the house.

Ralph now saw Conan's horse. "Whose steed is that?" He looked at the sullen Dizier, then again round the yard. "And a fat stag! What, hunting old boy, and so glad of a little meat that you forgot to be cautious? I had not hoped to find the gate open. But where got you such a horse? A serviceable beast, truly."

"Now!" said Conan to the woman. She glided into the house.

"By Saint Hubert!" cried Ralph, pleased. "The horse is too spirited for Odo, too light for Aymar. 'Twill carry me well. Dizier, the horse is mine now!"

Conan was peering from his place and watching the young man who was guarded by Ralph's followers. A recent wound marked the young peasant's cheek. He was powerful, slow of movement like his father, but with the same heavy jaw and determined face. He was slow of wit also; but knowing that the horse could not be his father's, he was scanning the courtyard for a sign of the owner. His problem was plainly evident on his features; but he had given no start, and his silent search was slow, unobserved by the others.

Ralph struck his hand on his thigh. "Well, Dizier, I brought your son on a visit, expecting a little parley over the gate. This is more friendly. Look at him, man. You see he is well and hearty. He will be well fed and warmly lodged until, like any of us, he gets his few inches of steel in a fight." Ralph laughed as he described what was, to him, the natural end of man. "Well, Dizier, give us the news, and the haunches of the venison, and we will leave you in peace. Tell me, how far has the building gone at the castle?"

Dizier had neared the door. If Ralph marked the movement, he was indifferent to it. The peasant said: "How do I know anything of the castle? I have not been near it for a year, nor any of us. But you have your spies."

"The spies," replied Ralph contemptuously, "have come to the end that all spies meet, first or last, for we have had no news for weeks. I could go myself and view the castle; but these men of Vézelay are a contentious lot, and would claim that we have broken the agreement. Come, man, tell us what you know, and we will be on our way."

"By our lady," replied Dizier, "I know nothing."

It was at that moment that the young wife reappeared. She came slowly from a shed beyond the house and was drawing behind her a short pole, the end of which rested on the ground. After her, three other women came silently from the same shed and took various directions, each dragging a similar short pole. And though the ends of these poles seemed harmless, Conan saw that to them were attached the blades of scythes, for as they dragged in the dust they picked up the straws of the barnyard. Dizier's wife made her way toward him; the daughter-in-law went toward her husband. Their movements, though slow and cautious, were yet determined. One of the women spoke to a staring boy; and he, taking his eyes from Ralph, looked at her, nodded, and taking a younger lad by the sleeve, led him into the shed.

Ralph was not angered by Dizier's second refusal. "Think, man," he warned. "Look at your son; see that cut on his cheek. An obstinate devil he is, like yourself, and we had to teach him obedience by a little roughness. What we did to him once, we can do to him again. Dizier, don't be a fool, for whatever you deny us we shall make him pay for. Come, what is the news of the castle?"

As the threat sank home the young wife stopped short and gave a little cry. Ralph laughed. "Be sensible," he said. "The young fellow is decent enough, and I will do him no harm — unless you force me."

But Ralph meant to have his way. For he gave a sign to the horseman beside the young peasant, and the man at once lifted a short club studded with spikes, ready to lacerate the young man's bare head. Plainly all this was planned. The young man squared his shoulders and awaited the blow.

"A bold young cock," said Ralph approvingly. "A pity to harm him — eh, Dizier?"

The young peasant spoke bravely. "Father, say nothing, unless you wish."

Ralph was quite at his ease. "That is right, Dizier, just as you wish. But decide quickly."

The pause that followed, while the old man struggled with the situation, was tragic for him. He might have lied, but any falsehood was slow to his mind. And his hatred of the Sauval, with his heavy wrongs, fought in his mind with his love for his son. His mouth worked, his brow was furrowed with perplexity.

Then Conan stepped from his concealment. In his shield hand he carried his javelin; his right hand was empty, and with it he saluted Ralph. "I can tell you about the castle," said he.

Ralph was hardly startled. "Luke, is it you? How do you come here?"

"I have been hunting," explained Conan. "That is my horse, and yonder is my deer. The masons at the castle grumble so much at the food you left them that I have had to hunt for meat. And the work is sadly behindhand. Come in ten days, and it will be ready."

"What?" demanded Ralph. "The full fifty days? That is hard to believe. But very well, come with me to Odo and explain it."

"Nay," answered Conan. "I must back to my work."

Ralph knit his brows, but as he was about to speak, there rose a clatter of hoofs and a commotion behind his back.

At Conan's sudden appearance every eye had turned on him; even the man whose club had been raised to strike turned his head and listened. And seeing his chance, the young peasant had now leaped from his saddle, and dodging past his guard, caught the scythe from the hands of his wife. On this, Dizier's wife ran forward and gave her scythe to her husband. The man shook the weapon with savage joy.

"Now," he shouted hoarsely, "take my son if you can!"

The situation had changed. Though Conan seemed neutral, against Ralph and his three men were the two peasants and their whole family. For from the hands of a boy, Dizier's wife took another scythe, and two other women uplifted theirs. And the short, broad blades of these heavy implements, wielded by women used to the work of the fields, might easily disable man or horse. Further, the larger lads now showed themselves, each with a club or pitchfork. — It had not been planned, this sudden threatening, but it was the more dangerous. For here was a breed whose instinct was for fight; and at the right moment each, big or little, male or female, was ready to swing weapon and fall on.

Ralph, while not daunted, clearly was taken aback. He and his men, though horsed, armed, and grouped, could be attacked from all directions. In such a fight, either side was sure to receive grievous harm. Ralph was angry, but he parleyed.

"Come," he said, "think what you do. Will you have all the Sauval down on you? Dizier, give up the boy; and do you, Luke, come with me."

But Dizier answered between his teeth: "I care not. My son shall never go with you again."

And Conan, his javelin now ready, said, "Neither will I ride with you. Go! Wait till I bring you a message."

What Ralph hungered to do was plain. To snatch out his sword and strike against any odds was the desire that was boiling in his blood. But he was faced too coolly from in front, and he knew that danger beset him from right and left. More than that, he heard behind him the horses of his men as restless as their riders, and one of the men-at-arms spoke uneasily. "Come! Away from this!"

Then Conan, while Ralph still lingered, strode to his horse, and with a quick turn and spring was in the saddle. He caught his feet in the stirrups, gathered his reins, and, as he swung the steed to face Ralph, hitched his sword into position for drawing. He said nothing, but his whole attitude bespoke defiance, as he met Ralph eye to eye.

Ralph was no bull, like Aymar, to bellow and charge. Controlling his anger and dropping his hand from his sword, he backed his horse a step or two. But then his eyes dilated with sudden surprise. He spurred his horse forward again, and faced Conan from close at hand.

"So you have been hunting? Show me your sword!"

Conan, as he raised the scabbarded weapon, kept his eyes on Ralph's face to see if here were any trick. But Ralph merely glanced down, smiled with a sneer, and wheeled his horse away. He did not look again at Dizier or his lost recruit, but with his men willingly going before him, without another word rode away through the gate. His sharp command was heard, and the horses' feet pounded into a gallop. This yielding and departure were so quick and unexpected that Conan remained fixed, wondering at it, oblivious of the shouts of the boys shutting the gate, or of the cries of the mother and the wife, casting themselves on the breast of their lost one, thus restored to them. Why, Conan asked himself, did Ralph depart so suddenly, without even a threat? He sat thinking, until he became aware that he was still holding the sword in the position in which he had shown it to Ralph.

And looking down, he saw very plainly what Ralph must have seen — the points of the carved gold of the pommel showing through the wax with which Pierre had covered them. In these rides of his, the wax had been worn away. Ralph, then, must have recognized his own weapon, must even have pierced Conan's disguise at the moment when his eyes suddenly widened.

In fact, it was Conan's knightly leap upon his horse, and his management of the steed, which showed Ralph that here was no mason, and no peasant.

As this became clear to Conan, he snatched out his bow and strung it. He turned to the gate, but the boys were just closing it. When, at his quick command, they slowly heaved it open and he rode out, he saw Ralph, far beyond bowshot, just entering the skirts of the forest, while his men, less well mounted, lumbered behind.

Conan drew rein. He could do nothing now. Hopeless to ride after those four men, not knowing how soon they might join a stronger group. But everything now was betrayed to the Sauval.

As he re-entered the yard, Dizier, who met him, read dismay in his face. "What is wrong?"

"Ralph knew me."

"Of course. He called you by name."

"More than that. Dizier, this is misfortune."

"I care not," said the stanch peasant. "Let them

come and burn the house, but we can escape in the marshes. If I have again Alard, my son, I am content."

"You mistake me," answered Conan. "Not your house, but the castle is in danger. Call your son here."

The young man, with his wife and mother still holding to him as if they feared to lose him again, came and stood before Conan. "Alard," said the squire, "you have escaped the Sauval, but you are not yet your own man, for you are still the Lady Anne's."

"It is true," admitted Alard. "We are all hers."

"Now Alard and Dizier, attend," said Conan earnestly. "The squire whom you supposed slain by the Sauval, Conan of the Prigny — that man am I."

The men exclaimed in wonder; the women cried out in joy. They listened with amazement, while Conan quickly unfolded to them all the plan for seizing the castle for the Lady Anne.

"Yet now that I am known, Ralph has gone with his story to the Sauval, who will surely rush to take the castle. Therefore we, on our part, must summon our friends at once. I go to Baron Roger's. Dizier, have you a horse?"

"One sickly beast," answered the peasant. "Too lean even for the Sauval to steal."

"Alard," directed Conan, "you must ride the horse till it drops. Then you must run, to Castle Prigny. Do you know the way?"

"I have never been there. But I can find it."

"Tell my brother what I have told you. He must come at once. Go and saddle. Lose no time!"

And the women, though they had just regained Alard, cried, "Yes, make haste!" They hurried the young man to the sheds.

"As for you, Dizier, you must rouse all the other vassals, Sandras, Louis, everyone. Send these lads or the women, go yourself, if necessary. Every man must turn out. Hide your families in the woods. The men must hang on the rear of the Sauval and the outskirts of any camp. Harry them. Pick off every straggler. Make every effort. Stop at no risk. For now is the time, and never again, to bring back the Lady Anne."

In haste he watered his horse and gave directions for keeping the dog. Then he tightened the girths, mounted again, and rode away.

XVIII

Conan Is Not Dead

CONAN, with his horse not yet tired, appeared again suddenly at the castle, and called for Pierre. While the horse was lightly foddered, Conan told his news. "How soon," asked Pierre, "will the Sauval be here? And how soon can you bring help?"

"Much is due to chance," replied Conan, "to the speed of messengers, the quickness with which men can be gathered and started. Because the Sauval are raiders from habit, the chances are with them. Yet my brother and Sir Roger should be already preparing, and perhaps they can be prompt. For my own part, much depends on my horse. The distance is long, and I can get no other."

"And we are still to continue getting the stone inside the walls?"

"Aye. For today you should be safe, for they cannot be here before tomorrow. But from tonight, keep the drawbridge raised. If men go out for the last loads of stone, raise the bridge as soon as they leave. Keep watch. Open to no one that you do not know. But the men know nothing, yet, of the meaning of all this. Tell them the whole story."

"Take a few minutes now, and tell them yourself," advised Pierre. "Then leave them to me."

Conan's speech, when once the thirty masons were grouped before him, was effective, because his life among them had taught him their very minds. Further, it was in his favor because they thought well of him. That he was not what he seemed, they had long ago surmised. They perceived that, horseman and hunter as he was, he could not be a peasant's son. And where did he get his carriage, his ready speech, and the leadership which had made all willing to work not merely with him but even under him, when often, quite unconsciously, he took the lead? But no speculation concerning him had hit upon the truth, and his opening words surprised them.

"Men, you have heard of Conan of the Prigny, said to have been lately killed. Well, slain he was not, for I am he!"

They stared at each other, not at first believing. For lords did not work, and this man had turned his hand to every task. But Pierre stood by, smiling and agreeing. Luke, then, was that lost young baron! Well, well! They began to smile.

Briefly he told them of the plan to outwit the Sauval, and its discovery. He ended, "The Sauval will be down on us tomorrow, but on the next day, help will come. What say you, will you hold the castle a single day?"

The men all shouted, "Yes!" And with that comfort, Conan started on his ride to Sir Roger's. At

best it was a half day's ride, from noon to sunset; but
the sun was already past the zenith, his horse was
not fresh, and he himself had had no food since
morning. And he had forgotten, now that he wished
to make speed, how hard was the going, how numerous the steep pitches, how stony the footing. Impatiently he longed to gallop, with thundering hoofs,
across this obstinate fact of distance; but he could
not risk it. He must use all his knowledge of horse-
flesh, must call into play each instinct gained by his
years in the saddle, to keep his steed going. Too long
a burst, or too heavy a strain at the outset, and the
beast would be done. But by deliberately slowing the
pace, by wise walking on hillsides or among stones,
even by Conan's going afoot to ease the animal on a
stiff grade — by all this and more, requiring constant
self-restraint, the horse was kept going and the miles
slowly unrolled.

But the ride was long and tedious. The time came,
as the afternoon wore on, when Conan thought it best
to stop and rest after a steep climb. And a little later
he stopped by a brook to let the horse drink and crop
a little of the grass. When he started again, he walked
the horse before he dared to put it at the trot.

Yet at last Conan knew himself to be in the domain of Sir Roger. Here was the tree under which
he had slain the boar, that time when Anne came
pushing in. It was not much more than a league,
now, to the castle. And he thought he could risk
setting spur to his steed.

But from beneath a tree two men started up, with the cry of "Stand!" They barred his way, each with poised spear.

Conan's hand snapped to his sword hilt, and he shifted his buckler for defense. Then as he looked from one to another of the men, he dropped his hand. "So, it is you, Granson, and you, Morat? Since when have you taken to stopping travelers?"

For he knew the men well, the oldest and trustiest of Anne's retainers. Shabby, morose, dogged, they had grown to be like each other in temper and devotion, and neither was ever far from his young lady. Taken completely aback, they lowered their points at his familiar authority, yet stared at him, unrecognizing.

A little impatient, he looked down from his horse, and demanded, "Do you not know me?"

Then the mouth of one of them opened wide in recognition. He bore a step backward, tried to speak, swallowed, gasped, turned white, and was silent. The other, when Conan turned his eye on him, stubbornly held his place, but was stricken with a like amazement. He stammered:

"Messer — Messer Conan?"

"The same indeed," answered Conan sternly. "What is it ye do? Have you turned thieves?"

"No," replied the man. "But — but you came so suddenly, we feared you might ride her down."

Conan leaped from his horse. "Lady Anne — is she here?"

The man pointed. "Behind yon thicket."

Conan tossed him his rein. "Hold my horse, Morat." He turned away from them so quickly that he did not see the movement which each of them made, as if to stop him from going forward so abruptly. But they checked themselves, shook their heads in deep perplexity, and stood still.

Conan knew where Anne would be: on a broad stone where often hunting parties had rested themselves after the chase. And there he found her, seen in profile, sitting dejectedly and so deep in thought that she did not hear his step, nor notice the jingle of his sword belt, as he approached. Unsuspicious, he did not mark her attitude, nor her paleness, nor, in his masculine eagerness to greet her, did he think of the possible significance of the broad black scarf which she had put over her shoulders. He was simply glad to see Anne again. Quickly he stepped close, and stood in front of her.

Anne looked at him as returning from faraway thought. But then her eyes flashed wide, her hands caught at her heart, she turned still paler, and seemed about to fall backward. Conan dropped on one knee before her and quickly caught her.

"Anne," he cried, perplexed, "it's Conan! Don't you know me?"

She looked into his face — such a doubting, hoping look. She made a pitiful failure of a smile. And she said, while two tears started to her lashes, "Oh, Conan, we were told that you were dead!"

He shook her gently, at first completely obtuse. "Dead, Anne? But you see that I'm alive!"

"Yes, yes," she replied. "But they said the Sauval —"

"I escaped them," he said, and did not notice, as he groped for understanding, that one of her hands came up and rested on his breast. "It is true, my death was reported in Vézelay. The news came here?"

"Yes." Her answer was gentle; the hand caressed him, ever so slightly; and the eyes, damp with their unshed tears, were tender. But Conan was in the depth of his thought.

"Surely Sir Roger received a message from me, to prepare to come to the Red Keep."

"Yes. But when we heard that you were dead — "

"You mean," cried Conan, "that you thought it had happened afterward? When my escape — my death! — was before I sent the message?" Conan started to his feet. "Anne, does Sir Roger believe that the plan to take the castle was given up?"

Her hand dropped to her lap. The tenderness faded from her eyes as she watched Conan, manlike, forgetful of her, struggling to comprehend the situation. "Why, yes," she said gently. "We thought it had to be."

"But we have been building!" he cried. "The castle is ready for defense, and we need but the men. But now, by unlucky chance, the whole plan has been revealed to the Sauval, and tomorrow they are sure to descend upon us. Therefore I have come to summon Sir Roger to our aid. Where is he?"

Color had come back to Anne's face, and seeing the emergency she likewise rose. "Sir Roger is away! He has just started on a journey to Semur, to be gone three days. And half his men are with him!"

Conan struck his hands together. "That this should happen!" But as he saw his plans threatened, his spirits rose to save them. "If I could get back, if my brother comes, and I had Sir Roger with but a few, all at the Keep by tomorrow noon, we could save it."

Anne shook her head. "To bring the baron so soon is impossible."

As Conan stood and frowned, Anne saw that she was still just his comrade, like another man. But that was welcome, anything was welcome, since she had him again. He said at length: "Will Lady Blanche send but half the rest of her men? Eustace could lead them."

Anne shook her head. "Eustace is sick. As for the castle, when Sir Roger left, Lady Blanche raised the drawbridge. She was scarcely willing to let me come riding. Sentinels are doubled, and no man can leave."

Conan set his jaw. "I must turn back and hold the Red Keep with the masons alone, till Fulke comes. And you can at least send me your own men; they are not under Lady Blanche's orders. Support me in this, Anne, at least."

She reared her head. "Support you?" she cried. "Conan, this is my own fight!"

"True," he returned. "I have so learned to hate the Sauval that this has seemed like my own affair. — Anne, what horses have you here?"

"Only my old gray. Granson and Morat are on foot."

Conan shook his head. "I had hoped for a fresh mount, but my own horse is better than the gray. I must turn back from here, to save time. — But your men? They have no horses, I fear."

Anne shook her head. "Not one that we can depend on. And Lady Blanche will spare us none."

"I would go with you if I could do any good, but if you cannot shame her into giving help, I cannot. — Now, Anne, gather every man and send them as soon as you can. Send none singly. For defense, they must go together."

Anne nodded. "But half of them are in the fields. We cannot muster until night, nor start until the morning."

"It is the best you can do," agreed Conan. "Tell them to keep watch as they go, and to approach the Red Keep cautiously. In doubt, let them wait at the knoll from which they first can view the castle, and raise a pennon on the oak tree there. If Eustace cannot go, put Granson in command. And now I must go. Good-by!"

He shook hands with her, still as if she had been another man. Then he was gone without looking back. And Anne gave him but one last glance. With

her spirits roused to meet the emergency, she called
her men and started for Fessart.

It was a full hour before Conan, on his return
journey, began to think of Anne. He had been coax-
ing his horse, or thinking of the news that Anne
gave him, planning what he should do. But when at
a long, hard climb he swung himself from the saddle
and walked beside his horse, his mind turned to
Anne herself. She had thought him dead, and was
so startled when first she saw him that she had
seemed about to faint. But why? He had long thought
that even a ghost would have no terrors for Anne.
So why should she have turned so pale?

It could not be — no, she could not have been
grieving because of him!

Quickly, in Anne's defense, he denied that she
could have been so weak, so impossibly foolish, as to
be fond of him.

And on his own part he felt shame at his pre-
sumption in thinking it of her, even for a moment.
He was glad to mount again and put his mind on
the further study of his horse's endurance. At last he
knew that its strength was evidently failing, and that
he must rest it. Forced to curb his own impatience
to proceed, he stopped for the night at a place where
there was water for the horse, and young grass. He
himself could have nothing but the water, and envied the beast its food. But at early dusk, as he laid

himself down, he fell almost instantly asleep, so tired was he.

He woke in the night, however, as the horse moved about. Then it was not hunger which kept him awake for awhile, but the remembrance of Anne's hand, unnoticed at the time, as it had lain upon his breast. That little action of hers had seemed almost like tenderness. Though again he was ashamed of himself, the thought would hold him.

On the morrow that same recollection was his undoing. He had been an hour under way, his horse now acting as if stiff and weary, when his mind wandered again to Anne. Her hand at his breast, that firm little hand of hers, but almost tender! He lost himself in the thought, and so was not ready when his horse stumbled. It fell, and threw him heavily. Bruised and dizzy, he rose and examined the horse. Its shoulder was so lame that it could not carry him another step. He must go the rest of the way on foot. Surely he had been punished for his presumptuous thoughts.

XIX

Anne Will Go

ANNE RODE BACK to Fessart, her horse lumbering at its usual slow gait, the two men loping behind. When she came out of the forest, and saw the castle before her, but half a mile away, she drew rein. The men behind her stopped. Anne said, "Morat."

Morat came forward and stood at her side. She was looking across the fields where laborers were still at work, near the little village where old Hughes had died early in the summer. "Morat, we are starting for the Red Keep at tomorrow's dawn."

He was startled out of his usual sour silence. "The Red Keep, my lady?"

"Aye. Are you willing?" She smiled at him — the smile, with dilated nostrils, of one who grimly says, "At last!"

"Willing," he answered, "and ready!"

She spoke over her other shoulder. "And you, Granson?"

He stammered in his eagerness. "To — to start this minute!"

"We must prepare," she replied. "Morat, tell each man, and the youths, David, Hugot, Jourde, to make ready. Bring them all in from the fields."

"Lazare?" suggested Morat.

"Your own son?" asked Anne. "He is not too young?"

"Madam, I offer him. I dedicate him."

Calmly Anne accepted the sacrifice. It was for them all. "Very well. Lazare, too. Let each man have his arms, and a day's food. Tell no one else. Be at this spot at first dawning."

She was sure of the silence of each of them. "Go at once," she said. Morat bowed and turned away. "Granson, when we are in the castle, quietly tell each of our men to prepare. They are to be at the gate together at cockcrow."

"Good, my lady! Good!"

As they approached the castle, the drawbridge, raised as in wartime, was lowered to receive them, and the portcullis was lifted. One big gate was opened inward, and Anne rode in. Granson took her horse when she dismounted, to lead him away. As Anne was going to her turret chamber, she was intercepted by a page. Lady Blanche wished to see her as soon as she returned. So in her riding clothes Anne presented herself before the chatelaine where she sat at her tapestry frame among her damosels, all sewing. Not one of these looked up to give Anne a smile, and it was evident that Lady Blanche had not been in the best of moods.

Only two persons were not completely cowed by Lady Blanche. One was her husband, and he was afraid of her at times. The other was Anne, who was not afraid of her at all. Anne had her own way, and her freedom, because of Sir Roger, but not always. When Lady Blanche insisted, Anne always yielded, after brief communing with herself. Lady Blanche knew that these submissions had been because Anne had never felt the occasion important enough to resist.

She eyed the girl's costume with disfavor, yet could say nothing in reproof. The skirt was short, but not too short; the ugly black scarf Anne had put off; and even the gold circle in her hair could not really be criticized. No one else in the castle wore such an ornament except Lady Blanche herself, and hers was a sign of her rank as seigneuress. Anne wore the thinnest circlet; it was her mother's; and Anne claimed a fief, though she did not possess it. Lady Blanche felt that for Anne, a charity child, to wear the circlet was uppish. But when once she had hinted as much to Sir Roger his anger had been genuine, and she had not forgotten his forbidding her to mention it, or even think of it, again. But at any rate, apart from this feminine ornament, Anne was always too mannish, forever running out into the woods.

Lady Blanche was still under forty, fair but sharp of feature, and dark of hair. A notable housewife she was, versed in every domestic art, and a little jealous, some suspected, that Sir Roger thought more of Eustace's power of healing than of her own. She made wonderful tapestries, and sat now with her needle suspended above the frame. "I am glad, Anne," she said, but without the appearance of pleasure, "that you came back before dark. Yesterday you were so late. It is not safe. And so I have decided that you are not to go out any more on these jaunts of yours until Sir Roger returns. What he allows then is his affair, not mine." By the toss of her head she anticipated her husband's indulgence of a spoiled ward, and washed her hands of it.

Full of her own thoughts, Anne scarcely noted the lady's familiar mannerisms. She replied simply, "Tomorrow will be the last time."

"Tomorrow?" repeated Lady Blanche sharply. "Anne, I said that you are not to go out again."

"Lady Blanche," Anne hurried on, "I must tell you. Today, in the forest, I met Conan — "

The damosels' heads flew up, their eyes flew open, and their mouths. Lady Blanche stared. But Anne gave no time for question or exclamation. Rapidly she told the story. "And so you see," she concluded, "that I must have every man you can spare, to save the Red Keep."

Nothing in Lady Blanche's expression showed that she realized the choice that lay before her — if such a situation is ever met by choice and not by the automatic action of old habits. To rejoice, or not to rejoice, that the lad whom she had fostered had come to life. To see, or not to see, the appeal in

Anne's hands, eyes, her whole quivering figure, as she stood expectant. To be moved by the generous desire to aid these two, the high-hearted determination to make the whole region safe against the Sauval, or to close her heart to these impulses. No, it was not choice, but the smooth operation of Lady Blanche's customary selfishness, together with the rigid intention never to risk anything for anyone whatever, which closed her mind and heart to the opportunity before her.

She said, with that correctness of manner which never failed her: "I am glad that the news about Conan was false. But do you not see, Anne, that in going back to the Keep he but throws his life away again? I cannot help him, nor can anyone."

Though Anne scarcely expected anything else, the cold answer bitterly disappointed her. She was determined, however, to make every effort. "Lady Blanche," she said, "this may be the last chance, the only chance. I beg you, give me men!"

Lady Blanche, with an air of patience, put her needle in the tapestry, and left it. "I cannot," she said.

"Then at least," urged Anne, "give us horses!"

"Us?" repeated the lady. "What do you mean by *us?* You do not think of going?"

"Of course I must go," replied Anne. "No one else shall lead my men."

She might have seen, in the eyes of some of the

damosels, flashes of admiration. But her look was fixed on the baroness, and in that face she read only a dainty horror. "Anne," remonstrated the chatelaine, "that is so unmaidenly that I cannot believe it, even of you. Think again. The idea is impossible."

This was worse than Anne had imagined, but quietly she clasped her hands as they hung before her. "My lady," she said simply, "I must go."

She was met by equal firmness. "No one," said the lady, "is to leave the castle until Sir Roger returns. I have made up my mind to that, and what you tell of the chance of fighting only confirms me." And when Anne would have spoken again, she added, "I think you had better go to your room."

Anne stood and thought. It was the old deliberate weighing of a situation which always had irritated the baroness. Then Anne said, as one calling witness, "I have given you your chance." And she left the chamber, still unconscious of the admiration in the eyes of the less wise of the damosels.

It was because of this admiration that she received a warning, two hours later, from the youngest of them all. Anne had supped with the rest, had borne herself cheerfully, and had quite coolly, when no one was looking, slipped into her lap and under her mantle a portion of bread and cold meat which she had cut and laid ready. She took it to her room with her, wrapped it in a cloth, and put it by. Then she was called to the door by a timid knock. There, full of agitation and with a finger on her lip, she saw the little maiden. "Rosalind," she said, "come in."

"I cannot," said the girl, with hushed voice. "But Anne, I came to warn you. Lady Blanche means to shut you in tonight. She means to close the door at the foot of the turret. As soon as all have left the hall, she will order it closed."

As soon as all had left the hall: that gave Anne a little time. She kissed the girl, who suddenly, in tears, clung to her, sobbing. "Oh, Anne, I would go with you, if only I knew how to fight!"

"Dry your eyes, dear," said Anne, soothing her. "You mustn't seem to have been weeping. Thanks for the warning. If Lady Blanche asks about me, tell her I have gone to watch with Eustace awhile. Father Gregory should be there too, at this hour."

Thus it was that Father Gregory, dozing by Eustace's side, was roused by the coming of Anne. She laid down by the door a long package, but kept her cloak closely round her. Its hood was over her head. "How is he?" she asked. The priest could know her only by her form and her voice.

"The fever is declining, he thinks," replied the chaplain. "He is as interested in himself as ever he was in any three sick men." He pointed to a scribbled parchment. "See, he has written down all his symptoms. In two or three days more, he should be on his feet."

Anne bent over the young leech and noted his

heavy sleep, his flushed face. Then she said quietly to the priest, "Father, I mean to spend the night here with you two."

For all his oddities and self-indulgences, Father Gregory was a kindly man and no fool. Having gone to the hall for supper, he had gathered the rumors that were whispered about. He looked keenly at Anne's closely held cloak. "My daughter, what do you plan to do?"

She answered, "Nothing in which I shall ask you to help, if only you do not hinder."

He crossed himself. "God forbid that I should hinder you in anything, or Conan. Get your sleep, Anne. I will watch."

And through the night the priest did watch, attentive to Anne's quiet breathing, Eustace's heavy sighs, and to any sounds that came from the passage outside. Once, led by these last, he took the candle and went to the door, to satisfy himself that he had heard aright. The form of a man lay across the passage, and the priest saw his open eyes reflecting the beam of the candle. It was a guard, and Anne was a prisoner! Shaking his head, the priest went back to his place. But toward morning he slept.

It was Eustace who, rousing at length, saw first, through the window, the faint gleams of dawn, and then, by the flickering of the dying candle, the form of Anne. In her sleep she had unclasped her arms, and for air had thrown back her hood. Eustace saw

her, therefore, reclining in a chair, her braids escaping from under her iron cap, her form sheathed in chain mail. He gave a gasp of astonishment.

With that, Anne roused and sprang up. She too saw first the dawn, and in haste shook her hauberk into position and adjusted her girdle, from which dangled her dagger. She stooped to her bundle, opened it, and drew forth her sword. As she hooked it to the belt, her eyes met those of the astonished Eustace. To his unspoken question she gave immediate explanation, while the priest, himself now awake, listened. That Conan was alive, that the Red Keep must be saved, that now she must get away from the castle — this she told rapidly.

"Bad fortune, Eustace, that you are sick," she finished. "But I must away at once." She turned toward the door.

"Anne," warned the priest, "Raymond is on guard."

But Anne merely drew her poniard, and stepped out into the passageway. Raymond — she knew Raymond well, a good fighter. She would see if he would stand up to her. Round her left arm she wrapped her mantle, and clanked toward the figure which, startled, yet barred the passage.

"Lady Anne," said the squire, "you must stay where you are."

"Raymond," she returned, "out of my way!"

As she stepped into the light of a torch, he saw the armor, the pointed dagger, but more formidable, the resolute face. She advanced upon him without pause, and — he gave ground.

"My lady — !" he expostulated. But still she came on, and again he retreated. "Lady Anne, I beg you — !" Once more he gave way. "I must call Lady Blanche." And he backed out into the courtyard.

"Call her," said Anne, and passed him. She heard his hasty footsteps, and herself sped across the court to where shadows, under the wall, ought to mean her men were there.

They were all there, in the dim light. Granson with her horse, and nine of the men of the Red

Keep, who rose from their places as she came, and murmured a greeting. Since long before dawn they had been waiting there. She gave a hasty hand to each, then turned toward the gate. None of them protested against her going first. It was as natural to her to lead as to them to follow.

The gleaming clouds in the sky threw more light down into the courtyard; night was all but gone, and she could see the guards as they clustered before the gate, listening to her coming. They were awake and quite ready, had been warned of her plans and been told what to do. They stood in front of the gate, and with crossed spears barred her passage.

"Who is in command here?" asked Anne.

It was Walter, good servitor, whom she knew well. To her demand that he clear the passage, he replied that it was forbidden. He must not open the gate, nor raise the portcullis, nor drop the bridge. Here was a different problem. Seven men against her ten, but she could not merely back them out of the path. There was a key to be produced, winches to be worked, time to be lost in opening the way. She had foreseen this, and had not known how to meet it. But go she must.

There was a clatter as a door opened on the other side of the court. Torches flickered, and people came hastily. First of all, Anne saw Lady Blanche, and behind her, Raymond and more men. The lady, long nervously awake, had responded instantly to the summons. And Anne felt easier; for it was to be woman against woman.

The lady cried as she advanced: "Anne, back to your room! No one shall leave the castle!"

Anne waited. She let Lady Blanche come between her and the gate. Then she gestured to her men to come behind her. This they did immediately, as if drilled to it. And, when Anne drew her short-sword, with accord they raised their weapons.

Lady Blanche shrank at the flash of steel. "Anne! Anne!"

"Lady Blanche," said Anne, "if you do not let us go, we will fight, and die, right here at your feet!"

Not one doubted that she meant it. Lady Blanche looked about on her men, and not one sword had come from its scabbard, not one spear had been raised. To fight — this would be wickedness, friend against friend. And for what? Every man there sympathized with the girl.

Walter spoke in the lady's ear. "Madam, these men are desperate. They will fight to the last one. Bethink you — if we fight, you will lose a score of men before these are finished."

It was a shrewd suggestion, and Lady Blanche caught at the idea that she was risking her own safety. She knew too well, also, these sullen devils of Anne's followers. Good riddance, then! She turned away.

"Open the gates. Let these men depart. But Anne, you shall not go."

Anne said nothing, but lowered her sword. Her men eased their positions merely half; they were ready at a sign, at a word. With relief the men of Fessart sprang to the work of opening the gates, raising the great grating, lowering the bridge. Not a word was spoken. When the way was clear, Anne gestured to Granson. He led the horse across the bridge, and one by one the men followed. But when Anne took a step to go, Lady Blanche once more spoke. "Anne, on your duty I order you to stay."

"Madam," replied Anne firmly, "I follow my duty." And she marched out.

Two more figures had approached, and stood waiting. As they stepped forward to follow Anne, all recognized them. Eustace was first, pale, with bright eyes, his clothing hastily donned, his cap askew, his weapons dragging. Behind him was the priest.

"Eustace," cried the lady, "what would you do?" But as the answer was plain, she commanded, "On your obedience, remain!"

"Madam," answered Eustace, "I owe you no obedience. All obligation I have long since repaid. I will answer to Sir Roger." And went forward.

The priest followed. He was short, heavy, clumsy, clogged by his robe. But there was dignity in him as he stepped out, as he would not listen to the command the lady threw at him, as, regarding nothing, he still advanced.

"Stop him!" cried Lady Blanche.

Only one man sprang out to obey the order. But

the priest bent on him a glance so sharp and stern
that the fellow stopped short. No one else moved,
and the chaplain went on. Anne, her men, Eustace,
and the priest, all were safely out of the castle. Lady
Blanche looked at their backs, as with determination
they marched away. Her voice shook when she spoke.
"Up with the bridge! Down with the portcullis!
Close the gates and let none stir out!"

She hurried back to the donjon. Unwillingly her
men worked at winch and rope and chain, swung
the doors, thrust home the heavy bolts. Not one of
them but wished himself free to follow Anne.

But out at the edge of the clearing, Anne mar-
shaled her little force. Eustace must ride; she would
allow nothing else, except that the horse might carry
her mail until they neared the Red Keep. Without it
she was light of foot, ready for the long journey. But
the poor priest!

"I will achieve it," said he manfully.

"Then forward!" commanded she.

And into the forest marched that little train.

XX

Strange Visitors

A HALF MILE from the Red Keep, in the forest, was that little stony knoll of which Conan had spoken to Anne. From there, with Sir Roger, years ago, he had seen the burning castle, while at the same moment the watchman set by the Sauval had caught the flash of the weapons of Sir Roger's men. Hard by this knoll, a little before noon on the day of Conan's attempted return, liveried servingmen had lighted a fire and warmed a meal, which their masters presently enjoyed.

These were three young men, of whom the two elder, perhaps twenty-five years of age, paid deference to the third, who might have been barely twenty-one. All three were handsomely dressed in garments fancifully cut and richly colored, such as the abbot of Vézelay sometimes affected but few others wore in all that region. Each had golden spurs at his heels, wore sword and dagger, and had beneath his surcoat a light suit of chain mail showing at the shoulders and around the hips. But they had no other protection, for their light caps seemed to conceal no steel.

They were in the holiday dress of gay young men, with just enough besides to show that they were trained to arms.

"It is strange," said the one who seemed the eldest, "that the abbot of Vézelay should have discouraged us from riding in this direction. True, it is not a rich region, but it is not too wild. And out there on the plain, with the masons building on the castle, it seems a haunt of peace. What can have been his reasons?"

He had ease and grace, a confident address, and a manly voice. It was no wonder that the youngest, to whom he deferred in manner, should in return defer to him in fact.

"But Enguerrand," said the youngest, "I did not suppose that the abbot tried to keep us from this place. To me he merely praised Montreal."

The third one, Bernard, laughed grimly. He seemed the strongest of the three, one who, in spite of youth, already had a set purpose in his life. "The abbot, Hugh, is double-faced. To you he merely made a suggestion, but to us he said it would be a waste of time to ride into this forsaken region. Which seemed to us a very good reason for coming. But if you think the castle peaceful, Enguerrand, so do not I. Why should the castle need repairs, and why is the drawbridge up? — But who comes?"

He pointed down an aisle of the forest along which a man was running toward them. He was coming at a slow trot, flat-footed and full of effort.

He seemed very weary, held his head low and let it swing from side to side, stumbled once and with difficulty recovered himself, but still came on. His weapons, sword and bow, shield and quiver, were bundled on his back. The ascent to the knoll forced him to walk; he plodded up the ascent, turned away from the shaded spot where the watchers sat, and, walking to the bare spur of outcropping rock, stood scanning the castle.

The weary runner was Conan. For miles he had been heavily trotting, feeling more and more the need of haste but less and less the ability to hurry. With enormous relief he perceived that the castle was still safe.

At the sight, all the pressure of haste was removed, and his fatigue and hunger descended heavily on him. Food he had none, but at least he could lie here for half an hour and rest before undertaking the last short stage of the journey. He unslung his weapons from his back, and looked about for a spreading bush under which he could lie unseen. His eye fell upon the three sitting figures. At once his weariness left him, and he began feeling, in the bundle of weapons, for the handle of his sword. What were such strangers doing here?

Enguerrand spoke to Hugh. "Here is one that we can question. Shall I offer him food?" Hugh nodded, and Enguerrand, turning to Conan, pointed to the dishes that still stood spread upon the cloth. "Friend," he asked, "are you too tired to eat?"

Slowly Conan came forward. Casual and friendly though Enguerrand seemed, the squire eyed him warily. "A little food would be welcome," he said. "Have you plenty?"

"We have finished," replied Enguerrand. "The rest is yours. What, you have not eaten for long?"

Conan smiled. "Not since yesterday morning."

Hugh uttered a word of surprise, and Enguerrand lifted his brows in a comradely smile. "I marvel," he said, "that you could run at all. Eat, then, but go slowly with the wine, for it is heady upon an empty stomach."

As Conan sat down he studied these young men, so well dressed, so assured of manner, and all so nearly of his own age. Suspicious, he yet felt a liking for them, though such men he had never seen before. He was used to the squires and young knights at Sir Roger's, all a little rough in manner, and with strangers somewhat given to aggressiveness in order to assert their own importance. But these men, ready to accost a stranger without formality or doubt of a welcome, possessed a dignity which required no assertion. As for their dress, its quiet richness seemed to proclaim a thing as yet unknown to him — fashion. Where could they have come from? Probably Avallon; scarcely from the ducal court at Dijon, so far away.

Behind them in the shadow of the bushes he now perceived their squires, and moreover three pages, one of whom came forward to serve him. But Hugh waved the lad back, and himself lifted and offered the dish of pasty. "Pour the wine, Enguerrand," he said, and the latter, overtaken in a look of surprise, obeyed. "Nay," said Conan quickly. "You are knights. I am but a squire. Let me serve myself." But as Hugh still held out the dish, Conan helped himself from it, and bowed to Enguerrand as he poured the wine. "You honor me," said Conan to them both, and felt that his words were true.

Yet in spite of that, what was the meaning of their presence here, and how might it affect his own plans? Wondering thus, Conan ate sparingly, with a precise knowledge of the position of his sword.

But Hugh, shifting his position as he laid aside the dish, frankly studied Conan's face, and liking it, urged him to eat, pressed more wine on him, and then began to ask questions. Had he traveled far? What had happened to his horse? — and to him, Conan perceived, every gentleman had a horse. And why, when Conan had been forced to go on foot, had he not discarded his weapons?

It was impossible to resist the boyish interest.

Conan smiled. "Are weapons so easy to come by, where you live, that you do not know the value, in this wild place, of a good sword and bow? I should have to travel many miles before I could get as good again."

"While," suggested Enguerrand, "if you had been attacked — ?"

"Even so," agreed Conan. "True, I had trussed all my weapons on my back, but unless completely surprised I should soon have had them in hand."

Hugh protested. "But, Enguerrand, who would attack a wayfarer here in Burgundy?"

Enguerrand echoed dryly, "Who, indeed?" His glance seemed to invite Conan to answer the question.

But Conan was cautious. He attended, therefore, to his meat and wine, very grateful for the warmth and power which they gave him. And he listened with growing surprise while Hugh, with mounting feeling, expressed his belief that here in Burgundy, if anywhere in the world, the roads and the countryside were safe. While Conan marveled at such simplicity, he admired the high-mindedness with which Hugh laid down the cardinal principle that every man, whatever his degree, had a right to expect from his suzerain the safety of his body and his goods. There was silence when Hugh finished.

But as his eager and almost anxious look required response, after a moment Bernard soberly replied. "Hugh, your goodness is evident with every word you say. Yet Louis, King of France, cannot travel anywhere in his domain without a strong escort. How then shall we hope for better things in Burgundy?"

Hugh pressed his hands together. "They are better! I know that they are better!" But this time, in spite of his greater earnestness, the others said nothing.

Yet Conan, feeling that they disagreed with Hugh, wondered if here were not a situation deeper than he had at first imagined. For he divined that Hugh's almost passionate words had been addressed to that unspoken disagreement, and that the young man felt his failure to remove it. Hugh sat and looked at his two friends, deeply disappointed at their silence, until he could bear it no longer.

"You do not agree with me!" he cried.

Bernard answered, "What, Hugh, shall we flatter you?"

He replied with deepest feeling, "No! Before God, no!"

"Then consider," went on Bernard. "Not my opinion will settle this question, nor Enguerrand's. Only one thing can do it, and that is fact. And fact is here at hand."

He pointed to Conan, and as Hugh turned upon him, the squire became the focus of all their searching looks. Bernard said seriously, "Sir squire, answer truly all we ask of you."

But Conan replied: "Not so fast. I am indeed indebted to you for your meat and wine, which I needed much. Yet I might have fasted a little longer, and may wish I had, rather than take part in your controversy. This is not idle talk of yours. I perceive that something lies on it. Ask me nothing."

Bernard shook his head. "So much lies on it that we needs must ask and you must answer. And first, who are you?"

"Returning crusaders have told me," returned Conan warily, "that an Arab will ask his guest nothing, not even his name. Tell me first who you are."

Hugh looked at Bernard. Bernard shook his head. It was Enguerrand who spoke. "Friend, one man may give his name freely while others for good reason conceal theirs. Be satisfied with this: Hugh is a young gentleman who, before he takes up the care of a goodly property, wishes to learn something of the world. And Bernard and I, his friends, differ with him in opinion, and we need proof. Now you, it is plain, have experience of life here in this corner of Burgundy. Answer, therefore, what he asks you."

His words were not satisfactory to Conan, who was considering his reply, when Hugh spoke impulsively. "I must have information, yet I may not give it. Your name I do not ask; but tell me, messer squire, that I am right in believing that in this region there is peace."

Conan could only echo, "Peace!"

But in his tone there was such irony that Hugh could not mistake. He faltered, then said: "At least in yonder castle there is quiet industry. What is the place?"

"It is the Red Keep, which sometimes, to myself, I call the Bloody Keep, when I remember the murder of its master there six years since."

"Murder?" echoed Hugh, and drew back. Then he returned to his inquiry. "Whose is the castle now?"

"It should belong," replied Conan, "to the Lady Anne d'Arcy, daughter of the slain lord."

"And you are of the household?"

The ignorant, innocent questions were stirring Conan's feelings. "There is no household," he said. "Since the murder of the baron, the castle has stood empty."

"Strange!" remarked Hugh. "Yet now it is being repaired. For whom?"

Conan answered bitterly, "For him who can take it!"

The young man, finding here more than he wished to believe, was silent. But Enguerrand took up the inquiry. "Is the castle for you, then?"

"If I were there, with men to help me, I would hold it for the Lady Anne."

Enguerrand was keen to draw out the facts. "And you came running to look, as if the castle might have fled in the night. Why?"

"To see if others had seized it."

"You are as mysterious as we," said Enguerrand, with that swift change to good humor which seemed a characteristic. He spoke with persuasive charm. "Tell us at least this — you are of noble blood?"

Without answer Conan took his sword, and held its hilt over the still hot coals of the brazier. At once the wax began to drip down. Conan looked at Enguerrand, and said, "I am of the small nobility, as I suppose you are of the great."

"But you are not yet knighted?" asked Hugh.

Conan smiled. "Foolishly, you may think, I declined knighthood until I had earned it." He turned to watch his sword, keeping the hilt above the flame of the wax which now was burning in the brazier, and shifted it until the wax was all melted away. Then, rising and gathering leaves from a bush, he rubbed the golden pommel and guard until their points began to shine. When he had finished, he looked at the silent three, and said: "This sword, which I wear because I won it, I will never disguise again, nor myself. I am Conan of the Prigny, brother of the baron."

Enguerrand exclaimed. "But in Vézelay I heard that you were slain!"

"It suited me to have it believed," replied Conan.

"Because of plans for this castle?"

"Yes," admitted Conan, surprised at the other's quickness.

Hugh, listening and looking from one to the other, was puzzled and felt hurt, and being so, became imperious. He rose and said, "What is this story you have heard, Lord Enguerrand, and why have you not brought it to me?"

His manner was aloof. The others had instantly risen as he rose, and Enguerrand bowed with an immediate abandonment of comradeship. "Your lordship," he said, "was not ready to believe it."

"Lordship this, lordship that!" thought Conan. "I am in high company, but as these people are nothing to me, I must away." He waited for an opportunity.

Then as Hugh stood divided, it seemed, between resentment and affectionate reproach, there came from a distance the floating note of a horn.

The sound came from the direction of the castle. In alarm, Conan turned and ran to the spur of rock. He hoped that the horn meant only a summons to surrender; but when he saw the castle his heart sank in dismay. The drawbridge had been lowered, and close at hand, almost upon it, was a little column of galloping horsemen, perhaps twenty in all. Following them were still more footmen, running. And the hoarse note of the war horn expressed certainty of success. Before the drawbridge could be raised, the foremost horsemen were upon it. Conan thought they were Ralph and Aymar. Certainly one in the middle of the line, closely attended, was Odo. The horsemen streamed across the bridge and under the raised portcullis, the footmen followed, and the workmen on the walls merely stood and stared.

Then Conan saw why all this had happened. Approaching the gate was a load of stone, slowly dragged by the masons' pair of horses. While the workmen went for this load, no one could have been on guard, but meanwhile the Sauval must have been lurking in the wood. Seizing their chance, they had dashed for the gate. The masons had been caught napping.

Conan stamped in fury. Behind him Enguerrand spoke. "And was that peace, my squire, or war?"

Conan saw that all three had followed him to the rock. "It was war!" he cried. He turned to Hugh. "In this peaceful Burgundy you have seen the castle of a girl seized by the robber neighbors who treacherously slew her father — who will take her fief now that they know themselves safe from the duke's justice!"

Enguerrand pressed Bernard's shoulder, pressed hard. "What," said the latter, "you impeach the duke's justice?"

"And why not?" returned Conan. "Six years ago I was with Sir Roger of Fessart when he arrived just in time, here at the castle, to save the girl from the slaughter which took the rest of her family. Again and again, since then, has Sir Roger sent petitions for redress, never to be answered. And now the Sauval, the murderers, have bargained with the abbot of Vézelay to seize the castle, while he takes the better lands. For the duke's justice — sleeps!"

"Sleeps?" cried Hugh.

"Being drugged, I think," added Conan, "with money!"

"What!" mocked Enguerrand's silken voice. "You accuse barons, and an abbot, and the great chancellor of Burgundy?"

Conan saw that the mockery was not against him, and followed where it led. "Yes, I accuse, a simple squire."

"And what hope," asked Enguerrand, still scoffing, "have you of redress?"

Conan snapped his fingers. "As much as that, while the duke is still in leading-strings."

"Enough!" said Hugh. He spoke with dignity, and the others were silent. "And this," he went on, "is the golden age of Burgundy, of which I have been taught to be proud!" He stood frowning, but while his glance passed from Enguerrand to Bernard, their eyes did not fall before his. He turned away. "I must see this abbot, and this chancellor. Attend me, lords, back to Vézelay." And he strode toward his waiting horse.

While Bernard followed, Enguerrand lingered. He asked earnestly of Conan, "What you have told us is all true?"

"True, every word."

"If I cannot depend upon it," warned Enguerrand, "it will cost me my friendship with the young lord."

"Lay your life upon it," replied Conan, "but believe not the abbot."

Enguerrand's intensity relaxed. "Perhaps," he suggested kindly, "our holding you here in talk lost you your chance to save the castle."

Conan had mastered his anger and disappointment. "Once I had seen you I had to find out if you were enemies. But also I was too tired to go a step farther. And had I merely rested a little and gone on, I should have been caught in the open, and cut down like a dog. Besides, what happened, happened."

Enguerrand put a hand on Conan's arm. "Come with us to Vézelay."

Conan shook his head. "My brother is coming with his men. A few old vassals may come from Fessart. I must stay and warn them."

"Stay, then," replied Enguerrand. "But take no risks. If I mistake not, we shall return soon."

"Return if it interest you," replied Conan. He would have added, "With fortune, I will show you how justice can be administered here, without the duke."

But Enguerrand was hastening away, and presently, with much trampling, the horsemen were moving away through the forest, leaving Conan alone.

He sat himself on a spur of rock and gloomily watched the castle. The load of stone had been drawn within, and the drawbridge raised. There was no longer any work on tower or rampart. Conan brooded long.

XXI

The Captured Keep

CONAN STUDIED not merely the castle but the open land around it. The strong situation of the Red Keep was evident, on its promontory surrounded by ravines, cut off from the plain by the moat. To besiege the walls, engines would have to be brought up under cover of great moving shields. Here was idle speculation, thought Conan, as he found himself wishing to batter the walls which he had just built up. He had no catapult or mangonel, without which he knew it would be impossible to force his way into the castle.

What was going on inside he could not make out. No workers appeared on the walls, even after two hours' waiting. Once in awhile a figure moved on top of the keep, a watchman. But at last an unexpected sight brought Conan to his feet. The drawbridge was being lowered!

He shaded his eyes to see the little figures. A horseman appeared on the bridge, leading horses. Other strings followed, with four riders in all. At a smart trot they headed for the woods. Conan under-

stood. In the castle was not fodder for so many
horses. They might be pastured on the plain, but
would there be raided by Anne's supporters. So they
were sent to be pastured in the hayfield of some
farm, to be kept there till wanted. The plan was
good.

But Conan smiled. Fulke had not arrived, but
there was Dizier to be reckoned with. If the peasant
was not already on the track of the horse-keepers,
Conan could follow them to their hiding place, and
bring word to him. So he circled to cut off the little
train, and striking their broad, fresh track, followed
it for a half mile, until confronted suddenly by a
man, who heaved up an ax to smite, shouting, "Ha!"

"Dizier!" warned Conan quickly.

The peasant lowered his ax. "It is well you spoke
so sharp. I thought you another of them."

Conan looked at the blade of the ax. "Clean it,
Dizier. What — did you get them?"

"All four of them. And but three of us."

"So few? Have not the other vassals turned out?"

"They are dribbling in. Tell me what to do with
the horses."

"Bring your men here. I will speak to them."

In a glade in the forest where the men of Sauval
had found no safety, the peasants gathered, already
half a dozen of them, excited, keen for more blood.
Conan noted the harsh triumph with which one of
them stepped on, not over, a body lying in his way.
Seeing an enemy lie dead, the squire felt such re-

spect for that complete misfortune that to insult it
seemed shocking. But suppressing his feeling, he
turned to the business in hand. Some men he told
off to drive the horses where they could be left in
the care of women. Others were to bury the dead.
As more came in, he assigned them to stations around
the castle, covering the complete circuit. None were
to show themselves, but all were to watch, and to
assemble at any point of danger. He himself, he
warned them, was going to study the castle from
every angle: let them not take him for an enemy. Let
them watch, too, for friends coming from Fessart
and Prigny.

At sunset he began his own prowling circuit. From
in front of the gate towers, one complete as of old,
the other still unfinished, he went to the left, peering every little while from a new vantage point.
When the castle was in his power, he told himself,
these young bushes that gave him cover should be
cleared away. Meanwhile he studied this side of the
tower, from the edge of the ravine which protected
its rugged and steep foundations, its straight walls
with no handholds, and its window-slits hopelessly
out of reach.

He came to the farther corner of the great triangle, and slipped down into the ravine to where the
bottom was freely grown with bushes, from among
which he looked up at the huge bulk of the square
donjon, the Keep itself. Gazing at its color, more
deeply dyed by the sunset, he wondered if its hue

were prophetic. Alone of all the buildings the keep had windows of fair size. But they were hopelessly above the reach of the tallest ladders.

He came to the next corner, guarded, like the other, by its slender turret. He climbed out of the ravine and studied this last side, noting how the wall which ran from the turret to the unfinished gate tower was also not quite finished, for it lacked its guarding battlements. But what use was that to him? In spite of this incomplete corner, Conan was balked by the massiveness and imperturbability of this great mass of stone. And he himself had put it into condition for defense! Anger shook him that his plan, so good, had failed, and that those robbers had once more succeeded.

But calming himself, he tried to use his wits. What were the Sauval doing? From the black arrow-slits were men watching? Or were they, feeling secure, already settling themselves in the great hall and the chambers near-by? The smoke that had risen from the kitchen chimney told him that they had dined long ago. By this time they should be getting sleepy.

He was suddenly alert when at the top of the keep he saw two figures whom he knew to be Aymar and Ralph. The baron lurched to the battlement with his heavy stride and stood looking across the ravine. Ralph, following, was nearly as tall, but leaner, and supple. The two looked for awhile, pointing here and there as if to master the lie of the land. So much Conan could

see in the dusk before they withdrew — except that
twice Ralph yawned and stretched.

"He has traveled far, with little sleep," thought
Conan. "But now he is well fed, while my stomach
is nobly empty again. That is well, for I must not
sleep, while I hope he will. He is too dangerous."

No one else came into view; no lights shone from
the donjon; and all was silent from within. Feeling

safe at last, Conan left his concealment and approached the unfinished tower. Here he let himself down into the ditch, now almost dry from the heat of summer. Moving across it slowly and cautiously, so as not to be seen or heard from the watchmen's slits close above him, he found himself below the drawbridge. This stood nearly upright against the face of the gateway — nearly, but not quite, for there showed, between fresh lumber and the deep tone of the wall, a black shadow which proved that a man, if he scrambled up, might find standing space just outside the portcullis.

"This shall be remedied," thought Conan grimly, "when the castle is ours." Stepping close to the foundation, he discovered a convenient footing, and reaching up, secured a handhold. "And *this* shall be remedied," he thought, as he swung himself up. In a moment, and without sound, he was standing between the drawbridge and the portcullis. From here, since the gates were missing, he looked through the arched tunnel of the entranceway into the castle court. This was not dark, but was lighted by a flickering orange dimness, as by a single torch.

Now first he heard the noises of the castle. Three sounds came to him continuously. His ear delicately detached them from each other, and he knew the meaning of each.

Across the court, in the keep, some few were carousing. A harsh voice croaked a song; and at the same time a thin, high tenor was cutting across the tune in a speech of monotonous assertion. "Drink," thought Conan, with much satisfaction.

Snores came from nearer at hand. Conan ascribed them to the door of the new tower, which opened to the right of the passageway. It was likely that here was the guard which the Sauval had posted to keep the gate. The snores cut across each other like the voices of the drunken men.

From quite as near, yet muffled, Conan heard voices muttering in a broken cadence. These came, he decided, from the old tower on the left, whose door was closed.

Besides these sounds he heard but once the crackling of the hidden torch. As he looked into the courtyard and could not see its flags or the bottom of the keep, he realized that his view was cut off by the heaps of cut stone which the masons had carried in and piled. He wished to enter, but the portcullis, that enormously heavy grating of wood and iron, was in his way. He tried to shake it, and it barely responded to his thrust and pull. He stooped and gripped a lower bar, and, with a slow heave, tried to lift the whole. It rose but a few inches, and he saw that he never could hold it up and at the same time slip under. As he let it down again, it grated badly.

He heard a voice. "Eh? Who's there?" It came from the open right-hand tower. But it was sleepy, and while Conan waited in silence he heard a grunt and sigh, as if the guard had gladly gone to sleep again. But his slumber was not deep. How then to find Pierre?

The question solved itself. For the door on the left opened slightly and a beam of light shot across the passage. A head thrust out and remained listening. Conan knew it, and whispered, "Pierre!"

Pierre stepped out and closed the door behind him. The light gone, he was a shadow in the passage, craning this way and that. Then, swiftly and noiselessly, Pierre was at the portcullis. Conan reached a hand through, caught his sleeve, and drew him close.

"Conan, I knew you would come, so every little while I would listen at the door. The watchmen have only just gone to sleep."

He spoke in a whisper, and Conan asked, "How many are there?"

"Three."

"What are the Sauval going to do?"

"They say they will force us to complete the castle, and laugh at the idea that we can go home without their permission. Conan, must we submit?"

"Hist!"

Inside the guard tower they heard a growling and the scratching of shoes, as of one man slowly rising, while yet the snores of his companions continued. He came to the doorway and snarled, "You Vézelay stoneworker, go back to sleep!"

Pierre answered, "I was doing nothing."

"You were whispering to yourself, unless — Oho, who is there talking with you?"

"No one can be here," returned Pierre.

"No one? Well, I'm coming to see."

"Come, then."

Pierre stood still; Conan crouched. The lurching shadow approached, grumbling. The man was not really suspicious, but was angry because of the disturbance. "I'll teach you to prevent a sentinel from sleeping!"

He came close and felt along the bars. Pierre moved aside. "Curse you, let me get my hands on you!"

Conan rose, reached through the portcullis, felt the man's clothing, jerked him close, and with swift certainty caught the hairy throat. The man, writhing, tried to brace himself and pull away, but was helpless.

"Pierre, a gag!"

"This is quicker!"

A blow sounded dully, and the man collapsed in Conan's grip. He let him go, and the body sank limply.

"My hammer," said Pierre briefly. "He will be quiet for awhile. Listen, now."

But there was no other sound than the near-by snoring. Conan said: "I must get in. Can we lift this portcullis together?"

"Of course."

They laid hold of the grating and lifted it to the height of the knee. "Hold it now, Pierre." Conan slipped under, rose, and helped to let it down in place. Again they made sure, by listening, that they had roused no one in the castle. "Drag him into your tower and bind him," directed Conan. While Pierre obeyed, Conan himself went and stood where the entrance archway opened on the court.

His opportunity had suddenly become clear to him — to build a wall across this narrow end of the court and hold the Sauval imprisoned! Here there was but the width of the archway and the two towers that flanked it — less than sixty feet — to be stopped by a wall built of these piles of square-cut stone. Yet overhead were two ways by which the Sauval could attack along the walls that enclosed the court, on footpaths which, some fifteen feet overhead, led to doorways in the second stories of the towers, doorways from which the doors had long since vanished. These, therefore, must also be stopped by stone. With good fortune, it could be done — if the masons would fight.

He went back into the masons' tower, where Pierre, kneeling, had just finished tying the watchman. The circular room was some eighteen feet across, and the masons, roused from their sleep, had mostly raised themselves on their elbows and were watching. On the head of one he saw a bloody bandage. He asked, "What happened to Landry?"

The man, with a curse, put his hand to his head. Pierre explained briefly. "He tried to raise the drawbridge against the Sauval."

"Lucky for him," said Conan, "that he was not killed."

"I ought to have been," growled Landry. "It was I that forgot to watch." Conan stifled an exclamation: the damage that this man had done was incalculable. "Why do you not yourself kill me?" asked Landry; and when Conan shook his head, added, "I will repay what I can."

"Come with me, then, and Pierre, and two more, and bind the other watchmen. Two to a man, and one to hold the light."

Five of them went, then, across the passage and into the other tower, where in the circular chamber some dozens of bags of lime were still piled, and the snoring watchmen were outstretched on straw. Pounced on and throttled, gagged and tied, they were rolled aside and left, and their companion laid by them. Again in the first tower, Conan found himself in a ring of men, eagerly waiting for his word.

"We have just a few hours to sleep and to act. If you wish, you can slip away. But if we abandon the castle, all the plans of the Sauval will succeed. They will hold this place. We cannot retake it. They will harry Vézelay whenever the abbot calls them."

Landry spoke eagerly. "Tell us what we can do."

"In the court are many loads of cut stone. A wall

across this narrow end will keep in the well and cut off their water. As soon as my brother arrives with his men we are safe."

"But we have not enough mortar to lay the stone."

"Lay it dry," replied Conan. "Its weight, with our spears and swords, will make the walls strong."

He waited for more objections; then as none came, he spoke again, with growing feeling. "This is a chance that will never come again. The worst enemies of our peace have shut themselves in the keep, but we hold the gate. The abbot cannot bring them food; we hold their water. If they attack us, we shall have the advantage. When my brother comes, and the men of Fessart, we can attack them." He thought of the secret passage which would lead him into the midst of his enemies; but of that he would not speak until he was strong enough to divide his forces. "Remember that if the Sauval keep this castle, they will always be a threat against your commune. And now, answer: are you men enough to build this wall and defend it a single day, for the sake of the Lady Anne, for hatred of the Sauval, and for the safety of Vézelay?"

In the faces that confronted him he saw doubt. These were not warriors, but men of peace. They looked at each other uncertainly, and the most that Conan expected to hear was one man saying to his neighbor, "I will if you will." His heart began to sink.

But Landry spoke suddenly. "I will, to pay my debt."

Pierre was the more manful. "Conan, we understand this threat to our freedom. Give us orders, and we will fight for you!"

And a quick, hoarse murmur showed that the men agreed. Conan felt weak with relief. Recovering, he said: "Let every man get his sword and spear and lay them near where I shall tell him to work. Pierre, come outside and plan with me."

Alone with Pierre, he said: "You understand the risk? If we are not able to finish the wall — !"

"I understand," replied Pierre calmly. "But it is for Vézelay."

"And for the Lady Anne," added Conan warmly. He pressed Pierre's shoulder. "Silence, now, and speed. Lay out the line of the wall to take in the well. Take all the men but eight, and drive the work. I will put the others to work in the towers. — One thing, however, Pierre. What of food?"

Pierre led him silently near the well, where above a fireplace roughly constructed of the loose stone blocks, Conan saw a great kettle, smoke-blackened. "They made us cook our own food. We have a whole day's supply."

He spoke with lowered voice, and Conan responded in the same tone. "Thus they put a weapon in our hands. — Here come the men."

The first man that came out was Landry, with his weapons. The second was one Baptiste, a good worker. To them Conan said: "Choose each of you three men, and wall up the doors which lead out upon the curtain walls, one flight up in each tower. You, Landry, take the new. Close up each doorway with a double wall, bonded well, finished to the full height. Lay your weapons near at hand."

Conan himself fell to work with the men who were building in the court. Once the line was laid out, and the first course laid, they needed no instruction. The stones were cut so nearly uniform that the work went fast. They "broke joints" by having no one joint above another. They "bonded" by laying the longer stones crosswise, in the wall of double thickness. By the wavering torchlight they went to and fro, and only the shuffle of their steps, the sound of occasional heavy breathing, and the grating of the stone rose in the place. One course was laid, and two, and three, by the time Conan guessed it was midnight. But these summer nights were short. And he wanted not four feet, nor five, but six feet of wall, with footings inside for the defenders to stand on, giving them the advantage. When two more hours had passed, with the men from the towers now working on the wall, he began to fear there would not be stone enough nor time enough.

From time to time Conan stopped and looked about upon the work. His broigne cumbered him; he wanted to lay it aside, but dared not. He looked over what the others had done; and he looked often, too, upon the silent keep, or on the torch, burning to-

ward its socket. At length he went boldly to the
torch, carrying a new pitch knot. This he lighted
from the first, and set it in its place. As he stood for
a moment beneath it, for the twentieth time listening for some sign of alarm, he gave thanks that the
Sauval still slept.

But he saw that the sky, above the open court, was no longer black, nor were the stars so bright. He joined Pierre at the wall and asked, "Will the stone hold out?"

"For two more courses."

"It is not enough. Level up this course and then build the wall single."

"It will topple when assaulted."

"Then that must happen." He gave the order in whispers, and the men of their own accord worked faster, with fortune still with them. Some men worked in the court, handing up the stones; others, within the wall, helped to set them. From end to end the wall was made level at last, and the stone was nearly used up, just as Conan remarked that the coming daylight had dimmed the torch. The men outside the wall came clambering over, and Landry laughed. "Are those Sauval dead? We have walled up their tomb."

But the wall was a scant six feet high, dry jointed, and with no place for the defenders to stand. Conan felt little confidence. He passed the word, "Let every man take his weapons and be ready!"

At that very moment a shout resounded in the courtyard. It came from a window of the keep; and Conan, with a smile, took his bow, strung it, and looked for the shouter. That one called again, "Ho, who is building that wall?" And he leaned out of a window to see.

"Every man that I can get out of the way," thought Conan, "I must." He shot, and the man lay upon the window sill, and was still.

Conan called aloud to his men, "Quickly now." They scattered to their places. Conan, ready with another arrow, and scanning the keep, saw that its battlements stood sharpcut and empty against the sky, and noticed, even in that tense moment, that the whole top of the keep was ruddy in the sunrise. Day had completely come, even in the courtyard.

Inside the donjon shoutings answered shoutings, echoing dully in its heavy depths. There were the pounding of feet and the clash of iron. But Conan could not see the door of the keep, and called to the nearest men to bring a lime bag, and lay it for him to stand on. When they did so, and he stepped upon the bag, he could see the door, but no one was so obliging as to come and stand in it.

"Beware," called Pierre. "You are too much exposed."

"Not yet," replied Conan. "Let the men bring other bags, and lay them for themselves."

They sprang at once to the work. While they were busy, and while Conan watched, a figure suddenly appeared at the top of the keep, between the battlements, looking down.

It was a narrow space which the court enclosed, not more, perhaps, than thirty yards across. The curtain walls at the side rose but fifteen feet, but the keep opposite, fifty. The man, at this height, could see Conan nearly to the knees, and the backs of the men laying the bags. He turned and beckoned to someone behind him; then raised a bow and prepared to nock his arrow.

"It is you or me," said Conan aloud, and shot again. Those of his men who watched heard the rush of the arrow, the *thuck* as it entered flesh, and the man's scream. He fell backward.

"Finish laying the lime bags," ordered Conan. His own eyes were fixed on the door of the keep, for he heard noises in the room behind it. Then a half-dozen men with swords and bucklers ran out into the court and stood hesitating, viewing the silent wall and the one man visible behind it. They seemed unready, disheveled from sleep, half blinking. Some looked back, as if expecting more to come. At that Conan called to his men, "Keep down until I order." and he sped another arrow. One of the Sauval dropped his sword, clutched at his side, spun about, and fell. His iron cap tinkled as it rolled among the stones. And every one of his comrades crouched, trying to cover himself with his buckler. Conan felt for another arrow.

It was then that Aymar, armed and angry, strode through the doorway. "What," he roared, tramping straight forward, "do these masons rebel? Follow me, and we will teach them!"

Conan, fumbling for his arrow, repented his haste in shooting. As he drew the arrow from the quiver the swordsmen cried, "Arrows, my lord!" On the warning, Aymar's great triangular shield came up and covered him. He stood still, peering over the top with a single eye.

It was a small mark, but Conan shot, putting venom into his wrist-snap. The arrow struck squarely on the steel cap, just above the eye, and its owner staggered from the blow. "Into the castle!" Aymar roared then. His men swiftly withdrew into the dark doorway. Aymar himself retreated out of sight. Once in the donjon, he was heard hoarsely shouting for more men.

Conan stepped down from his place. "We have a few minutes now. Divide your men, Pierre, into swordsmen and spearmen. But keep down. I must go into the towers."

In the old tower he found Baptiste and his men behind the walled-up door. The door was flanked by two arrowslits, one of which commanded the path on the wall, the other the court. "Shoot when the attack comes," he directed, "but at short range. It is not easy to shoot from a slit. And be ready with your spears if any man comes close."

To Landry and his men in the other tower he gave the same directions, then went up to the floor above. Here the unfinished tower was open to the sky, but the wall had been built highest on the outside, from which attack had been expected. Above the door which Landry was to defend it was not three feet high. On his hands and knees Conan crawled to this point, and lifted his head to look above the wall.

The court was still empty, the battlements of the keep bare.

But from the donjon came the twang of a bow, and from a black window a yellow arrow flitted across at him. It came so neatly, so precisely, with its feathered tail wavering ever so slightly, that it almost fascinated Conan into waiting for it. But, with a start, he dropped, and it whizzed by.

Lying on the scaffold, he looked for blocks of stone to build the wall higher. But all had been used. Then he called down to have bags of lime brought up to him.

One by one he placed them as they were brought, raising the little parapet by their height. He coughed from the dust of the lime, and his eyes smarted. Then, as he was working a bag into position, his face close behind it, the shining point of an arrow came slowly through, and stopped almost at his eye. But he finished two rows of bags to his satisfaction.

"Landry," he said when he went down, "I am so sure that the attack will come against your tower that I will send you one of Baptiste's men. Put the four at this door, but do you watch from the wall above. Shoot with your bow, or strike down with your spear. And if the Sauval crowd so close to the door that you cannot reach them, push the lime bags down on them."

He went to the court to wait the attack.

XXII

The Fight in the Courtyard

CONAN PLACED his men so as to be ready for
the assault, spearmen and swordsmen alternating.
Their weapons were not bad. Some had the spears of
the town watch of Vézelay, stout-shafted, broad-bladed
weapons some nine feet long. The swords of the
others were all short, best for close quarters. Conan
gave them their orders: the spearmen — when he spoke
and not before — were to leap upon the lime bags
and strike at heads across the wall. The swordsmen,
between them, were to strike upon men that clambered over.

One man there was a fair archer, and Conan posted
him within the archway, to shoot at the best marks
that he saw. "Shoot at bowmen if you see them. But
they keep well behind the windows, and are like
mere shadows."

There passed between them the well-known buzz
of an arrow, which split on the stones behind them.
Then — zz, zz, zzz — the arrows came in a thick
flight, and blunted themselves or broke against the

stones. Looking up, Conan saw new arrows sticking in the lime bags of the parapet. He called up to Landry.

"Do you see those who shoot?"

"No, they are all hidden."

The arrow-flight had ceased. Conan cried to his line of men: "The attack is coming! Be alert all!"

He had scarcely finished when from the old tower came the warning, "Men are coming from the keep!"

And Landry shouted down, "They are coming to attack along the wall."

Conan stepped upon a bag. Looking over the wall he saw men issuing into the court from the donjon door. Others, in single file, were running from the corner turret out upon the curtain wall that led to Landry's tower. A glance at the other side showed that there was to be no attack on Baptiste's tower. The men in the court came slowly, spreading out as they came, looking for support from behind. Those on the wall demanded Conan's attention, hastening toward the tower. The swish of an arrow passed close by him; he cared not. He raised his bow, sped his arrow, and the first man on the wall swerved and dove headforemost, out into the moat, exactly as if the act had been intended.

He looked down at the row of his men, who, all crouching, were watching him intently. He saw frowning brows and bared teeth, and knew that all were breathing quickly. "Not yet!" he warned, and looked among the men in the court for Aymar. To his disappointment the baron was in the rear, covered by his shield, rumbling out orders and threats. And with a slowness that amounted almost to reluctance, each man careful not to advance before his fellows, the men in the court came on. They bore swords, spears, and axes, and looked doubtfully at the dead wall before them, as if wondering why no opponents crested it as targets for their weapons.

Conan cast his bow behind him and drew his sword. "Keep low!" he warned his men. As he spoke, an arrow plucked daintily at his sleeve, and passed uselessly on. Conan turned to the archer. "Kill me that fellow in the keep." Then in a panic lest the Sauval should rush too soon, he cried to his spearmen, "Ready!"

The line of his men, with perfect confidence in him, ignorant of his panic, rose erect, waiting for his final order.

"Up!" he cried. They sprang upon the lime bags; and Conan, stepping down, gave his place to one who leaped at it eagerly. Behind him he heard his archer loose an arrow, but where it struck he knew not. He glanced along the top of the wall.

The wall was too high for the assailants to strike across it. At the same time their iron caps, all that were visible, were out of reach; and the spearmen, like statues set on pedestals, waited, intent. Then to Conan's left a head and arms appeared above the top of the wall, and the arms clung, while the head stared its surprise at the spectacle of a spearman waiting.

The arms relaxed, the head was about to fall back, when the thrusting spear scattered teeth, rove palate, held the miserable man a moment, before he fell to the ground.

The next instant another, lifted apparently on the back of a comrade, appeared above the wall waist-high, leaped from his unsteady footing, and thrust at by two spearmen at once, escaped them both, and lighted down between them on the ground. He swung his ax at the knees of one, when from behind Pierre thrust him through. Shrieking, he fell, and Pierre tugged in haste at his weapon, fearful that over the wall another might come leaping upon him.

By that time the whole wall was lined from outside with heads and springing bodies, some clutching for a handhold, some lifted by comrades, shouting war cries, snarling defiance. One man, astride the wall, defended his face with his shield, and struck desperately at the spearman in front of him, ignorant of the swordsman below, until the bitter blade pierced his midriff. Still another, leaping clear of the wall, lighted on his feet and rushed between the spearmen to strike at the archer in the passage. That one was unaware of his danger, but a backward slash of Conan's sword hacked through the bones of his assailant's neck.

Conan turned again to the wall, watching for Aymar.

Then a great hand, behind which appeared the conical cap which Conan's arrow had already dented, reached across an upper stone of the wall, and grasping its inner edge, drew it from its place. The stone moved outward, and fell with a crash. A second clutch Aymar made, and hauled from its bed a second stone. For the width of a yard, therefore, the wall was lowered at that place. "Here," roared Aymar. "Up and over!" He brandished an ax as lightly as if it were a sword.

While from within Conan made quickly to the spot, from outside two of Aymar's men leaped at the opening so hastily that they interfered with one another. As they were wedged, the spearman in front drove his point into the throat of one who, writhing, dragged his comrade backward in the effort to get away. Across their bodies, as they fell, Aymar struck at the spearman, who had leaned forward to the thrust. The ax split the leather cap and the skull beneath; the body, as it fell, dragged at the ax, while Aymar tugged to withdraw it. Conan, darting, struck at the shoulder of the Sauval; but as Aymar struggled, the sword glanced and turned on the armor. Roaring, Aymar released the ax and swung his hand to seize Conan. His fingers slipped along the arm and were grasping the wrist when Conan's violent backward swing wrenched his hand free. The effort lifted his sword high, and he brought it down with force on the Sauval's helm. The iron cracked, yet did not split. Aymar staggered back, and catching his foot, crashed upon his back. And Conan, overbalanced by this effort, leaned with his breast against the wall, unable at first to recover himself. For one second, for two, he was helpless against any attack.

But the assault of the Sauval had already broken. Seeing Aymar fallen, the nearest men shouted and fled; and others, seeing their support melt away, turned to save themselves. One, trying to climb down from the wall upon which he had sprung, was dragged within and stabbed. Another took in his thigh the hasty cast of a spear, and dragged it away with him, its end clattering on the stones. And two, seizing Aymar by the arms, were about to drag him away when, recovering, he shook them off, rose, and ordered them to attack. Instead, they fled. Finding himself alone, Aymar held his shield to protect himself and stalked to the door of the keep. He disappeared within, and left the floor of the court cleared, for a few moments, of all but the fallen.

Conan, as soon as he had recovered himself, turned for his bow. The body of the man whom he had slain lay across it, and Conan disengaged it and turned, only in time to see Aymar vanishing into the keep. At once the squire looked up to see what was happening on the wall.

That fight had been brisk. The first man of the attack had dived to his death; the others ran singly along the wall. There were six of them, the last of them Ralph, directing them all. He alone had pointed out to Odo that last night's walls, so hastily built, had no mortar and therefore were weak, and he had his own plan for breaking into the tower. Seeing the arrow-slits that defended the door, he commanded his men to block them with their shields. But as the leading man approached, an arrow pierced his leg, and missing footing, he somersaulted to the court. Another arrow met the next man in the throat; it turned aside, but the man, bruised and daunted, stopped. Jostled by the third, he dropped to his knees, and the others passed him by. Immediately the next two rushed on and carried out Ralph's plan, blocking the arrow-slits with their shields, thrusting in with their swords, and keeping the defenders so busy that they could inflict no harm.

This was exactly according to Ralph's calculations. While the kneeling man crawled back to safety, Ralph pressed close to the doorway just in time to escape an arrow from above, which splintered behind him. He pushed ahead of him the fifth of his men, and the two, swords in sheaths, attacked the blocked doorway with bare hands, and pressed with force against the uppermost stone. So powerfully did they thrust that the stone, though backed by another, gave way slightly. "Push!" commanded Ralph through his teeth. And at the next endeavor both stones gave way and crashed down inside, just missing the startled defenders.

"We have them now!" cried Ralph. "The next stone!" And again they tried. But Ralph's shout of triumph was too soon. As they pushed, the tongue of a lance flicked out above the stones, and the man at Ralph's side sprang back with wounded throat. As he stood swaying, with startled eyes questioning the meaning of the spurting blood, there dropped on him, from above, a dusty lime bag, which brushed him from the wall and carried him down with it into the court.

Ralph himself barely escaped from the second thrust of the lance. Too wise to step back, he swung to one side and caught at the shaft. It avoided him; and again the shining point, like a live thing, drew back and thrust. He escaped by crouching; but pushing on the narrow footing against the man at his side, he made that man give place. And then the second lime bag, slowly revolving, smote the man from the wall, and striking the edge of the stone as it passed, burst and filled the air with blinding dust. Ralph and his remaining man stood with their arms over their eyes, their mouths closed, not breathing till the dust should settle, quite unheeding the scream that came from overhead.

Then as they stayed rigid, crouching against blows, there fell on them headfirst a struggling figure. Overbalanced as he pushed the lime bags from the wall, Landry could not save himself, and it was only by good fortune that he came down upon the man at Ralph's side. Clutching, the mason brought him down, struggled to his knees, seized Ralph around the legs,

and in the wild endeavor to save himself a second fall, brought it about. Ralph toppled upon him, and the two fell together down into the court.

Beneath them two had already fallen from the wall. On them these two now fell, Ralph uppermost and unhurt. He rose from above the groaning mason, and with his first instinct drawing his sword, looked about him.

He saw the complete failure of the Sauval attack. Aymar was just vanishing in the doorway of the keep. On the curtain wall the last of Ralph's own party was racing to safety. Glancing across the new-built wall in the court, Ralph saw faces glaring at him, heard threatening cries, and next saw Conan, elevated above the rest, making the hasty motions of an archer who lays an arrow on the string.

For defense, Ralph caught up the groaning Landry and held him in front as a shield. And boldly, with his face to his foes, he began his retreat across the court toward the open door.

Conan, watching for a chance to shoot, felt helpless. But Pierre leaped with a shout over the wall and rushed against this too cool, too skillful helper of the Sauval.

Pierre had no chance. It was watchdog against wolf: the strong, well-fed townsman against the iron strength of the hardened outlaw. Nor did Pierre have the swift instinct of the born fighter. As he rushed at Ralph the body of his comrade was dropped at his feet, and Pierre stumbled. A lightning blow crashed on his head. Pierre dropped senseless. Another moment, and he was hanging head-downward from Ralph's shoulders, while as coolly as before the outlaw was stalking to safety, protected by his burden.

Conan stood raging. In the moment before Ralph caught up Landry, Conan had drawn his bow, but it had been broken at the tip, which had cracked when stepped on in the melee. He had snatched the light bow from the archer at his side, and had been ready for his chance when Pierre fell and Ralph stood over him. But as Conan drew the bow with his accustomed force, it split at the handpiece and the string slackened in his hand. Now the sight of Ralph retreating to safety was too much for Conan. He threw down the bow, snatched out his sword, and leaped upon the wall.

But the masons, with one voice, shouted to him to stay. His own good sense came to his aid. Ralph was at the very door, and beyond it lurked his mates. Besides, whatever Pierre's fate, the masons needed Conan to direct them. Sullen, he stood still.

There came a flight of arrows against him. One hissed by his ear, and unwillingly he stepped down into safety.

XXIII

Secret Entrance

CONAN FORCED himself to think no more of
Pierre. If he were already dead, then there must
be vengeance. But now Conan had to think of his
own battle, and his men. Up in the old gate tower he
knew there had been no fighting; he went up into the
new. There the defenders of the door had just been
checked in their jubilation, for they had discovered
the absence of Landry from overhead. His fall had
passed unseen through the arrow-slits. Conan explained briefly, and added, "At first he groaned as he
lay in the court, but soon he was silent."

The men accepted the obvious conclusion. Said
one, "He was my wife's brother."

"We must fight the harder," replied Conan, "for we
have also lost Pierre, the best of us all. So bring up
bags and rebuild the parapet above. Set one of your
number there to wait for the next attack. And replace
these stones thrown down from the doorway, leaving
room for a spear to thrust out between them."

Going to the court again, he estimated the situation at the wall. Some stones had been dislodged, and falling outside, could not safely be recovered. As to men, though one had been killed, and three were out of the fight because of wounds, there were yet enough left to man the wall. At the same time the Sauval had, as he reckoned, lost twelve, dead or disabled, so heavy a loss that the next attack must be less dangerous.

He set the cooks to getting breakfast. Water was handed about, the more welcome because the Sauval had little or none. Conan noted that when the little fire was built for the breakfast, smoke drifted across the court and into the windows of the keep. If that reminder of eating did not tantalize their enemies, he was mistaken.

A sudden call from Baptiste brought Conan hastily to the top of the old gate tower. Baptiste pointed out a rope that was hanging from the opposite slim corner tower that stood over the ravine. "It is hanging loose, but it has been tight. See, now they are pulling it up. There is a loop in the end."

"Then they have let down a messenger," reasoned Conan. "Watch. They may send down another."

And presently appeared, descending, a dangling man, who was lowered into the ravine. The rope came up again, this time not to reappear. But after a little two men clambered up to the edge of the ravine. On reaching the level, they began to run in different directions.

"One toward Sauval, one toward Vézelay," said

Conan. "But if the peasants are alert, they will not go far."

For one of the runners the distance to the woods was short, and presently he disappeared among the trees. But immediately there was shouting in the forest, and then silence. Next, Dizier himself strode out of the bushes, and set up, in full view of the castle, a spear. On its end was an object which was but too evidently of the shape and size of a human head. There were shouts of rage from the keep; but Dizier disappeared in the bushes with a scornful wave of his hand.

"But the other messenger?" asked Baptiste.

Conan took him to the other window, from which they could see the man racing to what he considered the safety of the forest. Ignorant of the fate of his comrade, he had no thought of danger as he ran toward it. Just before he reached the woods there rushed out upon him two men who, taking him unaware, together struck him as he ran head down; then, after standing over him for a moment, with defiance like Dizier's they saluted the castle and disappeared under the trees.

"The Sauval will send no more messengers," said Conan, "and they have lost two more men. If our friends will but come, we shall have the advantage. I know not what keeps them. Be on the watch for them, Baptiste." He showed him where to look for the signal from the men of Fessart, and went down into the court.

The breakfast was ready, and Conan ordered it distributed to the men, who ate at their stations. And presently the comfort of the food was enhanced by the muffled roar of Aymar's voice, coming from the keep: "Who asked for water? Eat your food dry, fools; and if you want water, fight better when next we go out."

It pleased Conan to see his men meet each other's eyes with looks of confidence. One said, "What we have done once, we can do again."

Then there sounded a voice close outside the wall against which they sat. "What! Eating, boys, without me?"

Conan jumped up. That was Landry! He saw, at

the gap in the wall which Aymar had made, a hand reaching in. "Help me over," said Landry, clinging to the stone. "I am a little shaky."

Conan leaped over the wall. Pale, with difficulty propping himself against the stones, the mason looked at him and essayed a smile. Conan lifted him, and the men on the inside dragged him in. As Conan clambered back, not an arrow was shot at him. Sitting with his back to the wall, Landry looked at the wondering faces.

One man said, "You stopped groaning. We thought you dead."

"Not even wounded," replied Landry, "but badly shaken up. When I found myself groaning I stopped, to make them think me dead. Food, someone." He took some from the dish and munched while they watched. "Water," he said next. "Ah, that is fine!" Then, with fire in his eye, he began to scramble to his feet. "Do you know what I heard as I lay there? Their men are wild for water. And do you know what I am going to do? I am going to make them wilder!"

He limped to the well. There stood on the curb a bucket of water, with a cup. Landry filled the cup, and threw the water over the wall. "Here is water!" he shouted loudly. "Ye Sauval, here is water to drink!" He threw another cupful, and another, and another, each time shouting "Water!" Listening, he heard a voice cursing within the keep. Dropping the cup, Landry then seized the bucket, swung it, and shot the water, in a great sheet and splash, over the wall and onto the stones of the court.

"Drink that!" he shouted. Panting, he leaned against the wall.

Inside the keep there was angry laughter. A single arrow came harmlessly over. Conan took Landry by the arm. "Man, you look sick."

"Maybe I am," agreed Landry. "But I am safe. Help me to the tower." And in the old gate tower he laid himself down, groaned a little, and declared that he would rest.

Conan sought for a bow to replace his own, and chose the strongest he could find. The archer whose bow he had broken was given a spear and a station at the wall.

It was then, when Conan was asking himself what more he could do to resist attack, that he found himself instinctively laying an arrow on the string while staring in surprise at a figure that suddenly appeared between the battlements of the keep. "If anyone is so reckless as to stand there — " And Conan drew his bow, almost satisfied with its strength in resisting him. He looked to see if the figure were armored, to know where to send his arrow.

And then he recognized Pierre! The mason's cap was gone, his forehead bloody, his arms bound behind him. Gasps came from the masons, and exclamations, for all could see the figure, high up, and looking down upon them. Conan lowered his bow.

Across the court boomed Aymar's rough voice. "Do you know him, you scum of Vézelay? And do you see what he has around his neck?"

"A rope!" cried out a mason. It was true — a rope ran from Pierre's throat, leading behind a battlement, where, it seemed plain, hidden men were holding it.

"Now you see!" rasped Aymar. "If we push him over, he is hanged, you dogs! Now, fools, listen! We give you an hour to march out of the castle and leave it to us. If you do that we will set him free to follow you. If not, he will dangle, and you may watch him die."

With one impulse the masons, from wall and tower, shouted threats and curses. But then the clamor subsided, as the men, feeling themselves helpless, turned to see what Conan would do.

He spoke to the three men nearest him. "Take the three men that are lying bound in the new tower, hurry them upstairs, and stand them where the Sauval can see them, on the open parapet. Have ropes round their necks, and be ready to throw them over if I give the word." But Conan's heart was torn as he wondered if this threat would be enough.

It was not. The two men that had been surprised in their sleep were placed, unhurt, in view of their comrades across the court; and the man whom Pierre had stunned was allowed to sit, still bewildered, on the lime bags. All had ropes around their necks, a visible counter-threat to Aymar's. And Conan shouted,

"Throw down our man, ye Sauval, and three of yours pay with their lives." The masons added their defiance.

But the answer was without hesitation. Not Aymar's harsh response, but Odo's thin, sneering voice cut across the court. "Those three have forfeited their lives, for they did not keep the gate. They are nothing to us."

Conan stood baffled. One mason spoke to him, a man who loved Pierre deeply. "The castle is not worth Pierre's life."

It was Pierre himself who made answer, in a strong, manly voice audible to every one of the hidden opponents. "Conan, hold the gate for the Lady Anne, and for Vézelay, and take no account of me. My brothers, think of me as dead, and avenge me!"

The rope tightened quickly about his neck, and he was dragged out of sight. The listeners heard the sound of blows, and asked each other in frightened whispers: "Is he dead already?" Then Pierre reappeared, thrust up into the embrasure. He sank wearily upon the stones and rested there, his head against the battlement. He had been blindfolded and gagged.

Odo's voice mocked. "You see that we mean it. An hour, you fools, and he will be dead."

"Conan, Conan," urged those near him, "we must save Pierre."

Conan laid down his bow and threw off his quiver. "Believe not," he said, "that we could save him by yielding the castle. They have marked him for death."

Shuddering, those who were at hand crawled nearer, under the shelter of the wall, to hear him better. "But we have an hour, and with good fortune it will be enough. I go to collect the peasants. If I can gather them quickly, we shall surprise the Sauval right in their own midst."

"What do you mean?"

"There is a secret way into the castle. We have been so few that I have not dared to divide you and use it. But now I must, even if I go alone. Do you keep watch and listen. If you see me on the battlement by Pierre, or if you hear fighting in the keep, leap the wall, every man of you, and come to my help. Will you do it?"

They cried eagerly, "We will!"

"Then keep watch!" Carrying sword and buckler only, Conan slipped under the portcullis, which four men lifted for him. He leaped down into the dry moat, crossed it and climbed out, and on the other side was just starting to run, when from the old tower the voice of Baptiste hailed him eagerly.

"Why do you halt me?"

"There is a pennon, of red and yellow, there at the very edge of the woods."

"The saints be praised!" Conan had feared that the hunt for Dizier might be long. But now he ran at top speed toward the spot where he knew Anne's men would be waiting.

But he found but a weak little group. There were barely eighteen, and few of them good fighters. Gran-

son; Morat; old Bethune; Gillement the lame harness maker; Sebastian the falconer; Stephen the smith,
a good man; Orri the cook, soft and evidently exhausted by the journey; Guyot the groom, little, but
strong and bold; and young Lazare, inexperienced
but eager, having in his eyes that same burning look
which among Sir Roger's contented household marked
all of Anne's exiled followers. These and others Conan
noted. There was no question of the spirit of all
these, but only of their power.

And who was this that came to meet him —
shoulder-high, slender, in light mail, with hair of red
gold straying from under the steel cap? Anne! Anne
herself, with buckler and short-sword, the least formidable there, except for the fire in her eyes and the
high seriousness in her mouth. Anne, who had always ridden to the hunt, shot with the bow, borne
herself knightly in pain and misfortune — she was
here as the leader of her men.

And behind her was the stout priest, worn and
weary, and leaning on him Eustace, drooping and
pale.

Conan gazed at Anne in dismay. Keyed for a desperate fight against whatever odds, he was checked by
her coming. He could not take her — and yet he could
not leave her. With him she would be a weight on his
sword arm; left behind, some prowling peasant, not
knowing her, might strike from ambush and kill her.
And she would not go back: he knew her too well.
Conan stood appalled.

She saw the knot in his forehead. "Conan, I did not come as on a frolic. Lady Blanche would give me no men; she would have kept mine. I had to force our way out. And we have had every misfortune on the road, for we lost the way and wandered, and were mired, and overnighted. But I am here at last with what men I have, to live or to die!"

"Perhaps to die, then," he said gloomily. He gave a hand to weary Eustace, then to the priest. But looking again on Anne, she was so sweetly brave that his fears vanished. "Anne, we hold the Sauval in the keep, but they have captured Pierre. He is dead if I cannot surprise and overpower them. There is a secret passage by which I thought to plunge with your men into the midst of them. But with you — !"

Anne saw his meaning. "Fear not for me. Take me with you!"

"You accept the risk?" he asked. "You forgive what may happen?"

She looked up with eyes full of courage. "Let us put everything on the chance!"

Here was no romance. Conan thought only of the coming fight. Anne, though she knew she loved him, was at that moment the feudal chieftain, mistress of her lands, ruler of her people, fighting for both. The electric current that passed between them was hard resolution, not a poetic thrill. As Conan turned away he said only:

"Follow next me, but give room for my arm."

He gave order for all to follow in line, and if they

saw any of the peasants, to halloo to them. Then he hurried the little band to the spot from which they must descend to the mouth of the passage. And though they learned later that Dizier and half a dozen others must have passed within a hundred yards of them, hunting for the man whom they had seen leave the castle, fortune kept them apart. Reaching the ravine, Conan led the way down the winding path, until he stopped on a shelf which overhung a steep fall. There seemed no further passage, and he turned to Anne, who asked with her eyes why he brought them to that place.

"Here we enter," he said to those who could hear his quiet voice. "Pass in one by one, form in line in the darkness, touching one another, and wait till I can take the lead again. Eustace, you first, then Anne."

Before their astonished eyes he swung the stone open.

One by one they entered, and scuffed forward in the passage, by its lessening light. At last Conan and the priest were alone outside. Father Gregory stood dismayed before the opening through which all had entered, but which seemed to forbid the passage of his bulk. His distressed eyes turned to Conan. "Can I — ?" he seemed to ask, and then to beseech, "Conan, do not desert me!"

"Let me go first," said Conan.

The humor of it did not strike him till long later: how like a boy he slipped through the opening, and turning, saw outside the unhappy face of the priest. But Father Gregory manfully essayed the opening, caught fast, and then Conan, with one powerful heave, pulled him through. With a swing of the stone he cut off the light, and all was a blackness in which he heard some of his followers gasp. He felt his way along the line, put Anne between himself and Eustace, gave the order, "Hold hands, all," and led the way forward.

The passage, when he had gone but a few score feet, began to seem endless. With bent head and exploring hand he advanced through the dark, which to his straining eyes seemed always solid before his face. Holding Anne's hand, he tried to keep her clear of the rough stones which, at the turns, bruised his hand and jostled his shoulder. The footing was irregular; at last he knew by wetness underfoot that he must be beneath the moat. After that, though he kept on, he could not tell whether he were ascending or descending, and his sense of direction had long been lost.

He had two contending feelings. One was of haste: he must hurry because of Pierre, sitting dazed above the courtyard into which his foes were waiting to hurl him. And his other feeling took its rise in the hand which, behind him, clasped the hand of Anne. In that darkness, though he was the leader and she the led, he was a little afraid to go on, yet she gave him courage. He knew that darkness, yet felt a dread

of it; while she, though she now knew it first, had
no fear, but trusted entirely to him. Her trust domi-
nated his fear, and he went on boldly.

He came at last to a place where the direction
was doubtful. A wall of rock met his hand in front,
but his feet struck stones to right and left. He felt
to the left: still stone. He felt to the right, and his
arm thrust forward to its full length, yet met nothing. Here was the stair. "Now we go up!" But in a
moment the stair grew steep, and began to twist. He
had to leave Anne to follow by herself, while he
went on and on.

The twisting stair confused him; it went endlessly
up, and the darkness seemed to have weight and
thickness. He knew that Anne was just behind him,
and he heard the shuffling of many feet in that close
and echoing place. No one spoke, though a few were
panting. But he could not slacken pace for anyone.

He was aware of a little light, and came abreast
of the tiny slit in the wall by which he once had
looked out on the countryside. He glanced but an
instant, saw the green landscape, and passed on. Again
he mounted, always twisting to the left. Once he
reflected how well the stair was planned for its owner,
had he but torchlight to fight by — his sword arm
free as he advanced upward or retreated downward,
and the enemy correspondingly hampered. But now
came dim light again, which meant the end of the
stair. He reached the little chamber, and in the dusk
the men pressed up close to him, then stopped.

Anne was nearest. "Now is the danger," he said to her. "For what may happen, forgive me!"

She caught her breath. "If this is the end, Conan — good-by!"

He bent down and kissed her, not as brother or companion, but as something nearer, he did not know what. Her kiss was frank and ready. "Swords out!" he commanded then. Gripping the handles of the great stone, he heaved at it; as it began to swing, he checked it when it was scarcely out of its bed. With his ear to the crack, he listened to the sounds outside, within the keep.

Nothing near at hand: no voice or footfall of men close by. Distantly he thought he heard some sound; but it seemed as if this upper story were deserted. Quickly he swung the stone wide and stepped into the outer passage.

He had expected it to be dark; but his eyes, used to blackness, found it tempered by the light that filtered in from either end. Listening, he still heard nothing near. He helped Anne through the wall, and passing her to the right, told her to stand. The others, as they came out (and last of all the priest, with silent heaving and hauling), he divided into two bands, setting some to the right, others to the left, making them as nearly as possible of equal fighting qualities. Granson he kept with Anne, as her best bodyguard. Morat he made the leader of the others. Leading Anne's band, he crept to the end of the passage and listened.

Still nothing was heard near, though more clearly came sounds from below. Cautioning the rest to stand still, with a sudden spring he was in the open, and crouching, looked about him.

XXIV

Surprise and Flight

THE OUTER CORRIDOR was empty. There was not even a sleeping sentry where the winding stairs ran up and down. Conan stepped rapidly to the doors of the chambers. Not even a bundle of clothes that might be a man.

He called out his two bands, and bade Morat station himself where the stairs ran down. "Anne, stay with him. You others, follow me. Eustace, come too. Now!" And quickly, but in silence, he sprang up the stairs.

He was in broad sunshine, on the flat roof. Overhead were drifting clouds; beyond the toothed battlements was the peaceful green of the trees. Conan's eyes, fierce for war, sought and found his friend and his quarry. Pierre, bound, blindfolded, gagged, sat — but no longer drooped — in the opening of the battlement. And beneath the protection of that wall, safe from arrows and in the shade, two unsuspecting men-at-arms lolled on their bellies and scratched with their knives in the lead of the roof, playing the ancient game of tit-tat-to.

Conan's rush brought him instantly above them. One rose on an elbow, his mouth wide in surprise, and took in the throat, without resistance, the point of Conan's sword. The other, as he saw his comrade collapse, put his hands over his head as he tried to rise. But the neck remained bare, and the sword chopped through the bone. Their heads almost touching, the two lay and shed their blood over the bright lines they had scratched in their idleness.

Conan turned to Pierre, but Eustace was already at his side, removing the gag, cutting the bonds. Conan lifted the bandage from Pierre's head. His forehead was bruised, his eyes blinking; unsteadily he rose to his feet.

"Oh, my friend," said Conan, "it is a joy to save you. But now we must save ourselves. Pull yourself together. Eustace, give him a shield and sword of those that lie here."

Mindful, next, of the masons across the court, Conan leaned from the embrasure. Down below, behind the wall, two of his men were staring up at him. He dared not call, lest he rouse the Sauval in the keep. He gestured, therefore, to the liberated Pierre, and pointed down at the door of the keep. Then he beckoned for their advance. They separated, to summon their fellows, and at once he turned to his own task.

There stood Anne behind him. "Anne, I told you to stay below!"

She answered simply, but positively, "I must take my own risks."

"In heaven's name," he implored, "take not too many!" But as he ran to the stairs she was next behind him. On the next floor he found Morat's band waiting, some of them strong only in their spirit. He drew both bands together, while he gave orders in low tones.

"Below is the great hall. Out of it, on the opposite side, two stairs lead down. Morat, you with your men seize the stair on the left. Granson, you take that on the right. Sebastian, Stephen, Guyot, strike with me on any in the hall. Now follow!"

He rushed down into the hall, regardless of the sounds he might make. The others poured after him. The hall was all but empty, for only three men were there, retainers. Neither Aymar nor Ralph nor Odo was in sight.

But the three men had been roused by the clatter on the stairs. One, the instant he saw Conan, plunged for the left-hand stair, and shouting, lurched against the wall and rounded the turn, out of sight. The second man, not so quick, ran against the very point of Morat's sword. The third man charged at Conan, who stood to meet him. In one moment, he thought, he would be free of the fellow.

But he had not counted on the other's desperation. The man, a seasoned fighter, having neither sword nor shield at hand, closed with Conan before point or buckler could interpose, and within guard, stabbed quickly with his knife. Only the toughness of Conan's broigne stopped the blow. The downward smash of the pommel of Conan's sword brought the fellow to his knees. Here he clung, and struck at the groin, only to be frustrated again by the armor. Yet still he clung, trying to strike again, his close burrowing head safe from Conan's blow. But then Anne, shrinking yet determined, pricked the man's neck with her point, and the head jerked back. Instantly Conan clove the skull.

Raging at the delay, he stepped clear of that antagonist, cried his thanks to Anne, and started for the stairs. His men let him lead, then followed. But as Conan rushed down the stairs, the shouts resounding from below told him that his enemies were fully roused.

For suddenly though the alarm had come, it found the Sauval partly ready. With the greater part of their men around them, Odo had been consulting Ralph, since Odo, never dependent upon Aymar for ideas, had found that Ralph was more than a mere fighter. So, some minutes before this, he had told Ralph what caused him concern.

"The hour is wearing on," Odo said, "yet those masons hold their wall. What if they will not budge?"

Ralph laughed. "Something will be done to save Pierre — if I know Conan."

"What can he do?" asked Odo. Aymar, with a

contemptuous laugh, seemed to indicate that the masons could do nothing; but Odo waited for Ralph's reply.

"He can attack us as we attacked them. Since they have not opened up the tower doors, they must come across the court."

"You really expect that?"

"Yes, and soon."

Odo had, therefore, drawn together most of his men in the lower room, and they were actually standing at rest, the foremost of them uneasily watching, when the alarm came from across the court. Weapons appeared waving, there were clatterings and shoutings, and figures began crossing the wall.

The huge Sauval grasped his sword and grinned. "They are coming. Well, let them come!"

But Ralph raised a warning hand; and Odo, leaning toward the near-by stair, motioned for silence. There were tramplings overhead, and then a racing figure dashed down the stair, shouting, "Foes are in the hall!"

Aymar was thundering "Fool!" when Odo's thin sneer cut him to silence. Odo turned, whitefaced but cool, to Ralph. "They are in the keep?"

Ralph nodded quietly. "A secret way." He gripped his sword.

"What to do?"

Ralph looked across the court at the wall, already straddled by many figures. But the real danger lay overhead — and now there were clatterings on the stairs. Ralph pointed into the court. "We must strike there, and get away."

"But the bridge — the portcullis?"

"Leave that to Aymar and me." Ralph smiled grimly. "Keep close, little Odo." His cry rang out. "Men, for your lives now, follow and strike hard!"

He was first in the charge; Aymar was second; Odo, a little scuttling figure, impotently armed, was third. After them streamed the rest. And the masons, just clearing the wall, were struck, trampled, hurled aside. The Sauval stopped not to slay. Ralph dashed into the entrance archway, and hesitating, peered upward into the darkness of the vault. Then leaping, he lashed with his sword; and Aymar, imitating, struck in the same way at the opposite side. The tight ropes of the drawbridge, thus hacked, gave way, and with a rattle and crash the bridge began to fall. Light streamed in, showing the black grating of the portcullis still blocking the gateway.

To get rid of this, Ralph called on Aymar to lend his great strength. With one heave the two raised the portcullis knee-high; with another they lifted it to their waists; and then, putting their shoulders under it, they straightened and held the huge gridiron at full height.

"The beam!" cried Ralph to the nearest man, and pointed to it lying.

But a louder cry sounded in the ears of the fugitives, a death-scream from their own rear, and then an unknown war cry. As Conan, emerging into the court, struck down the rearmost of the fliers, Anne's men raised, hoarse or shrill, the old shout of their beloved fief as they too fell on.

And the Sauval were struck with panic. The hindmost pressed forward, those in front gave way, and Odo clutched Aymar, crying, "Come!" A brave touch of reluctance Aymar may have felt, but only for a moment, as he yielded the old obedience to his brother. Deserting Ralph, he slipped from under the weight of the portcullis, and hurried Odo across the drawbridge.

And Ralph stood imprisoned by his burden. As it settled its weight down upon him, he knew that should he bend it would crush him. Nor could he slip aside and escape before it would grind him down. So standing rigid, a sneer on his face both at himself and at those who streamed by him in flight, Ralph bore the weight of that huge engine, knowing that if he did not presently break under it he would be slain. Grimly he saw the last of the Sauval pass and leave him to his fate.

The next moment Conan faced him. His sword was red, his eyes were blazing; he was furious that his enemies were escaping. But here was one — and he drew back his sword to thrust, or no, to threaten, as he called to his men, his eye never leaving Ralph's, to lift the beam and set it in place. It was raised, it was

butted against the ground, and Ralph knew that he could stoop and be free. But that moment Conan's arm tightened for the thrust.

"No, no!" Anne was clinging to his wrist.

Conan neither objected nor reproached. "Eustace, Pierre, take this man and let him not escape. Slay him if he resists!" From the stern threat he raised his voice and shouted, "Now out, men, out and hunt down every one that flees."

Ralph had no strength left to resist those two, one sick, one injured, who seized him by the arms.

He was tied and led inside the tower. But long before he was secured, the stream of the Sauval had been followed across the drawbridge by the rush of their hunters.

The theater of that hunt was an open plain, an irregular semicircle of a quarter-mile diameter. In their panic the men of Sauval lost their one chance, which lay in keeping together. Scattering in all directions they sought safety, each for himself, except for the few whom the grumbling commands of Aymar kept near him. And making directly for the nearest point of woods, into which he hoped to plunge and escape, Aymar, encumbered by Odo's slow pace, lumbered with many a backward glance. He saw Conan following straight after him. He saw some of his men throw away their arms to run more lightly. He saw some turn and kneel for mercy. And he saw, when he looked again, those begging men struck down even as they had once, with laughter, struck down helpless men. And in a strange bewilderment Aymar rolled his eyes for help, not understanding why he, who all his life had slain men for his pleasure, now should be fleeing before men whom he despised. Never had he met the thought of death or failure. It roused him to fury.

He looked to one side and saw his swiftest man, who had cast aside his arms, racing toward the appearance of safety. But out of the bushes leaped more peasants, who slew him and exulted. Aymar looked to the other side and saw, dashing from the forest, shouting horsemen. "Fulke's men," he thought. "Let them come. But first I will kill this vermin that pursues me." He stopped and faced back on his trail, and saw but a few rods away Conan loping easily, certain of overtaking him. Close behind was but a single little figure.

"We have him now," said Aymar to the few men who remained with him. "Stop and slay him."

But he had never mastered them except by fear, and the fear of Conan was the stronger. They sped on. And Aymar, tired from his pounding run, put Odo behind him with a lifelong instinct of protection. He leaned upon his sword. Conan dropped into a walk, and with head high came forward unbreathed, treading lightly.

Odo said, panting: "Aymar, he is not your match. Slash him! Kill him!"

"Oh, I will carve!" answered Aymar confidently.

"And I will stab," said Odo. Winded yet clear-minded, feeble but venomous, he prepared to do his part with his short-sword. Then he saw the little figure following Conan. "There is another!"

"Only a page," answered Aymar contemptuously.

Conan came on. Unconscious of his gait, sure that whatever his mind demanded his limbs would execute, he advanced with a tripping step like a boxer's, balanced, cautious, resolute.

Aymar swung up his sword. "Nearer, you dancer, nearer!"

And Odo, drawing a little to one side, prepared to stab beneath the shelter of his brother's arm.

Conan paused with narrowed eyes. To dash at the giant, swerve, and strike at the dwarf? — or to swerve the other way, and keep Aymar always between him and Odo? Then a swift patter of light steps, a figure glancing toward Odo, and Anne's clear voice. "Conan, 'ware Odo! Leave him to me!"

He risked one startled glance at her. She was so quick and stern and ready that he repressed his instinct to rush and protect her. Accepting her help, he cried, "Not too close!" His instant leap toward Aymar brought all the Sauval's attention upon him. They raised shields, gripped weapons, bent for the encounter.

And Anne threatened Odo. Her sword glanced bright, her light buckler was ready, as she drew near. Unwillingly Odo turned to face her, and clumsy on his thin legs, braced himself for defense. His puzzled face peered from behind the nasal of his helmet; his teeth were clenched. And seeing that he had no such skill even as hers, Anne motioned at him and withdrew, advanced for a more daring feint, and was poised to avoid any blow.

Then a soft rumble of hoofs on the turf, like a distant kettledrumming, swelled to thunder, and the air quivered with the rush of approaching horsemen. Conan in fright thought only of Anne, and circling Aymar and Odo with all the speed of his feet, swept her to one side to face this emergency. If this were Fulke, she was safe.

Not Fulke! Great noble horses, such as never were bred at Prigny, fluttering surcoats, gilded trappings, silks, furs — who, then? Conan gripped his sword, but knew that if these were enemies he must be ridden down and overwhelmed.

But reins were drawn, the necks of horses arched to the bit, and their planted feet plowed the turf. The nearest charger stopped not ten feet away, and the clamor of voices blended in one cry: "Peace! In the duke's name!"

Peace? The duke? Disgust settled in a cloud over Conan as he saw these horsemen spread in a circle to surround him. There were full fifty of them, one rank behind another, some of them mailed knights, and some in the gay clothes of courtiers. Such an array he had never seen in his life, and it could not have been more unwelcome. He looked down at Anne. She was unhurt, though breathing fast from her exertions, and smiled up at him. He turned to these interlopers again, and demanded sullenly:

"The duke? Is he here, then?"

"Here!" The horseman nearest him lifted his steel cap from his head, and from behind its obscuring nasal appeared the handsome visage of the young man Hugh. "You the duke?" Astonished, but still resentful, Conan dwelt for a moment on the fine young face, afire with a strange enthusiasm; then next him he saw Bernard, also in armor, and older men near-by. Not so near as to jostle their suzerain, but keeping themselves jealously in the foreground, these last were watching every movement and listening to each word.

Conan glanced at the Sauval. Aymar, as sullen as himself, was still in posture for fight. But Odo, quick and ready, had come from behind him, waiting only for an opportunity to speak, to smother with words. At that sight Conan collected himself, and finding Hugh's eyes still fixed on him, asked:

"My lord duke, you want peace in this country?"

"Yes," replied Hugh, "and I shall have it!" In the light in his eye and the ring of his voice, Conan saw in him something that was not there yesterday, the awakening of manhood.

"Then," Conan said, "bid these horsemen keep this ring for me unbroken. Give me five minutes with this Aymar of Sauval, and then half a minute with the venomous dwarf his brother, and I promise you a lifetime of peace in all this region."

There was an outburst from the circle — of laughter and applause from the knights and some of the courtiers, but of protest from the older men. One of these, white-haired, in silken clothes, laid his hand on the duke's arm, and speaking in his ear, evidently remonstrated strongly. Hugh, inexperienced and doubtful, looked to his other side, where Bernard, after listening, austerely shook his head. Hugh raised his hand, the clamor subsided, and at a nod from Hugh, Bernard spoke with weighty emphasis.

"Conan, yesterday you challenged the justice of the duke. Therefore, when from the chancellor at Vézelay [here Bernard glanced coldly across at the old courtier] he could learn nothing of the case, he has come again in person. Justice he promises you, but only through his courts and by his judges. The sword has ruled too long in all this region. Therefore, he calls on all who have been fighting here to lay down their arms and submit to his laws."

In the circle there was a murmur and a rapid exchange of glances. Conan saw some — and among these were the chancellor and the abbot of Vézelay — looking at each other as if in appeal for support.

He rested the point of his sword upon the ground. "You speak," he said to Bernard regretfully, "like a wise counselor of a true duke. — Yet my lord," and Conan turned to Hugh, "I am the last to fear your justice." He shifted his sword to his left hand, underneath his shield, and taking Anne by the arm, presented her before Hugh.

"And here, lord duke," he said, "is a complainant whom at last, thanks to you, your judges shall hear after six years of deafness."

"My lord — my lord — !" protested the chancellor. But Hugh paid no attention. "This boy?" he asked. Conan smiled. "But bid him take off his helm."

Anne removed her cap and revealed her face, ruddy and confused, but charming in its frame of red hair. A murmur ran among those who could see. But Hugh, though evidently surprised, again glanced at Bernard, and taking cue from him, sought to guard his face from all expression.

"This," said Conan, "is the Lady Anne d'Arcy, heiress of the fief on which we stand and of yonder castle from which I have just driven this Aymar and his misshapen brother, whose soul is more deformed than his body. She accuses them of the open murder of her father and mother, and I accuse them of the treacherous murder of my brother. Let your justice, my lord duke, give these men their punishment."

He spoke with deep feeling. But there were immediate protests. Odo cried sharply, "It is not true!" And the white-bearded chancellor, with the abbot of Vézelay, together were trying for the duke's attention.

But Bernard lifted his hand, the slightest gesture; and Hugh, on the hint, lifted his own higher. Again there was silence on the part of his followers, but Odo seized the moment to be heard.

He stepped closer to Hugh, a crooked and awkward figure; but when he spoke his flexible voice and smooth words were in his favor. "My lord, welcome to this part of your duchy, where your absence has been mourned. And welcome also will be your justice, which will help me lift from my brother and myself these false accusations. Give me the chance, my lord duke, to defend myself in court, and I will defy this boy to prove his evil charges."

Hugh looked at him as with instinctive mistrust. But again he looked to Bernard for his answer. And at the turn of Hugh's head Bernard was ready with his words — while on the other side of the duke the chancellor, so long the spokesman, visibly struggled to control his anger.

Bernard said coldly: "Your chance, Baron Odo, will be equal to that of your accuser. Be comforted: the guilty shall not escape."

Odo bowed. "I ask only that." But his eye, as he glanced sidewise at the abbot, was sharp and suspicious.

Conan stood perplexed. He did not understand all the play and counterplay of ambition and interest that were going on before him, the rise of the new forces of youth to struggle in the ducal court against the entrenched privilege of age. Yet vaguely he felt that an unspoken alliance had been made by all of the elders there, to throw the weight of their influence on the side of Odo, to save their own futures. He sensed that there still lay in his way the barriers of law; and he feared that the revenge and victory that had been in his hand might slip away from him by some perversion of the justice to which he had appealed.

And at his side Anne, as mistrustful as himself, shrank closer to him.

Though he gripped her hand, he knew not how to protect her against this new danger, and stood doubting, when there sounded a voice close in his ear. "Conan — nay, do not turn your head. I am Enguerrand, and you can trust me. This quarrel must not be taken to Dijon and the courts, to drag through a year of delays. Tell me: do you know that these men killed your brother?"

"I know that Aymar slew him from behind, on the testimony of a servant that died in my arms."

"Then repeat your accusation now and demand the ordeal of battle."

Conan saw that Enguerrand had pointed the way to the one appeal in which every man in those days profoundly believed, the conviction that God himself would strike down in the lists the champion of an evil cause. And as confidently as if judgment had already been delivered in his favor, Conan stepped nearer to Hugh, and cried:

"My lord, an end to this talk of law! I ask my right of these two men, and particularly of Aymar there, in that he foully slew my brother, Blaise. I accuse him of that murder, and I demand of him the ordeal of battle, in which he shall meet me body to body, with God to judge the right!"

The circle murmured loudly now, as each man spoke to his neighbor. And Hugh needed no prompting, devoutly believing that where God was appealed to, man must acquiesce.

"This thing," he said, "is right and proper."

But the abbot of Vézelay objected. "Holy church will sanction no battle ordeal except in case of doubt of guilt, where there are no witnesses."

Across Hugh, Bernard looked at him in cold scorn. "What is the verdict of holy church," he demanded, "upon her servants who pervert justice?"

But Enguerrand had the practical reply. "In the present case, my lord abbot, the challenger's witness who saw the deed and told of it is dead."

"It is an empty accusation!" cried Odo. "Let a man disappear, and anyone can be blamed."

"I pledge my honor," stated Conan calmly. "And I offer my life." And this he said though he knew that he who failed in such a battle must die a dishonorable death.

Then Aymar lurched forward, and spoke in spite of Odo's protesting hands. "I will fight the fool," he growled, "and prove whether I did it or no."

The abbot of Vézelay spoke. "This is now in the hands of the church. I will act as spiritual counselor for the baron of Sauval."

"Conan," said the duke, "here is a bishop to take you in his charge. Will you accept him?" He pointed to a churchman by the abbot's side.

But both bishop and squire looked at each other in active distaste. "My lord," replied Conan, "with all deference to the bishop's holy character, I beg you to excuse me. There is a simple priest, a good man, long time my confessor, into whose hands I beg leave to put myself." And Conan bowed to the bishop, who did not know whether to consider himself insulted or relieved.

Odo made one final protest. "My lord duke, these

men may not fight, for my brother is a knight and the other but a squire."

Hugh replied: "Knight must meet squire, as lord must meet peasant, in such a case. But this difficulty shall be removed." He leaped from his horse, and beckoning to Conan, bade him kneel at his feet. Conan knelt, saw the sword drawn, and bent his head for the accolade. The blade smote his bowed shoulder. "I dub thee knight," said Hugh. "Rise, Sir Conan. — Lords and gentlemen, tomorrow, at high noon, these two shall meet in the courtyard of yonder castle. There let guilt be punished, or the accuser die!"

XXV

Peace at the Castle

THE YOUNG DUKE issued further orders. "Enguerrand, take every man you can and stop the fighting that is still going on." At once Enguerrand vaulted into the saddle, and calling to the knights and men-at-arms, snatched them out of the circle, to send them away in all directions. Only a few men in armor remained by the duke, his bodyguard, captained by the Count Ferrand who, uneasy, was wondering whether his patrons the bishop and the chancellor could save their places and, incidentally, himself. It was to him that Hugh turned next.

"Count Ferrand, I give into your care these two brothers of Sauval. Make sure that every courtesy is shown them, give their sponsor the abbot access to them at all times, but be answerable to me that they remain until they are cleared of all charges."

Odo, always persistent, made subtle objection. "Does your grace imply that the abbot is my sponsor as well as my brother's? Surely the burden of this challenge does not lie on me."

Hugh, by his silent look, passed the question to

Bernard, who, bowing first to the duke, spoke to Odo with quiet sternness. "The duke knows well, Baron Odo, the difference between a challenge and an accusation. But he gives you opportunity, while your brother is preparing for the combat, to make ready your own defense with your friends."

Odo still protested. "I may need to go and summon witnesses."

"Rest easy," replied Bernard. "Name your witnesses, and they shall be summoned. The duke intends that all men remaining in your castle shall be brought to Vézelay, and the castle itself carefully guarded in your absence."

"But this," cried Odo, "is force!"

"If with all your experience you recognize it," returned Bernard, "you are doubtless right. Let me commend you to Count Ferrand, who has not the habit of failing in his duty."

The count, taking hope, was grateful. He smiled grimly upon Odo, and with a soldier's sternness, was silent. Odo, in growing disquiet, sought the abbot's eye, but found no comfort in his shifting glance. He was about to protest again, when interruption came.

A sound of running feet, a clamor of hoarse voices. "Where is she? Is she safe?" Into the broken circle came hurrying a line of men on foot, weaponed, splashed with blood, breathless. The leader ran straight to Anne, and fell on his knee before her. "Oh, my lady, we thought you had stayed behind at the castle."

"Otherwise, surely, Morat," responded Anne, "you would have defended me. Who are these following you, who kneel to me, but whom I do not know?"

Morat rose and named the huge square man who knelt there, tears rolling down his cheeks. "This is Dizier of your Marsh Farm."

"Oh, my little lady," cried the great peasant, "to see you here again, on your own land, among those who love you!"

She went and gave him her hand, which he took as though afraid to touch it, and adored for its littleness and frailty. He was bloody from fighting, still hot with anger; but his fierceness drained away as he looked at her face and saw its sweetness. All his rough nature was purified within him.

"Welcome, Dizier," she said, "whom I have not seen since I was a child. And all those behind you, whose names I have yet to learn — they are welcome too."

There were kneeling Sandras and his sons, and a dozen others, wild, rude figures, their faces agape with happiness. They had been fiercely slaying, but now they were rapt as they saw her. This lovely young thing, their mistress longed for through the hard years of misery! She was more beautiful, more comforting than they had dreamed.

Dizier lumbered to his feet. "My lady, there stands your own castle, waiting for you. Let us take you and put you there, and not the Sauval, nor the duke himself, shall ever take you out!"

Tears were flooding Anne's eyes. She looked at Hugh and saw that in his eyes, young like hers, there was kindness. "My lord," she said, "pardon them!" For she knew that the faces of the abbot and bishop and chancellor were hard and contemptuous. She kept her gaze fixed on Hugh, begging for his support.

Dizier gripped his clotted ax. "Who is that?" he asked hoarsely.

"The duke himself," answered Conan in his ear. "Be still. You have spoken well, but say no more."

"Lady Anne," said Hugh, not looking anywhere for prompting, "sleep tonight, unafraid, in your father's castle, guarded by your own men. I and my following will bivouac here in the fields, for the night will be fine."

She thanked him. Then Hugh, with his courtiers round him, turned and rode away. The bishop, the abbot, and the chancellor felt satisfaction as they crowded nearer to the duke than Bernard, who did not strive with them for place. There remained the Count Ferrand with four of his men, and he indicated to the two Sauval that he was waiting only for their convenience. It was a polite command. Odo, sneering, made his bow to Anne, a caricature of Hugh's salute. But Aymar shook his sword.

"Tomorrow, Conan, I will crush you!"

"Tomorrow we meet," Conan answered. "But it will not be you and I, Aymar, who fight."

Aymar glowered, astounded. "Who, then?"

"God and the devil, and God will win. On whose side will He be? Make sure of the answer!"

Aymar stared, not furious but confused, until Odo caught him by the sleeve, and muttering angrily at him, led him away.

Then Bernard came riding back, a striking figure, tall, thin, and stern. He bent on Conan his steady glance, which revealed the austerity which underlay all his thoughts. "Conan, a word upon the meaning of your combat."

Conan assented. Anne, drawing a little nearer, felt herself chilled by this calm horseman, whose aid, though on her side, had been dispassionate and detached. A master of policy he might be, but too cold in every calculation. And yet, as he began to speak again, there was a gleam in his eye. With the beginning of animation, he bent toward Conan.

"Sir knight, remember that until this fight you are no longer your own master, but a man set apart. Live with that thought in mind. Put aside the things of the world. You have called upon God. Live as a suppliant for His grace. Do you understand?"

"Yes, yes," answered Conan hastily. He was impressed by Bernard's high seriousness, even a little awed by what seemed repressed passion. Bernard was unknown to him; Conan had not yet heard the story of his wild youth suddenly changed, by some unexplained experience, into a lofty devotion. But Conan divined that his own situation appealed to a deep emotion in Bernard.

Bernard's voice had the thrill of warning. "Forget worldly thoughts. Let the priests teach you to pray. Go to the combat pure of all selfishness, forgetting everything but that you have asked God to show His favor. — Farewell!"

Conan stood staring as Bernard rode away, a martial figure, made strong, he perceived, by some inward power. He was deeply impressed. But Anne shivered a little by Conan's side as she dwelt on the severe advice which would make him put out of his thoughts everything worldly, even his friends.

"Come, Conan," she said a little wearily; and he

started out of his reverie to follow her toward the castle. The circle of the little plain was almost cleared of the invading horsemen. But near the edge of the forest lay motionless bodies; and there came hobbling to meet Anne, from more than one quarter, those of her men who had been hurt. Conan recognized the compact group of the masons, who on seeing the coming of the horsemen had drawn together for defense, and had thought it wise to remain by themselves. At one side of him Morat, and at the other Dizier, began a rapid statement of what had happened. It could all be summed up in one sentence: the fleeing Sauval had been slain almost to a man. A few had broken away, but there were many in pursuit. There remained of them the small garrison in their own castle, the three captured watchmen — and Ralph.

"He is new in this country," said Dizier, "but he has served the Sauval in their own manner. He is in the gate tower. Say the word, Messer Conan, and I will slip ahead. The lady will never see him again."

"Hush, Dizier," answered Conan. "The man is her prisoner, not mine or yours. Trust her, and save yourself blood-guilt."

Anne, proceeding toward the castle, greeted her men as she met them, asked their condition, gave sympathy and praise, and directed that the wounded be brought to the castle, where Eustace would treat them. In fact, in the basement of the old gate tower there was already a little hospital, where Eustace was at work. Pierre was neatly bandaged, two other men were attended to and were lying on pallets, and another man was under Eustace's hands. The priest, with gown kilted up above his great knees, was helping. The busy surgeon smiled when Conan asked him how he did.

"I do not know whether I could again cure a fever by ignoring it. I am well, but it was a hard cure.— There, stand aside, man, and next time get yourself wounded in a place where it will not hurt so much. You men in the door, which one needs me the most?"

Leaning by the wall Conan saw Ralph, with hands tied behind him. His air of indifference was not assumed; genuine recklessness was in his eye, even though he saw Dizier, who had such cause to hate him, glowering at him and clutching the handle of his ax. The young outlaw had the hardihood born of bitter experience; he had dealt death carelessly and he would receive it without fear. Life had not meant so much that he would cling to it shamefully. For Ralph had his honor.

Anne spoke to Pierre and the wounded men. Pierre declared that he was sound, was merely bruised on the head, and that his dizziness was passing off. And then Anne saw Ralph and went to his side.

"You were taken prisoner," she said, "because you risked yourself for your friends."

Ralph looked at her with a stirring of respect which was an emotion almost new to him. Beyond mere admiration for her beauty, he wondered at her spirit and fearlessness. No such being had ever come into his ken. And in his confusion he merely bowed awkwardly, unable to find words in which to put aside her praise.

"The fighting is over," said Anne. "Give me your promise that you will remain here this night with the Sauval, and you shall be unbound."

Dizier cried out, "My lady, he will never keep his word!"

Anne did not take her eyes from Ralph's face. "Will you promise?"

Ralph's eyes were held by hers. "You gave me my life, and you may ask it of me again. I promise."

"Unbind him then, Conan," she said.

"Ralph," said Conan as he cast off the bonds, "I have no accusation to bring against you. If the duke grants you life, you may begin again elsewhere."

"Without my sword?" asked Ralph sharply. "If I am free, will you fight me for it?"

"Tomorrow I fight Aymar," replied Conan. "Until then it must be mine."

"You have challenged him?" cried Ralph. "Good news! For he deserted me. — Listen, Messer Conan. I know this Aymar well. He has enormous strength, but little endurance. You have one chance. Fight away from him, keep him following you, and wear him down."

Conan agreed. "Most likely that will be best."

"I see," said Ralph, "I must go away; but when I have made myself a place, I will return. And then will you fight me for my sword?"

"There is a better way," answered Conan. "The day you come to me honorably knighted, I will give it you."

Ralph jerked back his head, and put his hand to his brow. "Honorably knighted — I?"

Anne cried eagerly, "Ralph, you could win it!"

He looked on her gloomily. "Because you are good, you see hope in me. I am not worth your trying." He turned as if to go.

"Dizier," said Anne, "take this man, and deliver him safely to Count Ferrand."

Dizier swallowed hard, muttered to Ralph, "Come then," and strode from the room. Ralph, with a deference that surprised himself, dropped on his knee, caught Anne's hand and kissed it, and followed the peasant. It was nothing to him that scowls from the masons followed his passage. But there were no mutterings from Anne's peasants. Their lady had spoken.

Without a word, without a glance at the man who stalked at his shoulder, Dizier strode out into the open, until he came near the waiting Sauval. Three of their men had been brought, cowering, for Ferrand's protection. Dizier stopped and pointed at the group. "Go," he growled. "You are safe now, even from me."

He failed to notice that Ralph answered without a sneer. "Be comforted, Dizier. I may be of more value alive than dead."

Dizier, turning away, snarled over his shoulder, "It was she who saved you."

"Therefore," replied Ralph, "I bade you take comfort." As Dizier tramped away, Ralph, very thoughtful, joined the Sauval.

Anne took possession of her castle. Not without tears. When Conan led her into the great empty hall, where the storms had swept through, the birds had nested, and only lately the masons had made a rude housecleaning, then Anne's emotions choked her. "I remember," she said brokenly, "I remember — Conan, how terrible! Can I ever forget it all?"

"Think of it as past," he answered. "This day your enemies are defeated. Tomorrow — "

"Oh, Conan," cried Anne, "I am afraid of tomorrow. Can Aymar be too strong for you?"

With trouble in his face, he replied: "God has begun His vengeance. As for my part in the rest, you heard what Bernard said. If I put away thought of myself, and pray, will not that vengeance be completed?"

"Pray with me, then," she begged. And crossing themselves, they knelt and repeated that best of prayers, the Our Father. At the last words, she said: "Deliver us from evil? Oh, Conan, will He do it?"

"I will not doubt it," he replied.

"I must not," she added. Yet her face was clouded by the thought that Conan might too completely forget worldly affairs.

He told her then the story of the secret passage, and calling together the survivors of that little inva-

sion — twelve only of them now — made them promise on the blade of his sword, for vengeance, and on
the priest's crucifix, as a sign of still more dreadful
punishment if they broke the oath, never to reveal
their knowledge of the secret entrance.

Outside the castle rose bugling and shouting. Fulke
had arrived with his men. There was much talk, bustle, and business for all, preparing meals and sleeping places, until nightfall. The duke and his meinie
slept in huts made of boughs; Anne in her old room
— with Granson and Morat outside the threshold.

Conan (after long confession) slept near-by. The keep was full of men. Outside the gate the peasants camped on the ground, jealously watching the new tower, where Count Ferrand had put the group of Sauval.

XXVI

Ralph Refuses

EARLY IN THE MORNING Conan waked in a silent keep. Outside he saw the first rays of the sun on the treetops. He had slept in his clothes, and hastily making himself neat, silently went upstairs to the roof of the keep, where he hoped to clear his mind of thoughts that had made his sleep uneasy. As he passed the door of Anne's chamber, Granson and Morat, alert, greeted him without speaking. And on the flat roof, watching the sunrise, stood Anne.

She told him that she too had not slept well, and blurted out a thought. "Aymar is terrible! Conan, you could ask for a champion."

He had thought of it himself, and had his answer ready. "It is allowed. But if God takes part, I need no champion. And if my champion should fail, then I must be beheaded like a criminal, in cold blood. Such is the law. No, I must fight my own fight."

"Then you must have armor," she said.

"Yes," he agreed. "It is true that a child, with God on his side, should be able to slay Aymar with a touch. But I must have a hauberk. Probably I can borrow one. I will ask Enguerrand. But both he and Bernard are smaller than I."

A little wind blew across the ravine and fluttered Anne's hair. She shivered. "Come down to the hall," he said. And though she knew that her chill was fear for him, she liked to have him command her, and obeyed.

There were sleepers in the hall, lying like logs on the bare floor. Conan led Anne across to a window, and would have placed her on the sill. But at the first glimpse down into the court, she drew back and pointed. "Look — the Sauval!"

From the opposite tower a figure came stealing out into the empty court. The stone barrier had already been broken down, and the man crossed it — a follower of the Sauval. Another came, then Odo himself, then the abbot of Vézelay. Three more men came, and last Ralph, sauntering indifferently. There were no more, for Aymar, as afterward appeared, was still asleep. Odo, with pointing finger, made his five men stand back, then drew the abbot and Ralph away from them and led them toward the keep, where he paused not thirty feet away from the two who watched from the window above. They might have heard him speak, but he lowered his voice and hissed fiercely at Ralph's ear, while the abbot, a little aloof, looked fearfully around him. It was Ralph who, speaking carelessly, let the listening pair hear him plainly.

"Fight in Aymar's place? What, is he afraid the devil will not fight for him? For I know the talk of the castle. He killed that Prigny."

The abbot held up his hand for caution, and Odo hissed again. Again Ralph answered aloud. "If Aymar believes that God will take a hand in this, I do not. I believe there is no God. The abbot ought to know it."

"Quiet!" begged the abbot earnestly.

"Well, then," said Odo, beginning to speak louder, "if there is no God, will you not fight? You will have great payment. You can win your sword."

"I will get my sword in my own way," said Ralph. "Besides, though there be no God, there yet is a devil. No, let Aymar fight for himself!"

Then Odo tossed his head as if changing his method, and beckoned Ralph nearer. In one step Ralph was towering over him. Again Odo spoke low, and all that came to Conan and Anne was the murmur of brusque question and answer, until Ralph, suddenly stepping back when Odo gestured toward the keep, spoke loudly.

"Kill Conan in his sleep? Never!"

The abbot, with imploring hands, tried to silence him. But with a sweep of his arm Ralph pushed him aside and scornfully spoke to the glowering dwarf:

"I am for Conan! I will be his bodyguard against any stabbers that you send. And when he has killed your brother, who abandoned me, though I served

him well — then I will tell the duke all the plans
which you and the abbot made, to share this fief
between you. Remember, I sat by when you schemed.
I know where your papers are hid. And what will
happen to you then, wizened devil?"

And he struck Odo contemptuously on the breast.

Odo reeled back, but he cried to his staring men:
"Ralph would betray us all! Kill him! Kill him!"

The abbot slunk away, but the bodyguard rushed
upon Ralph. He drew his blade, and put aside the
first blow that was struck at him. A pass with his
point, and the man went staggering away. The others
swarmed upon Ralph; their swords flashed above his
head. But with a swing of his sword he seemed to
gather all their blades together and sweep them aside,
then with the return swing he slashed fiercely at the
nearest throat. The man threw himself back, his only
defense; the sword nicked through the windpipe, and
the man reeled on, a broken cry gagging. But Ralph's
sword, passing swiftly down after that slight resistance, struck against a stone. The snapped blade fell,
glittering, and rang upon the pavement.

Ralph, weaponless, shieldless, but free of his assailants for that moment, might have fled by the
door into the keep. But his blood was up, and holding the hilt of his sword as if he would yet strike
with its inch of blade, he moved toward the wall,
under Conan's window, for protection, looking about
as if for some weapon wherewith to renew the fight.

"Now," cried Odo passionately, "he is yours!"

His men spread slowly apart, as if to move upon Ralph from different directions. Then Conan, leaning far out the window, and holding in his hand the sword that he did not remember drawing, so naturally did it come there — Conan cried, "Ralph, your sword!"

Ralph looked up, and knew him. He cried in joy, "Mine!" and held up his hand.

Conan dropped the sword. Hilt down, falling like a plummet, its flight was swift to the waiting hand. Ralph took one short step; his palm met the force of the fall; his fingers closed. And feeling in his hand the once familiar weight, Ralph spun on his heel, faced the three men just bending for their rush, brandished the sword, shouted in joy, and ran to meet them.

One of them turned and fled for the gate tower. The other two gave ground backward; then one, his courage failing before Ralph's approach, stepped back, whirled round, and with his shield held behind his head, darted away. The last man doggedly stood still. Ralph struck him a tremendous blow that sheared through the gauntleted arm raised to receive it, and passing on, split the skull. Ralph, tugging at the sword to withdraw it, was completely exposed to attack.

Conan shouted, "Beware!"

Ralph did not heed. And Odo, with his short-sword held stiffly in his two hands like a lance, ran upon Ralph from behind and thrust him in the back.

"Ah!" said Ralph grimly.

His sword at last free, he tried to turn; but Odo at first clung to his weapon. Ralph wrenched, and tore himself away. He said to the little man, staggering from that struggle, "You should have struck deeper." And he drove his point into Odo's breast.

Then he withdrew the sword, and said, "Die slowly, Odo!"

Odo fell. And Ralph carefully stepped backward, one hand held out behind him, until he met the wall. Against it he leaned, and watched the man before him.

Amid the clatter of sleepers springing to arms, Conan ran down into the court and hastened to that bloody corner. Ralph, with tight lips, looked down at Odo. The fallen baron, holding his hands upon his bleeding wound, saw Conan, hated him with his eyes, yet spoke through rigid jaws.

"That monk! Bring him!"

Conan, looking about, heard heavy breathing, and found the abbot gasping behind a pile of stones. He looked at Conan as if expecting death, but Conan dragged him by the wrist to the baron's side.

"In God's name," gasped Odo, "shrive me!"

The abbot fell on his knees, pulled his rosary from beneath his robe, and pressed it into Odo's hands.

"In God's name?" gibed Ralph. "But Odo, there is no God!"

Odo turned his head and glared at him with such spite that the abbot spoke a second time before he commanded Odo's attention. "Do you repent of all your sins?"

"I do," replied Odo. Yet once again his eyes shot hatred at Ralph.

Ralph mocked. "So you hope to cheat the devil?"

"Silence him!" cried Odo. "How can I confess when he sneers? Hew him down! Where are my men?"

Ralph flouted him. "You are alone — dying alone!"

"Not dying!" cried Odo in terror. His voice thickened, and with a hand at his throat he turned to the abbot with a scream. "Shrive me! Say the words!" He choked, was flooded to the lips with the welling of his blood, and in that gushing, died.

After a moment, Ralph said, "That was worth seeing!" But his voice was weak.

Conan hurried to his side. Ralph was leaning against the wall; by him he had stood his sword upright. With both hands, held behind him, he was supporting himself. Though he tried to laugh, and failed, he still could sneer; but his face was drained of color, and his lips were gray. In spite of his supporting hands, he was sagging where he stood. Conan, who knew how deadly was his wound, cried:

"A priest! Abbot, here!"

"No," jeered Ralph. "That monk could not pass my soul into heaven. And it is too late. Conan, the sword: you gave it back to me?"

"Yes. To a brave man."

"To a brave man," repeated Ralph. "Not honorable. Well, in hell I shall find my father, and other brave men that I have known, good company all. Will you take the sword, and send Aymar after me?"

"If I can."

"Take it then. Let me see you sheathe it. Nay, wipe it not — let Aymar see his brother's blood. There, bear it at your side till you draw it against him." He

was holding himself rigid, nor did he venture to turn his head. "Where is the lady?"

"Here." Anne stepped before him. "Ralph, speak not of hell, nor that it is too late. Repent!"

"Nay, I repent not!" But as Ralph looked upon Anne, his sneer was gone, and he spoke with a wry smile. "My wrongs have been bitter, but well have I repaid them. My only sorrow will be, when in hell I meet Odo and other villains that I have sent there, that I cannot slay them again. Look down from heaven, Lady Anne, and see that I burn gladly. I — "

The light faded in Ralph's eyes, and Anne cried out as his body lurched forward. Conan caught it and lowered it to the ground. The lifeless face, when Conan turned it upward, was again scornful.

The abbot had slipped away, but the noise of the fight had roused the castle. Too late Odo's sleepy guards came running, and from windows and doors faces peered into the courtyard. Anne took Conan by the arm and led him into the keep, to the little old chapel where the altar still remained. The clash of arms had stirred him; the sight of those deaths had not daunted him. When Anne said, shuddering, "That was terrifying," he answered, "But such fighting!"

"Conan," she said with energy, "draw your sword. Take my handkerchief and wipe away that blood. You must go to your battle with a heart empty of trust in your own strength."

Accepting her rebuke, he crossed himself and answered humbly, "I forgot." He cleansed the sword and returned it to its scabbard. She asked then, "Will you go to the priest?" Much as she hated to give him up, she thought only of him.

"Pray with me first before the altar," he begged. "You can help me more than anyone else."

Kneeling, conscious of the fervor of her prayers by his side, Conan struggled to subdue his pride and forget his strength, and to put himself like a child into the hands of God.

XXVII

Judgment of God

THE CASTLE and the camps had been roused by the battle in the courtyard, and the news of it prepared all minds for the still more important fight that was yet to come. The duke gave command to prepare the courtyard for it by moving the loose stones into a low barrier, circular, within its walls. There was ample room for fighting, and even, as Enguerrand made sure, space to give Conan opportunity for the running fight which, all assured him, was his only chance against the strength of Aymar. Conan spent a long time with the priest, confessing himself and receiving the sacrament. It was still mid-morning when he was called out to receive a visitor. Sir Roger had arrived.

The baron, returning from his journey before he had expected, had learned the news and had galloped for the Red Keep with scarce a pause for refreshment. Just as he started, the youngest of the ladies-in-waiting had thrust a bundle into his hand.

"Clothes," she panted, "for Anne."

Sir Roger understood this when he found Anne

351

in her armor. She received the bundle gratefully, and disappeared to make use of it. But the baron, perceiving Conan still in his broigne, was deeply disturbed. Was there no hauberk for him? The answer was that the duke had given order to measure among all his men, but that while some of the hauberks were broad enough and some long enough, not one combined Conan's breadth of shoulder and his length of arm.

"It matters not," said Conan. "I will fight as I am."

Sir Roger was deeply anxious. "If only Isaac had brought one!"

"Isaac?" asked Conan. "Has he returned?"

"He came to the castle when I did. He began to follow us here, spurring his jade hard, though we left him behind. — Yet here he comes now!"

Worming his way into the castle was indeed Isaac, securing what he wanted by the persistence peculiar to his race. He saw Conan, hesitated, but evidently forcing himself to the act, came forward and laid at Conan's feet a bundle. It was wrapped, and in fact sewed, in oiled silk, and evidently was flexible but heavy. Isaac stood erect, crossed his arms on his breast, and looking at Conan with a boldness that he had never before showed, seemed to ask permission to speak.

"What is it, Isaac?" asked Conan.

It was plain that Isaac had prepared a speech. He delivered it with a sort of desperate bravery, for among lords he had never spoken before.

"Messer Conan, once you saved my life. ["May-hap," interjected Conan dryly.] And I failed you, like a coward. [Conan said nothing, but looked grim.] Jews were once brave. David, who slew Goliath, was a Jew. [Conan, surprised, now first realized that historic fact.] But now my race are forbidden to bear arms, and we have been forced to learn when to flee, not when to stay and fight. But when I saw what I had done, I went south once more, to Italy, to Milan where the best armor is made, and I have brought you," he pointed at Conan's feet, "a hauberk so good that not even the duke has better." He knelt, and amid the exclamations of Sir Roger, quickly slit the silk and drew forth a glittering mass of rings of steel which, drooping over both his hands, he held up to Conan. "Take it!" he begged.

Conan held his hands still, though he longed to reach for the mail. He said, "I have no money to pay for this."

"It is a gift," said Isaac.

"I know," said Conan, "that every journey you take is at a great risk. You have done this to bring me a gift?"

"No, no!" cried Isaac. His ready tears were on his cheeks. "To show you that a Jew may be grateful, even though he may be a coward. My risk was nothing, and now I am repaid for it. For here is your armor for your fight."

Anne was at Conan's side. "Take it," she urged. "It is all you can do for him."

"Isaac," said Conan, "you teach me that there is more than one kind of courage. I see that the armor cannot be paid for, and I accept it gratefully. Open out the hauberk, and let me see it."

Isaac rose, letting the rings cascade from his hands as he did so. He gripped them at two points and shook the mail out into its proper shape. "See, my lord, a hood is part of it, to go under the cap and protect your throat and neck. The skirts are split, to give freedom; but they are long, to cover the knees. And the sleeves come to the wrists, which older hauberks never did. Besides — the quality of it! — Ah, Sir Conan," as the weak hands drooped, "it is heavy for me. Do you take it."

Conan took the hauberk from Isaac's failing hands. He felt the substantial weight of the mail, yet also its suppleness and practical lightness. Once on the shoulders the burden would be nothing. He looked closely at the workmanship, saw its uniformity, the perfect pattern of the interlocking small links, and recognized the look and texture of good steel. This was the best suit that he had ever seen, and he turned to Isaac with flashing eyes.

"Isaac, perhaps I saved you; but more likely still, you will save me!"

The youth's tears came again. "Then I shall be happy."

"Ha!" cried Sir Roger. He took the hauberk and measured it across Conan's shoulders. "Never was such good fortune; it will fit! Slip it on, my boy."

And when the hauberk was in place, the fit was good. A little broad, for growth, but giving both protection and freedom. "Put a good long gambeson under it," said Sir Roger critically, "and you will be perfectly defended."

Conan considered, and then shook his head. "No. The gambeson protects the legs when on horseback, but clogs when on foot. This is to be a fight without horses, sword to sword and shield to shield. I will wear under this only my broigne, to break the force of the blows. But my legs will be unencumbered. Against Aymar, I shall be armored just as I need!" He turned and gave his hand to Isaac, whose eloquent eyes were shining with delight. "Isaac, my thanks!"

Isaac, pale from his emotion, stammered and began to draw away. Conan dismissed him kindly. "At need, fail not to call on me to help you."

But Conan's eyes shone. Pride entered him as he felt the hauberk on his shoulders; he was impatient for his fight. Father Gregory rebuked him. "Come again to the altar. Think only of the sword of the spirit!" And he led Conan away.

The bustle of mid-morning quieted down as noon approached. The courtyard was ready, with a dais and chairs erected for the duke and his great lords; one was intended for Anne. Gradually all work was suspended, as people sought places from which to watch the coming fight. Closely packed around the circle of stones were peasants and masons and folk from Vézelay and the ducal court, Fessart and Prigny. Some were on the top of the unfinished tower, more along the curtain walls, more in every window and on the roof of the keep. At last Sir Roger came to Anne where she sat, cold and trembling, in her little chamber.

"The duke is in his place. Come, it is time!"

And Anne went down the stairs. She was a woman of her time; hers was no modern delicacy; she had no fear of wounds and death; she too had wrongs to be avenged. Moreover, she told herself that if God were true, Conan must win. She went to see his victory.

She sat at the duke's right hand. On his left was Bernard; close by crowded the nobles. Anne looked round the circle of people, and saw those on the walls and the roof of the tower. She looked down, and saw on the opposite side of the circle two stools, and between them — horrible! — a coffin draped in black. She closed her eyes and prayed, offering her sacrifice.

"Holy Mary," whispered poor Anne, "if Conan may but win, I give him up! I lay down all wish for myself; I put aside all hope to be his wife. Oh, blessed Mother, make him win, and strengthen me!"

There was a stir, and through the crowd Aymar, attended by the abbot, made his way into the empty circle, and sat on one of the stools. He was armed in dark mail; his surcoat was blood-red; his great shield was scarred and dented by many blows. On his head the new steel cap, with its nosepiece, covered all his face but his cheeks and his eyes, which glared fiercely. Nothing greeted him but a buzzed whisper that did not cease. — But next came a bustle and a shouting, and Conan entered the lists. His mail was bright, his surcoat white, and on his head he wore as yet no cap. His shield, smaller and lighter than Aymar's, bore the falcon of the Prigny. Anne noted his curling hair, his open, ruddy face, his manly glance. Small wonder, though she was frozen and could make no motion, that the bustle, the craning, and the applause continued.

The duke at last rose, and the clamor died. "Herald," he commanded, "proclaim the cause."

The herald proclaimed the challenge and the acceptance. Then first Enguerrand and afterward the abbot, sponsors, declared that their men were waiting and ready. "Let them take oath, then," directed the duke, "that this battle shall be fought honorably and to the death, and that neither of the combatants bears magic or spells upon his person."

Before the duke's chair was an altar. To this the abbot led Aymar, who in his harsh voice made the oath and returned to his place. Without waiting to be conducted by Enguerrand, Conan strode forward to make the oath.

He had conquered his proud heart. Penitent and prayerful, he had banished from his mind the recent events. It was right, he knew, to banish also the thought of Anne, and to put aside all worldly wishes.

He came to the field, then, not as the avenger of his brother but as the champion of truth. He knew himself to be nothing, and yielded to the guidance of God. Earnestly, therefore, he made his oath — of right, of willingness to fight to the death, and of guiltlessness of magic. Then stepping back, Conan held up the cross of his sword hilt.

"By the cross of Christ," Conan declared with ringing voice, "I call down judgment. And though hell threatens me, I do not fear it."

He too went back to his chair, while the murmur of the onlookers rose again. Enguerrand then adjusted Conan's cap of twisted rope, raised over it his hood of mail, and upon them both laced down the steel cap. The nasal of this was narrower than Aymar's, and Conan's face could still be clearly seen, his eyes shining. Conan waited patiently. He had mastered himself; he had made before all these people his declaration and his claim. Now an end of humility!

Aymar was fretting where he stood. To increase that strain Enguerrand had brought Conan to the field with his head undefended. "He is impatient," he said to Conan. "That means he is alarmed. When you made your appeal, it disturbed him. He is not entirely a brute, for he has a memory. And he is yours if you fight away from him. All is ready now, Conan. Trust me: the cap cannot come off." He pressed Conan to his heart in an embrace, then stepped aside and signaled to the duke.

Hugh, in turn, made a gesture to the herald.

The herald cried: "Are they ready? Are they ready? Are they ready?" There was no answer. He blew a blast upon his horn. "In God's name, let them go!"

The duke sat down. Enguerrand and the abbot quickly left the barriers; and with long steps the two champions advanced to the middle of the lists.

Over the top of his shield Conan saw advancing his foe's sinister figure, grotesque in armor, in helm, with face concealed. What was beneath the cap, behind the nasal, shadows hid. The young knight had a moment's giddiness. "That is death!" How could he meet it? Then Aymar, with a muffled roar, flung high his sword and rushed against him.

Aymar had had no friendly adviser, no support from companionship. The news of Odo's death had smitten him. Much as he feared that venomous brother, he had always had his backing, and it was withdrawn. Dead! And what if God should intervene in this fight?

He had taken his place in the lists among a hostile crowd. Their murmur, their pointing fingers, had been hateful. Then those same people had applauded Conan. Alone then! But damn them, he did not care!

Conan's appeal had shaken him. Christ and hell — was it possible that they could punish? But no! Let him fight! He feared not that boy.

But shaken, he was hasty. He had little science to use, and he threw it away. He advanced, he shouted, he charged. Just a few of his terrible blows, and it would be over.

Conan could have avoided him. Ralph, Sir Roger, Enguerrand, all had told him to parry and keep away. His lightness and speed would wear the other down. They had warned him that otherwise there was no hope. He had believed it himself; he had meant to keep Aymar at a long sword's length. But in the instant when he conquered his momentary fear, his intention changed. Some instinct, some insight, would not let him give ground. The broken bellow from the helm of his foe told him that he was dealing only with a man. Obstinate, Conan raised his shield, and withstood the onset.

Anne, cold with fear, shut her eyes as she saw Conan meet the first blow. She tried to pray. But her mind was intent upon the fight, and though she could not see, in the sudden silence of that crowd she could hear.

Blow after blow Aymar rained down. The force was electric, the speed was frantic; so fast did he strike that Conan could only defend himself. Letting his shield give slightly beneath each blow, he cushioned it; and changing the angle of the shield beneath each stroke, he deflected it. Thus he was not beaten down; and thus Aymar's blade could not bite. One could not tell whether this were greater skill or courage. The shield thus deadened blow after blow —

Until one, glancing from its edge, fell heavily on

the shoulder of Conan's sword arm, and failing to cut the light, thin steel, passed on and struck the wrist. The arm went numb to the knuckles; it was uncut, but bruised. Conan gritted his teeth with the pain. He had a single thought, "Isaac's armor has saved me!" None other in that place would have withstood that stroke. Another such blow and his arm would be useless. Nor could he now strike back until the arm had recovered.

But determined not to slip aside, he still confronted his enemy, and shifted his shield under, and under, and under, blow after blow after blow. His shield arm grew tired, but he knew that he must parry and ever parry until this frightful storm had spent itself. For he would not give ground!

There was silence except for that combat. Anne heard only that clatter of blows. Not far away from her, the young duke turned an anxious eye upon

Enguerrand. The count shook his head. He could not understand why Conan was so recklessly standing up to that tempest. If the storm could last — !

It could not. Aymar had enormous strength, so great that he had never been called upon to exert it long. Not soft, if Conan had fought away from him Aymar might have been wary enough to struggle into his second wind. But in the craze of that hammering his breath began to fail. Anne, listening, detected longer intervals between the blows. Conan, enduring, marked them.

He made sure. The intervals lengthened. He heard his foe panting. Then he knew why he had stood to that close fighting. In a longer interval yet, now that his sword arm was limber again — crack! At last Conan struck in return.

The crowd gasped. Anne's eyes flew open. She saw the two figures standing close, Aymar all bulk, Conan, almost as tall, all litheness. They stood front-foot to front-foot, hacking and hewing. And now for each blow that Aymar smote, Conan dealt one in return.

The swords flashed; the shields shifted; there was fierce and dogged interchange; not only the fighters but the watchers were panting deep. Stroke upon stroke, hard, relentless, monotonous. As if the men were machines they struck, parried, struck in return, parried, struck. Could flesh and blood endure?

Conan knew that there was change. Aymar was still slowing. The knowledge gave Conan strength —

nor was Aymar's shield-work good. Conan struck shrewdly, passed the shield, hit squarely upon the helm. The next blow Aymar stopped with his shield, struck slowly in return. Conan struck harder, quicker. Again his sword met the helm, did not glance. Could he keep that up, the steel cap must split under Ralph's sword. He struck faster, faster, always upon the same spot — and now the crowd was shouting.

Ah! The crowd gasped into silence as the huge Aymar lifted his whole frame for a mighty finishing blow. The sword swung up, descended; it should have come like a thunderbolt. But that heave of preparation gave Conan his opportunity. He sprang close under, took upon his shield not the sword, but the elbow, jabbed with his own sword, sprang away. There was a long pace between them, with Conan poised for action.

Aymar stood, his head high, struggling for breath in his throat, where Conan's sword, though it could not pierce the mail, had savagely thrust. Something was torn; Aymar could not breathe. His arms drooped; his guard was down.

Conan strode past his side. The sword, with accord of weight of body, power of arm, snap of wrist, swept not downward, nor even level, but a little-upward. It cleft the nasal, passed under the brim of the cap, split the bone, bit upon the brain. And that mighty bulk of a man fell stiffly, slowly, like a statue, like a crashing spire.

As the toppling body dragged at his sword, with

a quick twist Conan wrenched the weapon free. And there he stood above that sprawled bulk, while a shout from every spectator rattled the very roofs.

Conan turned to the altar, and kneeling on that trampled ground, held up the cross of his sword.

XXVIII

Judgment of the Duke

JUDGMENT OF GOD — judgment of God! The peasants shouted it, the masons shouted it, knights and gentlemen shouted it. And if in all that crowd there were some, like the chancellor and the bishop, who could not shout with joy, they pretended to. Even the abbot put on a smile. For he was safe now. No one could betray him.

The duke went up into the hall, and all who felt that they had a right there, crowded after. No courtier risked absence; no one who sought promotion through ducal influence, in the overturn which now was certain through Bernard's influence, but followed along as fast as he could. Conan's friends, many of whom he had never seen before, conducted him. Anne was protected through the crush by Sir Roger, and found herself in her father's hall, where, alone upon the empty dais, the duke stood and waited for silence. When the room was full — and that took not long — each told his neighbor to be quiet, and soon was silent himself.

Hugh spoke. "There are here two cases that require judgment. In one the hand of God has taken part, and Aymar of Sauval has followed his brother Odo to death. They were the last of their line. The fief is vacant. I will appoint Count Enguerrand de Bourg to judge the offenses of their men who are in his ward. And I am here to receive the proposal of any who offers himself to be lord of the fief of Sauval."

Now there were in the court landless men, knights of various ages, men desirous of a footing for themselves. They were not modest; no one lives long in a court without learning that he must seize his advantage when he can. But from the crowd of men who heard the duke's words, not one raised his voice to ask for the lordship of a barren fief, lost on a hilltop in the wildest part of Burgundy, remote from the joys of Dijon.

The duke smiled. "Not one? Yet I had expected at least one applicant. Conan of Prigny, stand here before me. What, man, have you no desire for the castle of your enemies?"

Conan could only ask, "What — I?" His surprise was evident.

Not merely the duke but many others smiled at his simplicity. Hugh asked, "Could you not hold that castle, manage those lands?"

Conan stammered, "I was but yesterday a squire."

"If by that answer," said Hugh, "you mean to decline, I will say no more. My lords, the matter remains open till some worthy applicant appears. — For the second case let Sir Roger of Fessart bring before me the Lady Anne d'Arcy, the claimant of the Red Keep."

And Anne stood before the duke. There was a murmur as she rose from her knee, when first those around could see her clearly. She wore no jewels; nor any decoration except the thin ring of gold which was the sign of her claim to her fief; it was almost lost in the red of her hair. Her two long braids, twined with ribbon, hung down in front below her waist. She bore herself well. And the face, youthful and fine, showed only anticipation as she waited for the young duke's words. For surely he, who was wise in things so far, would deal rightly with her.

Hugh addressed his courtiers generally, rather than Anne. "There is nothing obscure about this case. Injustice has been done by ignoring the plea; punishment was not given to those who committed the crime of attacking a neighbor where no feud was declared; years have been allowed to pass. At last this girl, in order to press her claim, was forced to don armor and appear with men in the field of battle. By that action the justice of Burgundy was impeached; I am ashamed that my courts have failed in their duty. The Lady Anne still claims the fief of her father. Nevertheless," and the duke turned his eyes on Anne, "custom and law unite in denying a fief to a woman, except in the case of a widow claiming the inheritance of her husband as guardian of her son. Anne, I grieve that I cannot give you the castle for which you have suffered and fought."

It was bewildering. Anne had not expected the conclusion, so kind yet so denying, so friendly and yet so legal. But she did perceive that the duke must proceed by law and the customs of the duchy. Anne turned her eyes on Sir Roger, and saw that he had no protest to make. She looked to her other side, to Conan, and saw that he too was without recourse. There was no one to plead for her.

But the sight of Conan — sorry, perplexed — told her what to say. She had given him up; she had promised the Virgin not to wish for him any more. And how could she now? She was so sure that no wish for her had ever entered his mind that she felt it wrong, almost immodest, to dream of him again. She cast that hope away.

There remained only that other hope that could not be torn from her except with her very heart. She must consider her people, her men-at-arms sharing the years of her exile, her peasants counting the sad seasons till her return. They had suffered for her, fought and bled for her — some had died for her. Were those who remained to go into the hands of strangers? Anne could not bear it; at any cost she must try to prevent it. She raised her eyes and answered the duke.

"My lord," she began, and her low voice moved those who heard. She paused; her words were to be unmaidenly, but they were according to her vow, and they were for the sake of her people. Anne collected

herself and spoke on. "My lord duke, you saw yesterday men who fought for me, who after waiting years,
offered their lives for me as my father's daughter. I
cannot desert them. It is the law that a fief may be
held only by a man. Very well." Anne flinched, but
spoke again, "I ask of you a husband, who shall hold
my fief and let me work among my people."

Breathless, she paused. Ashamed, her face flam-
ing, she yet would not lower her eyes again, but
gazed steadily into the duke's. And she saw not
scorn nor laughter, but honest admiration.

Hugh raised his hand, and the murmur that her
words had raised were instantly stilled. The duke's
eyes were kindled with the enthusiasm of his youth.
"Lords," he cried with ringing voice, "braver words
heard I never! What the Lady Anne asks, I will
grant. What, shall this case too be taken under ad-
visement? Or shall this fief, bringing with it a chatelaine and a noble one, find a claimant here and
now?"

There was a stir in the ring. The courtiers were
not all cautious.

A fief, a brave and noble wife, the duke's favor —
"My lord duke! My lord duke!" There were three,
there were five, there were more, pressing for his
attention.

Hugh swept the circle with his eye. "I like it
well," he said, "that there are so many of you. Otherwise, I should ask what is wrong with the chivalry

of Burgundy. I see that there is nothing wrong but your method. For," and he laughed joyously, "you who apply to me have come to the wrong place."

He turned his eyes on Anne. Confused, proud, breathless with happiness, she was looking down on Conan, who, kneeling at her feet, his hands clasping hers, was asking what the crowding circle could not hear.

"Conan," cried the laughing duke, "what have you to ask the court?" Conan rose and faced them all. He was not afraid, but he could not speak. He took Anne's hand, led her to the dais, and they knelt together before the duke, who bent to the kneeling pair.

"Anne," he asked, "do you accept him?"

And Anne answered "Yes."

Glossary

Chatelaine — mistress of a castle

Collop — a slice of meat for frying

Corselet — armor which covered the wearer's torso

Croup — the hinder end of a saddle

Damosel — young unmarried lady of noble birth

Donjon — the principal tower of a castle, commonly used as the stronghold

Fief — an estate held on feudal tenure

Gambeson — a thigh-length military tunic of leather or thick cloth, used under the hauberk to prevent chafing and bruises

Hauberk — a sleeveless, knee-length coat of mail

Mangonel — a military engine of war used for casting missiles against an enemy position

Meinie — a company or retinue of men

Paladin — a knight or hero; one of the twelve knights of Charlemagne

Pennon — a tapered and swallow-tailed flag

Poniard — a dagger

Portcullis — a strong grating at the gate of a castle which can be lowered in case of assault

Quoits — a game in which an iron ring is thrown at a fixed peg in the ground

Sedges — Any of the various grass-like plants growing chiefly in marshy areas

Seigneuress — a woman who excercises feudal authority

Servitor — a manservant, especially one who waits on tables

Squire — a young man of aristocratic birth in service to a knight

Suzerain — a lord who has political control over the foreign relations of a feudal state

Thews — well-developed muscles

Tocsin — an alarm bell

Varlet — an attendant or page in service to a knight

Vassal — in the feudal system, a person holding lands under the obligation to render service to his superior

Villein — a feudal class of people who served as serfs to their lord, but had the rights of free men in respect to all others

About the Author

ALLEN FRENCH (1870–1946)

Allen French was a careful, scholarly writer of history. Several of his historical works on the Early American period are still in print today. More than once he traced undiscovered primary sources which shed new light on the happenings of the American Revolution. Yet, meticulous as he was, history was always to him more than dry facts. Whether Allen French was writing scholarly works or exciting tales for boys, his endless fascination with the past allowed history to come alive. His wife, Aletta, once wrote that while deeply immersed in what was to be his final major historical work, *The First Year of the American Revolution,* her husband also wrote a children's book on the Romans in Britain and a novel about the Puritan Migration to America. She says, "His imagination fired his mind to the point where it blazed and he would take to fiction to let off the heat!"

She further writes, "I think there were two elements in his devotion to history. One, a deep desire to proclaim the truth, avoiding no damaging details and letting the honors fall where they might. The other an enthusiasm for the drama of history which required heroes and villains and all the 'props,' and which logically led to stories of knighthood and chivalry such as *The Colonials, Sir Marrok, Grettir the Strong, The Story of Rolf and the Viking's Bow, The Red Keep* and *The Lost Baron.*"

Long-time family friend and author, T. Morris Longstreth, writes of Allen French, "It was hard for him to sit through a meal without our talk driving him to the encyclopedia. Yet there was no pedantry in all this, but rather a sense of adventure, the same romantic sense that led him to write his boys' books. History was for him a living glory."

In writing *The Red Keep*, and later, *The Lost Baron*, which derived from the same research, Allen French sought to provide exciting stories which sprang from the best sense he could gain of the medieval times. He and his wife spent six weeks near Vézelay to gather "color" for *The Red Keep*. He wrote: "Of the writing of history I have only this to say: that as my fiction was constructed out of imagination guided by common-sense, my history is common-sense illuminated by imagination. Common-sense: one should always be controlled by the facts of the case, ascertained by the most careful study, and set forth fairly to both sides. And imagination should try to make the facts living and interesting — not romantic nor sensational, but human." He finishes by saying, "If a man takes his work seriously, and himself not too seriously, he has a good chance of doing something worth while."

About the Artist

ANDREW WYETH (1917–)

Andrew Wyeth, known primarily now for his modern American realist art, created the illustrations for *The Red Keep* while still in his early twenties. Born in 1917, he received his schooling under a tutor at the same time he was being instructed in art by his father, N.C. Wyeth. The elder Wyeth, a student of Howard Pyle, is best known for his illustrations of such classic works as *Treasure Island* and *The Last of the Mohicans*. He also did the full color picture for the cover of *The Red Keep*. Andrew Wyeth worked for a few years in the field of illustrating, eventually leaving it to concentrate on his more serious painting.

He currently lives in Chaddsford, Pennsylvania, his residence of many years.